# A BAD DEAL IN MORMON LAND

# A BAD DEAL IN MORMON LAND

a novel

T.I.M. WIRKUS

TYPE EIGHTEEN BOOKS

Library of Congress Cataloging-in-Publication Data

Names: Wirkus, T.I.M., 1983–, author.
Title: A Bad Deal in Mormon Land / T.I.M. Wirkus.
Description: 300 pages. – First edition. | Laguna Hills, California: Type Eighteen Books, 2026.
Summary: "Spirit medium and ex-vaudevillian Madame Ilsa von Hoffmann accepts a mysterious job in Salt Lake City and gets caught in a web of church politics, competing interests, and vengeance."—Provided by publisher.

Identifiers: LCCN xxx | ISBN: 9798993351926 (paperback) | ISBN: 9798993351940 (ebook)
LC record available at https://lccn.loc.gov/xxx

Published by Type Eighteen Books
www.typeeighteenbooks.com

Printed in the United States

*For J & A*

# 1

As a younger woman, Madame Ilsa von Hoffmann (formerly Mabel Fairfax of Appleton, Ohio) had imagined an illustrious future for herself as the nation's most influential spirit medium, the Napoleon of Necromancy, the Cleopatra of Clairvoyance. Lionized for her prowess in communicating with the dead, she would lecture to packed auditoriums the world over, would capture the imagination of the masses through sensational demonstrations of her phantasmal powers, would dine with presidents and kings, all by the time she turned thirty.

Instead, at thirty-five years old (*midway through life's journey*, as that hack Dante would have it), Ilsa found herself in the odiferous back room of a dubious pharmacy with a pair of religious fanatics who wanted her to do the impossible for a sum of money she would have sneered at only a few years earlier.

This was not a few years earlier, however, and, having not been offered even a fraction of this sum for months now, she was eager to do whatever necessary to hook these prospective employers.

"How have you found our city?" asked the older of the two fanatics.

The city in question was Salt Lake; the year 1908. It was a

dreary, autumn Friday, the gray sky spattering cold rain on all those unfortunate enough to be out of doors, and though Salt Lake seemed to be a city on the rise, with two new train depots, a grand cathedral, several tall, commercial structures, and a slew of mansions under construction in and around its downtown, Ilsa couldn't help but view it all through the mournful veil of her own reduced circumstances.

Wanting to ingratiate herself with these men, she said the city was quite charming, and she couldn't wait to get to know it better. The men seemed pleased by this, and as the small talk continued, Ilsa took stock of her interlocutors.

The older of the two, Roger Marsh, was in his mid-fifties, hearty, with the mustachioed face of a respectable burgher; in fact, Marsh had been expelled from a position of authority in the Mormon Church for harboring beliefs too outrageous even for that wild-eyed institution.

The younger man, Adam Wolfe, functioned as both bodyguard and secretary to Roger Marsh. He was in his early twenties, pink-cheeked, upsettingly well-scrubbed, and larger than he appeared at first glance, a strange optical effect brought about, Ilsa supposed, by his unnervingly boyish face.

And what did these men see, she wondered, when they looked at her? Nothing more than a short, pudgy woman in an outdated black gown, her face made up to emphasize rather than subdue her dramatic features?

At a break in the pleasantries, Roger Marsh leaned confidentially toward Ilsa and said,

"We can speak freely here. This pharmacy is owned by an ally."

He sat behind a stack of patent medicine crates like they were a desk, while Adam Wolfe towered nearby with his meaty arms folded across his broad chest. Ilsa sat exposed, no pseudo-desk or table to shield her travel-weary body.

"Very good," she said. "Shall we discuss the Summoning you wish me to perform?"

Roger Marsh nodded solemnly, while Adam Wolfe fixed Ilsa with a sharp, threatening gaze.

"Not long ago," Marsh began, "I was excommunicated from the Church of Jesus Christ of Latter-day Saints for refusing to renounce the practice of Celestial Marriage."

"Polygamy?" asked Ilsa.

"Yes," said Roger. "For convenience's sake, call it polygamy. At the time of my excommunication, I was a member of the Quorum of the Twelve Apostles, a body of men holding the same divine keys the Savior Himself entrusted to His Apostles in times of old."

"I see," said Ilsa, liking the situation less and less with each word that left Marsh's mouth. This job was going to be a rough one, she could already tell.

"I could spend the rest of the day explaining why I defied my Brethren of the Quorum, and the First Presidency," said Marsh, "but in brief, I believe Celestial Marriage is an inextricable component of the Lord's true and living Church. When God revealed the practice to the late Prophet Joseph Smith nearly seventy years ago, He was endowing us with the final tool we needed to usher in His kingdom on the Earth."

Ilsa tilted her head noncommittally while, from behind Marsh, Adam Wolfe flared his nostrils at her like she was a glass of milk gone sour.

"And I have a sure knowledge," Marsh continued, looking earnestly into Ilsa's eyes, "granted to me by the Holy Spirit that my Brethren, and not me, labor in error at this time. In renouncing our religion's most true and sacred practice, they have acquiesced to the jeers of a faithless world."

"Well," said Ilsa, as Marsh seemed to expect a response. "How do I figure into all this?"

Marsh beamed at her.

"In short," he said, "I have been commanded by the Lord to restore His Church to its proper form, and it has been revealed through a dream that you, Madame Ilsa von Hoffmann, will play a vital role in that restoration. Tomorrow night you will aid the spirit of the Prophet Joseph Smith in crossing the veil to address, as if in the flesh, a few of the Lord's most faithful disciples."

This was all so much worse than Ilsa had feared, but she couldn't afford to lose this job.

"In terms of a full-body apparitions," she said, "the spirits can be very fickle. I would hate for you to get your hopes up for something the spirits may be unwilling to provide."

"What you refer to as *the spirits*, I know as the hosts of Heaven," said Marsh. "A lifetime of discipleship has taught me that these hosts can be commanded—if the cause is just— by the sacred Power and Authority of the Holy Priesthood of God, an Authority I still possess, in spite of what my benighted former Brethren may believe."

This was very, very bad.

"I admire your faith, Mr. Marsh—" Ilsa began.

"*Elder* Marsh," Adam Wolfe corrected, eyes sparking with animosity.

"I admire your faith, Elder Marsh," she said, "but the spirits are often *very* reluctant to reveal themselves in full. You're much less likely to be disappointed, I think, if what you anticipate instead is an aural manifestation of your prophet."

Marsh smiled with masterful benevolence, and Ilsa cringed inside.

"You know, I've followed the progress of spiritualism with much interest over the years," Marsh said. "I like to think of our respective religions as cousins, maybe even sisters, both demonstrating a greater permeability between this world and the next than many people believe possible. What I'm saying, Madame Ilsa, is I think we can learn from each other, and I'll tell you again, when a worthy request is made by the Power and Authority of the Priesthood, the Heavenly Hosts are bound to honor it."

He paused here, peering intently at her face. Adam Wolfe adjusted the cuffs of his shirt, demonstrating the considerable mass of his shoulders and arms. Madame Ilsa could see that these two men, each in their own way, were not to be trifled with.

"And if your faith isn't strong enough right now to believe," continued Marsh, "then you can lean on mine. Because I have total confidence that tomorrow night you will assist Joseph Smith in crossing over from the spirit world."

Marsh's request would have been impossible for Ilsa even at the height of her powers— impossible for anyone working without an accomplice, really—and Ilsa was hardly at the height of her powers, having committed near-fatal mistakes (botched palmings, forgotten names, spilled ectoplasm) in every single one of her recent Summonings.

She didn't know what was wrong with her. Or rather, she knew exactly what was wrong with her, still had nightmares about the incident that had kicked off this latest losing streak, but couldn't bring herself to name it.

Ilsa considered her present options as her stomach tightened with hunger and fear. She had no money. She had to take this job, in spite of its impossibility, but what would be the consequences when she failed to deliver a walking, talking Joseph Smith?

"I look forward to our collaboration," said Marsh, having apparently interpreted Ilsa's silent panic as an agreement to take on the job.

"Yes," said she, unable to muster anything more.

After a brief discussion of her fee and other such practicalities, Adam Wolfe stepped forward and rested a heavy hand on Marsh's shoulder.

"I'll see Miss Hoffmann out," he said.

"It's *Madame von* Hoffmann," Ilsa managed as she rose.

At the front door of the pharmacy, Adam Wolfe paused. Leaning close to Ilsa, he said, "I want you to look me in the eye."

She had to crane her neck to do so. Wolfe towered above her, and she saw in his young face a thirst for violence that caused a queasy flip in her stomach.

"Yes?" she said.

"I need you to understand," he said softly, "that if you fail to live up to your end of this agreement, you'll be very sorry. Do you understand me?"

Clearly, this job would not be the easy financial victory she'd been hoping for.

"Of course," Ilsa said, with vastly more confidence than she felt.

# 2

Several blocks away, Roger Marsh's wife—well, one of his wives—sought opportunity to betray him, not for thirty pieces of silver, but to better the station of her fellow Mormon women. This altruistic motive notwithstanding, the language of Matthew's Gospel concerning the betrayal of the Lord did flicker darkly through Diantha Marsh's mind as she prepared to give one of Roger's greatest enemies the details required to snuff out his nascent religion.

She believed in the rightness of her course, though, so here she was, in the parlor of her friend Vilate Dowland, or more precisely, in the parlor of Vilate's husband, Hyrum F. Dowland, Acting President of the Quorum of the Twelve Apostles, and Roger's former colleague and current nemesis. Each knew perfectly well the purpose of this afternoon's meeting, but so far, they'd spent the visit discussing everything but the business at hand. Nobody, it seemed, wanted to be the first to sink the proverbial knife into Roger's back.

"What I wish people understood about the Word of Wisdom," Hyrum Dowland was saying, "is that it's about so much more than not consuming certain substances. It calls for maintaining a sound and robust physique, a temple for the Spirit of the Lord."

"Which is why Hyrum and I do our exercises together twice daily," said Vilate, finishing her husband's thought.

They were one of those couples who looked like siblings, both tall, sharp-featured, and graying, although Hyrum's hair was all on his face in the form of a shrubby beard, and Vilate's was all on top of her head, tied into a loose bun. They were around Roger's age, in their early fifties, two decades older than Diantha.

The Dowlands had always been kind to her, though perhaps a bit distant since Roger's excommunication. Diantha had faced no disciplinary action herself but still ended up effectively alienated from her orthodox friends and acquaintances, occupying a strange no man's land that was neither excommunication nor full fellowship.

"Do you exercise?" Hyrum asked.

"You used to roller skate, didn't you?" Vilate said.

"I did," Diantha said. "These days, I go for walks."

Hyrum rose from his seat.

"You see, the trick with any exercise," he said, "is to perform each motion to the fullest extent. For instance—"

He swung his arms out so that he resembled a child's letter T.

"You see?" he said.

"No, dear," said his wife, before Diantha could respond. "You're holding your arms at too much of an angle."

Now it was Vilate's turn to stand and fling out her arms, punctuating her action with a yelping *Ha*!

"The sound is not necessary," Hyrum explained to Diantha.

"Not *necessary*, no," said Vilate, "but it engages the diaphragm and gives the motion a certain zest."

"You try it," said Hyrum, motioning for Diantha to stand.

"With or without the sound?" Diantha asked.

"With," Vilate said firmly.

"Without," Hyrum said, just as firmly.

Diantha stood but glanced at the clock on the mantlepiece. She had a meeting with that journalist Francie Bream in a little less than an hour.

"We should talk about Roger," she said. After a brief, melancholy pause, they all sat back in their chairs.

Hyrum tented his fingers under his chin. "What have you been able to learn, my dear?"

In a previous meeting, Diantha had broached the possibility of supplying Hyrum with the specifics of Roger's traitorous plans, and she'd also communicated—very politely—that she'd expect something in return.

She'd since articulated what that something might be in a fifty-eight-page, handwritten document describing changes, procedural and ideological, that would aid the Church in its ministerial mission as the earthly surrogate of the Lord Jesus Christ. Hyrum had promised to read her recommendations and bring them before the Quorum of the Twelve Apostles for consideration.

"Have you had a chance to present my proposal to the Brethren?" Diantha asked.

"I've read through it," Hyrum said, as if this act alone represented a surfeit of generosity.

"And?"

"Why don't you tell me what you know about Roger's plans," Hyrum said, "and then we can discuss your proposal on a more leisurely timeline."

"Leisurely?" Diantha looked to Vilate, who looked away, having already verbally withdrawn from the negotiations between her friend and her husband.

"Yes," said Hyrum. "What I mean is, we must act quickly to prevent Roger from committing further, graver errors, as much for his own welfare as for anyone else's."

"I agree," Diantha said, with what she hoped was a patient smile. "Which is why we need to discuss my proposal right now, so you can present it to the Brethren. You're having a meeting with them at the temple tomorrow morning, correct? After *that*, I can share the information I've gleaned about Roger's current enterprise."

Hyrum seemed to weigh the odds of successfully brushing off

Diantha's request, and, with a shake of the head, he left the room, returning a moment later with the document Diantha had given him. He withdrew a pair of glasses from his pocket and perched them at the end of his long nose.

"This first sentence," he said. "'As all are alike unto God, all—regardless of sex or race—must have equal access to the governance and blessings of His Church, including the ceremonies of the Holy Temple.'"

Hyrum looked over the lenses at Diantha.

"To begin," he said, "you mention access to the temple for all, regardless of race. I'll put it as simply as I can. Our African brothers will not at any point be given the priesthood, nor will our African sisters be admitted to the temple."

Diantha had included the stipulation on race as something she could tactically concede to preserve the more vital elements of her proposal; she knew as well as anyone the Church's position on that matter wasn't going to change.

"I'll repeat," Hyrum continued. "Priesthood for the African saints is never going to happen."

"All right," Diantha said. "What else?"

Hyrum pushed his glasses up, glanced at the document, and then took the glasses off, sighed noisily, and tossed the proposal onto a side table.

"The rest is all of a piece, isn't it?" he said. "You're bringing the language of women's suffrage to bear on Divine matters, and I don't know what to tell you."

Diantha took a breath.

"If you'll recall," she said, "the final paragraphs of my proposal suggest the formation of a committee to thoughtfully and prayerfully consider the ways in which women's voices might be more fully incorporated into the governance of the Church. Just a committee, Hyrum. That's all I'm asking for."

Hyrum again tented his fingers below his chin, and after a lengthy silence, raised his head.

"Before I present this to the Brethren," he said, "I would like a token of sorts from you, something to reassure me you truly have the information you claim to have."

This didn't seem completely unreasonable.

"I'll tell you this much," she said. "At a séance, a medium hired by Roger will be summoning the spirit of the Prophet Joseph to give the new church his blessing."

Hyrum and Vilate looked well and truly shocked at this revelation, Hyrum's cheeks ballooned out, and Vilate put a hand to her chest; this gave Diantha a perverse bit of pleasure.

"After the Quorum meeting," Diantha said, "I'll tell you when and where it's happening, and give you a list of those who plan to attend."

Vilate looked away, and Hyrum nodded gravely. Diantha hoped he'd hold up his end of the bargain.

# 3

They say hunger is the best seasoning, but in Madame Ilsa's vast dining experience, good seasoning was the best seasoning. A maggoty porkchop from a third-rate diner or a bowl of rancid stew from a fleabag boardinghouse tasted no less disgusting on an empty stomach. If anything, a poorly prepared (or rotten) dish was all the more dispiriting when one was hungry.

Thankfully, the Wasatch Diner prepared their food with cleanliness and competence. Her current meal may not have been the best lunch she'd ever enjoyed—this wasn't Delmonico's—but it was far, far from the worst. Which was a good thing, because over the past thirty-six hours, Ilsa had eaten nothing more than a bruised apple and a stale loaf of bread.

The sad fact was, she was broke, which was the main reason she'd agreed to Marsh's proposition in spite of her considerable misgivings. In addition to her promised fee, triple what she'd been paid for years, Roger Marsh also provided her with lodging at the Armitage Hotel, and food in the form of an open tab here at the Wasatch Diner.

As she polished off the last of her corned beef sandwich and tucked into her Nesselrode pudding, her thoughts turned from her immediate, corporeal needs to the task ahead of her. What Marsh wanted was, quite frankly, impossible for someone working alone, which she was. Even with an accomplice, it would be more than a stretch to conjure a walking, talking apparition recognizable to those in attendance as Joseph Smith—about whom Ilsa knew next to nothing.

What would happen, Ilsa wondered, if she failed to live up to her end of the bargain? Marsh didn't seem like a violent man, but many violent men didn't seem like violent men until something seriously displeased them.

Adam Wolfe, on the other hand, appeared as disposed to violence as a bell was to ringing. This was someone who wouldn't hesitate to hurt her if he didn't get what he wanted, and in spite of the diner's warm interior, Ilsa shuddered at the thought of an enraged Adam Wolfe.

She was in a bind, and a critical voice within her reminded Ilsa that all this could have been avoided, that she'd had another option she'd decisively turned down.

A few weeks earlier, Ilsa had run into her former mentor, Lucy Lammermoor, female impersonator extraordinaire and legend of the small-time vaudeville circuits. A decade and a half before, Lucy had given Ilsa her start in a musical comedy double act, Lucy playing the malaprop-prone daffy aunt, and Ilsa (then under the name Mabel Fairfax) the levelheaded niece. The straight man, as it were.

Both were competent singers and comediennes, but the biggest reaction from the audience invariably came at the end of the routine when Lucy and Mabel removed their wigs to reveal their true sex. Although whether their de-wigged state actually reflected their true sex was up for debate, as Lucy and Mabel generally maintained the act (if that's what it was) offstage as well.

There were a handful of others on the vaudeville scene like Lucy and Mabel, female impersonators for whom the term *impersonator* was not entirely accurate, and they formed a loose coalition known (for reasons none of them could remember) as the Crimson Swans. Mabel felt some discomfort at their earnestness and unabashed flaunting of themselves, but she valued the way they looked out for each other, sharing lodging when possible, and passing along information about how various bookers, venues, and cities might treat women like them.

Mabel/Ilsa had largely lost touch with the other Crimson Swans after she left vaudeville to pursue a career as a respectable medium, although she did run into a few here and there over the years—the most recent encounter being right before she received the offer for the Salt Lake City job.

She had been in San Francisco stocking up on spirit gum, flash powder, wigs, and other essentials at Thalmann's Costume and Theatrical Supply Company. She knew the owner—he'd had a mind-reading teakettle act when she was starting out—and he always gave her a generous discount.

After ringing Ilsa up, he cast her a sideways glance and said, "By the way, Lucy wants to talk to you."

"Lucy Lammermoor?" Ilsa said as she paid with some of the last of her meager cash reserves. "Is she in town?"

"She's upstairs," Thalmann said, handing over a receipt. "The apartment above the store. Been staying with me the past few months."

As she ascended the staircase, Ilsa wondered if this living arrangement was more practical or romantic—Thalmann was not a bad looking man—but more pressingly, she wanted to know why Lucy needed to see her. She reached the door, but before she could knock, Lucy opened it and pulled her inside.

"Still going by Madame Ilsa?" Lucy asked in a cigarette-roughened voice.

It had been years since Ilsa had last seen her old mentor, but Lucy still looked essentially the same: buxom, overdressed, and glamorously weary of this world.

"I am," said Ilsa, as the older woman drew her in for a theatrical embrace. "Are you in town with a show?"

Lucy shook her head as they sat down on a stained, silk divan, and Ilsa noticed that Lucy's clothing was more threadbare than it had appeared at first glance. The fabric was thin at the elbows, and the hems were at the cusp of fraying.

"I've retired, my dear," Lucy said, producing a cigarette and a foot-long cigarette holder from somewhere within the folds of her clothing. She lit up and took a long drag.

"Voluntarily?"

"Never one to beat around the bush, were you?" Lucy said with an affectionate chuckle. "Yes, voluntarily. I haven't exactly been raking in the money the past few years."

She shrugged extravagantly, tapping the ash from her cigarette into a tray on the side table.

"No," Lucy continued, "it seems a distant uncle of mine has died and named me his heir. I've inherited a small farm in Wyoming."

"Congratulations," Ilsa said to her smoke-wreathed former mentor.

"Thank you, my dear girl," said Lucy. "But that's only the half of it. I've decided to invite the Crimson Swans—you remember the Crimson Swans, don't you?—to come live on the farm with me. Work the earth, live by the sweat of our brow, that kind of thing."

The proposition sounded to Ilsa like an absolute disaster.

"You're starting a commune, is what you're saying," Ilsa said.

"If you like," said the older woman.

"Lucy, communes never work," Ilsa said.

"You should join us," Lucy said, sailing right past the critique. "You bring a lot to the table, and the girls would love to live with you. *I* would love to live with you. You know, I've always thought of you as the daughter I never had."

She said this last bit with the disarming blend of irony and sincerity Ilsa had always found oddly comforting. Still, joining a commune with the rest of the Crimson Swans was the last thing Ilsa wanted to do, for two reasons:

First, as far as Ilsa knew, the Crimson Swans had little to no collective agricultural experience, and she had a hard time imagining their farm staying afloat for more than a month or two. Ilsa had grown up on a farm in Ohio and knew what a challenging life it could be. Lucy and the Crimson Swans likely pictured some rural idyll and would receive a rude awakening when their first Wyoming winter arrived.

Second, and more important, walking away now from her career as a medium would be a concession of defeat she was not yet prepared to make. She'd worked so hard to build the little that she had and felt confident she could alter her current trajectory and avoid being quite literally put out to pasture with a group of former colleagues.

"I don't think that's for me," Ilsa said. "Sorry. But thanks for the invitation."

Lucy handed her absurd cigarette holder to Ilsa.

"Hold that, please," Lucy said, and began to dig through the handbag on the floor next to the divan. She brought out a loose scrap of paper and the nub of a pencil and wrote something down.

"Trade me," she said, taking back the cigarette holder and handing Ilsa the paper. "That's all the information you need to find us if you change your mind."

"I won't," said Ilsa, slipping the paper into her own bag. "But again, thank you."

Sitting now in the Wasatch Diner, Ilsa wondered for a fraction of a moment if she'd made a mistake in turning down Lucy's offer that afternoon in San Francisco.

But no—the thought of living on a ramshackle farm with a cadre of failed vaudevillians caused her visceral pain. She'd find a way to manage this current job.

Her rumination, and her pudding course, were interrupted by a realization that someone was standing right next to her booth.

"Can I join you?" asked the someone, a young woman with a look of self-aware gumption. Ilsa recoiled in mistrust, but the woman sat down before she could muster a response.

"My name's Francie Bream," the young woman said.

Madame Ilsa recognized the name immediately. Bream was

younger than she would have expected, mid-to-late twenties, and had the kind of face that would disappear in a crowd, an asset, Ilsa imagined, for someone in Bream's line of work.

"Francie Bream, the journalist?" Ilsa said. "Of the *Dubuque Standard Examiner*?"

"Formerly of the *Dubuque Standard Examiner*," Francie Bream said. "More recently of the *Pittsburgh Gazette*, but yes, that's me."

"'The preposterously named Ilsa von Hoffmann gave the people of Dubuque their money's worth last night at Granger Hall,'" Ilsa said, quoting from memory. "'That is, if their money's worth entailed a catalogue of parlor tricks so tired they made the dreary Madame Ilsa seem peppy by comparison.'"

"So, you remember that." Francie attempted a self-deprecating laugh.

"I remember every hack who's ever done a hatchet job on me," said Ilsa. "That article cost me a fair bit of work."

"I acknowledge that my language wasn't as measured as it could have been," said Francie, "but I was a much younger, rasher woman then."

"It was three years ago," said Ilsa, "and you called me a feckless charlatan."

"Yes, well," said Francie. "I suppose that's all in the past, isn't it? Now, what brings you to Salt Lake City?"

Ilsa wasn't going to play the other woman's game, whatever it might be.

"What do you want, Bream?" she said, shoveling a spoonful of pudding into her mouth as punctuation.

"You know, it's fortuitous, me running into you like this," said Francie. "I'm in town working on a profile of Mormon women post-polygamy, but I envision it as part of a larger project. A kind of survey of women in religion in these United States. And in a way, Miss von Hoffmann, you could make a compelling subject for an article of your own."

"It's *Madame* von Hoffmann."

Francie laughed at this, which only irritated Ilsa more.

"I'm serious, though," Francie said. "Let me profile you. It could do us both some good. I'll follow you around for the next few days and write a fair and sympathetic portrait of what I see."

"I'm sure you would," said Ilsa. "Who's your current victim, by the way?"

"My current subject is Diantha Marsh," said Francie. "I believe you're working for her husband?"

Ilsa detected a note of urgency beneath the studied casualness of Francie's question.

"Where did you hear that?"

"Is it true?" said Francie.

"As a rule, I don't divulge information about my clients," Ilsa said.

"So you are working for him," said Francie.

"That's not what I said," Ilsa replied. "Now, let me finish my dinner in peace."

Francie considered this.

"I'll do that," she said, scooting out of the booth.

"Thank you," Ilsa said.

Francie remained standing nearby.

"Whether or not you're working for Roger Marsh," she said, "my offer stands. Show me what your job is like, and I'll write sympathetically about it for the eager readers of the *Philadelphia Gazette*."

"Respectfully, Miss Bream," Ilsa said, dismissing the journalist with a wave of her spoon, "I want nothing to do with you."

# 4

As Adam Wolfe understood it, his relationship with Elder Roger S. Marsh arose from the contradictory necessities for a Prophet of the Lord to both keep his hands clean and to get things done. In order to cultivate the companionship of the Holy Ghost, Elder Marsh needed to live a consecrated life filled with prayer, fasting, and good works. He could not expect to continue receiving divine revelation on behalf of the children of God if he spent his time, say, spying on his former colleagues, or issuing threats to those who would derail his divinely sanctioned pursuits.

Sometimes, though, colleagues needed to be spied on, and threats needed to be issued, and that's where Adam Wolfe came in. If Elder Marsh was the Word, then Wolfe was, if he could allow himself this small blasphemy, the Word made Flesh.

And what fleshly duties occupied him at the moment? Breaking into the Hotel Royal—a just-better-than-seedy establishment—to search the room of that shifty journalist Francie Bream.

Wolfe didn't want to be seen entering the Royal, so he slipped around back and found the service door, which was locked but yielded without much resistance to the toolkit he'd purchased from a locksmith in Reno.

The air in the Hotel Royal smelled like cabbage and dust. Wolfe removed his shoes and crept up the stairs.

Bream was in town, she claimed, to write an in-depth profile about the state of Mormon women post-polygamy. Sister Diantha Marsh (herself a problem) was a key interview subject, and the two women had met half a dozen times already.

Wolfe could guess the type of article the woman would produce—its tone condescending at best and vicious at worst—but that wasn't the only reason he regarded Miss Bream with suspicion. He'd been keeping an eye on her since she'd first made contact with Sister Diantha, and there was something uncannily proper in the way she'd behaved in her off hours. Although, *proper* wasn't quite the right word for it.

The thing was, she did nothing that would give even the most circumspect observer pause, and in Adam's experience of observing people, nobody behaved *that* carefully when they were alone, which could only mean that Francie Bream suspected (not incorrectly) that she was being watched. Which meant, further, that Francie Bream had something to hide.

It was up to Adam to discover what that something was.

In his stocking feet, he moved as quietly as possible down the second-floor hallway of the Royal. After watching the hotel's windows from across the street for three evenings straight, he knew which room was hers. Wolfe paused now in front of her door and listened. Hearing nothing but the occasional, muffled movement from the room across the hall, Wolfe removed the lockpick kit from his pocket and set to work.

Adam was not a violent man, but he was an imposing one who had no problem letting people believe he'd use his considerable mass to cause them equally considerable harm. Sometimes he had to prove that willingness by roughing someone up a bit, but as far as true violence went, the really ugly stuff, Adam generally steered clear.

Before he confronted Miss Bream, he needed at least some notion of the obscure but doubtless sinister task she was pursuing in Salt Lake. More specifically, he needed to know if she posed a threat to Elder Marsh and his fledgling religious enterprise.

The door's lock clicked, and Wolfe slipped inside.

Francie's room was drafty and poorly heated, the floor cold beneath Adam's feet. Before he proceeded, he catalogued everything in the room so he could leave it exactly as he'd found it. There wasn't much: a sad, brass bed; a dilapidated steamer trunk; and a portable typewriter abandoned in the corner.

Miss Bream had packed lightly, which pleased Adam because it confirmed his suspicions that something was amiss. No upstanding citizen traveled with so few possessions.

He started his search with the steamer trunk. Examining its contents took only a few moments and yielded nothing, though he did linger over Francie's nightgown (he hadn't been with a woman since Betsy had died), justifying the lingering with the thought that a nightgown was as good a place as any to conceal something malevolent.

From there, he searched the bed from stern to stem, again finding nothing. And then he stood in the middle of the room, hands on his hips, breath short from his furtive exertions.

He sat down on the bed, waiting for his breathing to slow. It had been a long day already.

Earlier that afternoon, he'd discreetly visited the homes of Marsh's avowed supporters to let them know the séance would be happening tomorrow evening, and they should prepare themselves accordingly with fasting and prayer, demonstrating to the Lord they were ready to receive a miracle.

Marsh's followers (or rather, the followers of God's true voice, as Marsh would be quick to remind him) were a mix of plural marriage die-hards disillusioned by the Church's renunciation of the practice, and those who'd lost faith in the current Church President after he'd told the United States Congress that he received no direct revelations from God, that he led the Church by common sense, plain and simple.

In all, they were a politely volatile bunch, and Wolfe worried about Marsh's ability to keep them corralled once the movement really got going. After all, a person who'd dissented once before was more likely to do it again.

Wolfe's breathing had returned to normal by now, and he leaned back on the bed.

It was then that he noticed something pinned to the ceiling, right above where Francie Bream would lay her head each night. Wolfe stepped onto the bed, its springs squealing, and inspected the object more closely: a threadbare scrap of fabric twice the size of a man's handkerchief. It may have been bright yellow once, but was now jaundiced ivory, its stitching nothing more than a series of faint indentations with the occasional fragment of thread still clinging to the surface. If he had to guess, Adam would say it was part of an old quilt.

Why would Miss Bream want or need to pin something like this to her ceiling? It had to be a memento or reminder, but of what? Frustrated that his visit had not clarified Bream's motives one whit, Wolfe decided to act.

Procuring a grease pencil from his jacket pocket, he scrawled a note on the thin fabric: *We've been watching you, Francie Bream. Get out of Utah or you'll be sorry!*

Miss Bream was a woman alone in a strange city, without friends or allies, and Wolfe hoped his note would do the trick. If not, he was certainly willing to do whatever necessary to keep Francie Bream out of the way.

# 5

For a journalist, Francie Bream seemed too good to be true. Diantha had already sat for a handful of interviews with the woman, during which she'd been treated not like a specimen, Polygamist Woman Exhibit A, but like a human person with thoughts, feelings, and experiences all her own.

Tonight, as they strolled the damp grounds of Temple Square together, Bream's questions continued in the same solicitous vein: How did Diantha see Mormon suffragists fitting into the national movement? What factors had most shaped her current political thinking? What did she wish people understood about the experience of women like her in Utah?

No reporter could be this sympathetic, though. Bream was up to something.

The two women paused their walk near the Temple itself, and Diantha watched Bream crane her neck to take in the building's towering granite spires as the statue of the Angel Moroni gleamed in the October sunlight.

"Beautiful," Bream murmured.

Looking at her focused expression, Diantha wondered what the journalist really thought of the building. "Can I ask *you* a question?"

Bream turned to face her. "Of course, but let's keep walking."

They started down the curving sidewalk on the Temple's south side.

"What are you trying to accomplish with this story?" Diantha said.

Bream raised her hands in a gesture of openness. "I want to profile you because you're a woman of many apparent contradictions, and I find that compelling. In terms of ulterior motives, I also believe apparent contradictions make for sellable copy. And that's that."

Diantha was flattered by this, and suspicious of the flattery. "I know how reporters write about us," she said, "and it's never that simple."

Bream laughed softly. "I seem to be running up against a lot of distrust of journalists today."

"What does that mean?"

"Nothing," Bream said. "Listen, though. I'm genuinely interested in your perspective, and I hope to represent you as fairly as I can. I promise, you have nothing to worry about with me."

"You must think I'm very naïve, Miss Bream," said Diantha.

The journalist didn't immediately respond, and they rounded a bend in the sidewalk without speaking. Diantha recognized this silence as the investigative trick it was but rose to the bait anyway.

"Do you know what Mark Twain said about us?" she asked. "I can't remember his exact words, but he said he came to Utah ready to condemn polygamy until he saw how ugly Mormon women are. Any man willing to marry one Mormon woman—according to Twain—was a generous soul, and a man willing to marry sixty was truly a saint. Or something like that. And I know—I understand—it's a joke. I know that. It's not that I don't have a sense of humor. But—" She shook her head.

Bream laid her hand on Diantha's forearm.

"Trust me, Mrs. Marsh," she said. "That's not the approach I'm going to take."

"No, you'll be more subtle, but the message will be the same condescending tripe," she said, her irritation growing. "You must see, Miss Bream—and this is why I hate the way polygamy is discussed in the rest of the country—most anti-polygamists don't truly value the rights of women. Quite the opposite."

"Is that right?" said Francie.

"Yes," said Diantha. "These are the same men who want to continue denying women the right to vote, denying women access to property and education and good employment, and do you know the best way to do that? Find a bigger villain than yourself to distract everybody while you double down on your own oppression."

Francie jotted down notes as Diantha spoke.

"I'll tell you," Diantha continued, "no one is more disappointed that polygamy in Utah is finished than the fine legislators and activists of this country who've been using Mormons as a smokescreen, hiding their own refusal to advance the cause of women."

"So, you think polygamy isn't the real problem," said Bream, looking up from her notebook.

"I hate polygamy," Diantha said. "But sometimes I think I hate the anti-polygamists even more."

"Can I quote you on that?" said Bream.

"You can be honest with me," Diantha said. "I know you're hiding something. I just don't know what it is."

"I'm not," said Bream. "I'm really not."

They stopped beneath a tree, and Bream shaded her eyes against the autumn sun.

"You need to trust me if this profile is going to work," she said. "Can you do that for me, Mrs. Marsh?"

Diantha looked at the other woman's face shadowed by the afternoon light. "Not fully," she said. "No."

"Then I think we should call it a night," said Bream.

This move surprised and irritated Diantha, but she shook

Bream's hand without comment. As the reporter turned to go, she asked, "Are we still on for tomorrow morning?"

"We'll see," said Francie Bream.

# 6

DELUSIONAL THOUGH HE MIGHT BE, ROGER MARSH HAD put Madame Ilsa up in an eminently decent establishment. More than decent, really. The Armitage Hotel was the nicest place Ilsa had stayed in years, and she almost didn't know what to do with herself. Where was the grime, the stench, the population of vermin?

This room had a bed with freshly laundered sheets, attractive, non-peeling wallpaper, and a clean window looking out on a cheery stretch of city street. Best of all, it had an ensuite bathroom with hot, running water and a bathtub nearly as deep as it was long.

What Ilsa really needed to focus on was a plan to carry off Roger Marsh's impossible Summoning tomorrow night. Either that or pawning more of her equipment—her brass trumpet, maybe, or the crystal scrying bowl—so she could afford to skip town, but that would only mean pushing her financial problems a little farther down the line.

A little voice reminded her of the open invitation to Lucy Lammermoor's farm, but Ilsa had no intention of joining that wretched commune. Things hadn't gotten *that* bad—not yet anyway.

Instead of further picking at this knotty professional conundrum, Ilsa walked into the bathroom and turned on the bathtub faucet; the water emerged steaming hot. She would take a revivifying bath while thinking of nothing, and *then* she would face reality.

At her dressing table she removed the heavy makeup she always wore in public and took off her high-necked black gown, corset, and the rest of her various underthings. Next, shaving kit in hand, she repaired to the bathroom. Standing at the sink, she let the water run—two faucets at once, what decadence!—and considered her face in the mirror, bare of makeup, with a faint beard visible after a day of travel.

With relief and pleasure, she wet her face with the hot water, lathered up, and shaved away the stubble. And when she lowered herself into the tub a few minutes later, relief and pleasure expanded into untrammeled physical bliss. Why couldn't she always live like this?

Her life, especially over the past several months, had been filled with discomforts and indignities, although some, she had to acknowledge, were of her own making. Because of a series of poor decisions, for instance, she couldn't close her eyes without seeing the lifeless visage of her erstwhile business partner, Billy Lovelace.

She could see Billy now, in the steam rising from the hot bathwater, his once beautiful face caked with blood and mucus and pleading tears. Ilsa closed her eyes as tightly as she could, but the image remained before her.

Right now, she couldn't afford to be haunted by her crimes. She had a more immediate concern: this job. She couldn't afford to do it, and she couldn't afford to walk away.

So, how could she make it work?

She ran through a variety of futile schemes in her mind until the bathwater had cooled and her high spirits had abandoned her. Wearily, she lifted her body from the tub, dried herself, and set about the tiresome labor of dressing again.

# 7

DIANTHA MARSH KNEW BETTER THAN TO REST ALL HER hopes on the bony shoulders of Elder Hyrum Dowland, which was why she had been corresponding for the past several weeks with Gilbert Snaith, Utah's Copper King, a man whose life trajectory would have put any one of Horatio Alger's creations to shame.

Born in Missouri and orphaned by the age of two, Snaith scraped together the resources to attend college, eventually receiving a degree from the Missouri School of Mines. Within a decade of his graduation, Snaith had pioneered a revolutionary process for extracting copper from the low-grade ore found in Utah's Bingham Canyon and had become, almost overnight, a multimillionaire.

Snaith's mansion on Brigham Street—a French-inspired Chateauesque—stood as a limestone testament to his success, while the mansion's contents reflected an appreciation for beauty and a sense of play Diantha was drawn to in spite of herself: a library with walls of black Flemish oak and a floor of African red marble, a bowling alley in the carriage house, a ballroom that filled the entire third floor, chandeliers from Tiffany of New York, a heated greenhouse where exotic plants bloomed year-round, and a skating rink with an on-site calliope.

A handful of times, Diantha had encountered Gilbert Snaith in passing at various social functions over the years, but at a Liberty Park ice cream social a few months earlier, Snaith had made an astonishing proposal.

They stood in the shade of a cottonwood tree; the July heat was unbearable otherwise, ice cream or no. Snaith wore an immaculate linen suit and a self-satisfied smile that was not wholly unearned: he was a handsome man in his early forties possessed of an easy social manner and a significant fortune.

"Mrs. Marsh," he said to her, apropos of nothing. "How can I convince you to run my new charity?"

"And what charity would that be?" Diantha said, finding her ethical disapproval of Snaith melting at the edges in light of his considerable physical charm.

"An organization that provides resources and support to women trapped in polygamous marriages," he said. "I thought you'd be a perfect fit."

Diantha was shocked by his directness but refused to let it show. "I wasn't aware you'd established such a charity."

"I haven't yet," said Gilbert. "It would need the right person at the helm to have any chance at success."

Gilbert had a winning smile. He also had a propensity for exploiting his workers more brutally than anyone else in town, which Diantha found far less winning. She also couldn't tell how serious he was about this offer.

"And why do you think I'm that person?" she said.

"I suspect you're not entirely happy in your marriage," he said. "I've also seen your powers of persuasion at dozens of city council meetings, and I know you'd be a force to be reckoned with."

Though propriety dictated she deny his allegations about her marriage, she chose instead to let it pass.

"I'm flattered," she said.

"I meant every word," Gilbert said.

"Did you? What I mean is, are you flirting with me, or do you truly intend to found this organization?"

By this point, they had moved so close together that she could smell the warm, woody aroma of his shaving soap.

Gilbert gave her another of his winning smiles. "I'm a man who puts his money where his mouth is," he said.

Diantha looked into his eyes. "Would it be presumptuous to ask what you'd expect from me in return if I accepted your offer? Beyond my professional duties."

He gave her an exaggerated look of innocence.

"Nothing," he said. "This offer has no strings attached. I merely think you're the right woman for the job."

She didn't dismiss him outright that afternoon but said she'd have to think about it. Diantha had no doubt there were strings attached; the only question was how binding they'd prove to be.

Snaith had written her a handful of letters since that summer afternoon, renewing his offer in each one. Diantha had responded noncommittally, but now Gilbert had grown impatient. His most recent letter—which she kept hidden with the others in a hollowed-out copy of *The Pilgrim's Progress* on her bedroom bookshelf—read as follows:

*Dear Mrs. Marsh,*

*Given the urgency of my new charity mission, I'm afraid I must remind you that I can't wait forever for you to decide. I still very much hope you'll accept my offer, but I need to know soon either way.*

*Affectionately yours,*

*Gilbert Snaith*

Her response had promised a decision by the following Saturday, which was now only a few hours away. Diantha still didn't know what to do. She knew Snaith was serious about the charity, and while it was not exactly the type of work she'd hoped to be doing, it could doubtless serve as a steppingstone to something grander, something on a national scale.

What gave her pause was Gilbert's romantic interest in her. Though they hadn't stated it directly, his letters had strongly implied that if she accepted his offer, she would naturally leave Roger, presumably for the waiting arms of Gilbert himself. And while she *was* attracted to the man, she could never envision making a life with someone who treated the people in his employ worse than animals, who gathered up power to himself like a third-rate despot.

All that said, her gambit with the Dowlands could prove to be a dead end, and even a woman like her did not have an overabundance of options if she decided to leave Roger. Given her quasi-excommunicated state with the mainstream church, she couldn't count on support from them, and though Roger would likely *want* to be generous to her if they divorced, she also knew that his finances had been decimated over the preceding years.

Which left Gilbert Snaith.

She suspected Gilbert would approach her for an answer first thing in the morning. She would have to put him off until after her next meeting with Elder Dowland. She wanted to know exactly which options were available to her before she committed to any of them.

# 8

Six of the richest men in Utah, along with New York railroad tycoon E.H. Harriman, sat in a private room of the Alta Club, the most fashionable after-hours meeting place for Salt Lake's secular elite, debating how to best squelch their nascent labor dispute with the city's disgruntled streetcar drivers.

Mr. Harriman owned the Utah Light & Railway Company, and his presence inspired in the local magnates two concurrent impulses: to curry favor with one of the most powerful men in America and also show Harriman that here in Salt Lake City, they were as ruthlessly ambitious and capable as any East Coast titan of industry.

While two of them argued over which strikebreaking service was more reliable, a third turned to Gilbert Snaith, the Copper King of Utah, and asked if his undercover operative had any insight into the Carmen's Union's internal discussions.

Normally Snaith would have relished an opportunity to talk about the spy he kept on retainer, as none of the other men had such a highly placed informant at their beck and call, but tonight he could hardly be bothered, because tonight Gilbert Snaith was in love!

As he relayed the information he'd received from his spy, his mind and heart were consumed by the lovely, the fetching, the angelic Diantha Marsh.

The first time he saw Diantha was at the governor's Christmas party a few years back. Right away he was taken with her—the darkness of her eyes, the brightness of her smile, the fullness of her lips—and when he learned she was the plural wife of Mormon Apostle Roger S. Marsh, the attraction only deepened.

For years now, Gilbert had been a secret and avid consumer of dime novels featuring his neighbors, the Mormons. Tales from within this subgenre never failed to excite and delight him with their familiar litany of plot points: A beautiful young maiden is ensnared by licentious missionaries and lured to their Salt Lake City stronghold to be married off to an aging elder in the Church. But then, not a moment too soon, a handsome, non-Mormon hero—usually a federal marshal or an intrepid newspaperman—would swoop in and rescue the maiden, fighting off the homicidal polygamists, and then enjoying the fruits of the young woman's quivering, ecstatic gratitude.

That basic plot, unchanging though it was, never failed to entrance Gilbert. He would turn the final page in whatever dime novel he'd most recently acquired—*Old Cap Collier in Salt Lake City, The Bradys Among the Mormon, A Study in Scarlet, California Joe's First Trail*— and fall back in his bed, eyes closed, imagining himself in the role of the brave and worthy rescuer.

The thought of snatching Diantha Marsh away from her lecherous old husband thrilled him to his core.

Gilbert was so preoccupied with a piquant fantasy of a trembling Diantha pressing her grateful body to his that he barely noticed when the meeting with his fellow Salt Lake City millionaires ended. He managed to wish them a semi-coherent farewell and dreamily agreed that swift and violent action would be the best approach if the Carmen's Union called for a strike.

Drifting into the hall behind the other men, Gilbert was imagining his favorite part of the fantasy—the moment when he and

Diantha crossed the threshold of his bedroom after their joyous marriage—when a vaguely familiar voice called his name.

"Snaith!" the voice said again, and Gilbert turned to see Elder Roger S. Marsh in the flesh barreling down the corridor.

Gilbert was no coward, but the unexpected arrival of his beloved's husband catalyzed within him an undeniable panic. Was Marsh armed? Was Gilbert in immediate physical danger? To his shame, he stood rooted in momentary fear, and if the other man had wanted to kill him, he would have had an easy job of it.

Instead, Marsh grabbed him by the arm and shook his hand with alarming vigor. Marsh was smiling, though, and Gilbert quelled his nerves and smiled back.

"Elder Marsh," he said. "So good to see you."

"Please," said Marsh, "call me Roger."

"Of course," said Gilbert, and, deciding to take control of the situation, "I was on my way to the dining room for a late supper. Would you like to join me?"

The eagerness with which Roger accepted filled Gilbert with both uneasiness and contempt. The man was too friendly, which didn't sit well. There was something unmanly about it, something dog-like. Gilbert suspected it might serve as cover for more sinister attitudes and intentions, especially in these current circumstances.

Midway through dinner, then, in the club's main dining room, Gilbert was relieved when Marsh arrived at the purpose of their meeting.

"I have to admit," said Roger, "running into you was no accident."

Of course it wasn't an accident: Mormons tended to steer clear of the Alta Club, as the heavenly powers they possessed held little sway with the club's elite membership.

"Is that right?" said Gilbert carefully.

"Yes," said Roger, "and while this isn't something I'd feel comfortable doing under ordinary circumstances, these are not ordinary circumstances."

Gilbert eyed the exit. The encounter could still turn violent, or at the very least, intensely awkward. "Go on."

"I'm approaching you tonight in your capacity as a potential financier," said Roger.

Gilbert felt his fists unclench beneath the table, unaware that he had clenched them in the first place. Never had he been more relieved to hear that someone wanted money from him.

"I realize you must get similar requests all the time," said Roger.

"I do," said Gilbert. "But for you, I'm all ears. Please, continue." Within him, contempt edged out unease, and he leaned back in the chair.

Roger glanced around the room. "Can I trust you to keep this in the strictest confidence?"

"Of course," said Gilbert.

As Roger spun a fantastical narrative involving prophetic visions, harems of pious women, ecclesiastical maneuverings, and the resonant voice of the Almighty Himself, Gilbert could almost see how he and men like him had managed to build an eccentric yet durable empire for themselves. Rather than acknowledge this, however, Gilbert gave his standard line.

"Let me meet with my financial advisors," Gilbert said, "and we'll see what, if anything, may be feasible right now. Let's plan to discuss this again next Tuesday."

Roger looked distressed by this proposed delay. Of course he did.

"I had hoped it could be sooner," Roger said, "but I understand you're a busy man."

"I appreciate your understanding." Gilbert set his napkin on the table and began to rise. Though no physical blows had been exchanged, he had decisively bested his romantic rival, and he glowed inwardly at the thought of Diantha seeing her husband in a clearly diminished state.

"There's one more thing," said Roger.

Gilbert sat back down, realizing he'd let his guard down

prematurely. Could it be that Roger *had* outmaneuvered him? *Did* he know about the letters to Diantha?

"Tomorrow night," began Roger, and paused, glancing around the dining hall. He lowered his voice. "I'm holding a kind of séance, and I would be honored if you'd attend."

Gilbert almost laughed at this. Roger was completely in the dark, and so, feeling triumphant and more than a little sorry for the other man, Gilbert agreed to attend the séance.

# 9

Ilsa was stepping out of the Wasatch Diner after enjoying a dinner of broiled sweetbreads with peas—two hot meals in one day!—when a massive hand encircled her arm. She looked up to see Adam Wolfe, Roger Marsh's repugnant stooge, looming above her.

"Good evening, Miss Hoffmann," he said, his grip tightening as she tried to pull away.

"It's *Madame* von Hoffmann," she said, "and it would be a much better evening if I could spend it alone."

His youthful face, still spotted with acne, leered down at her.

"I thought you and I could get to know each other a little," Wolfe said, "before the big night."

He was trying to roughen his clear, tenor voice with a growl that was both unconvincing and unsettling.

"That's quite a grip," Ilsa said, keeping her tone light, maybe even a little maternal.

Wolfe squeezed her arm even harder and Ilsa winced.

"I could yell," she said.

"And get the attention of the police?" he said. "No, you don't want to do that."

He looked pleased with this line, an overgrown boy playing the tough guy.

Wolfe was right, though. She didn't, for many reasons, want to involve the police.

"Do you like moving pictures, Miss Hoffmann?" he said.

"Depends on the company," said Ilsa.

"Well, the two of us are going to see a picture together," Wolfe said.

He maneuvered her across the street toward a theater sandwiched between a grocer and a shoe store. Above the entrance a sign read Starshine in sparse lightbulbs. Wolfe purchased two tickets at the booth and shoved Ilsa through the double doors.

They sat down in two hard, wooden chairs at the back of the long, narrow auditorium. On the screen in front, a frightened-looking man raced around a drawing room pursued by a colossal mother-in-law type to scattered laughter from the audience. The theater was about half full—too late for the daytime crowd, too early for the night crowd—and Wolfe and Ilsa had the back few rows to themselves.

For a moment, they sat and watched the picture; the frightened man jumped onto the drawing room davenport, which was subsequently overturned by the rampaging mother-in-law. Wolfe giggled along with the on-screen antics, and Ilsa wondered if he truly had wanted to see a picture with her, a possibility more disturbing somehow than others she'd had in mind.

Then Wolfe reached over and grabbed her wrist, squeezing it in his meaty hand.

"What's the best picture you've ever seen?" he said, and Ilsa thought she could feel the bones of her arm grinding together.

"I don't know. I haven't seen that many," she said.

He squeezed harder, and her hand tingled from the pressure. Onscreen, a harried maid had arrived with, for reasons unclear, a live chicken. The chicken slipped from her grasp and now the drawing room hosted two pursuits—mother-in-law chasing son-in-law, maid chasing chicken—which amplified the chaos and the audience's amusement.

"I saw a picture once," Wolfe said, his face so close she could smell his oddly sweet breath, "about a medium—you know, a woman who talks to spirits—and she gets hired by some good-hearted folks, just simple, honest people who are hoping to make contact with a deceased loved one."

Ilsa's hand was shaking now.

"Well, the medium meets these good-hearted folks," Wolfe continued, "and she decides she's better than them, and rather than hold up her end of the agreement, she tries to skip town."

"This is sounding quite elaborate for a motion picture plot," Ilsa said.

"But her client has a helper," Wolfe went on, ignoring her, "who's been keeping an eye on the train station. Well, he sees this medium trying to leave town, and do you know what he does?"

"Apologizes for saddling her with an impossible job, pays the medium her fee, and sends her on her way," Ilsa said with a bravado she didn't feel.

This drew a blast of hot, sugary breath against her cheek. There was a roar of laughter from the rest of the audience as the mother-in-law crashed into the maid and the son-in-law crashed into the chicken. The mother-in-law swatted the maid with a folded fan; the son-in-law, mistaking the chicken for his hat, placed the bird atop his head.

"No," said Wolfe. "He scares some sense into her, and she turns right around and does the job for the client, as promised. It's a happy ending for everybody."

This attempt at a subtle threat was so clumsy it worried Ilsa. When someone threatened her, she preferred competence. Amateurs like Wolfe were too likely to panic, to let the situation get away from them.

"What do you think of that?" Wolfe said, in his ridiculous growl.

Ilsa appreciated her vulnerability in the moment. She needed to respond with delicacy and precision but couldn't bring herself to do it.

"I think you need to find a different line of work, my friend," she said. "You're an unconvincing tough."

Wolfe seemed thrown by this flippant response, and in that moment of confusion, Ilsa did something really dangerous. She laughed: a soft, contemptuous chuckle.

The effect was immediate and terrible. Wolfe's smooth face flushed a deep red, and before Ilsa could react, he grabbed her pinkie finger and bent it back until it snapped.

Ilsa's involuntary cry of pain was drowned out by a peal of laughter from the crowd—on the screen, a policeman had arrived in the drawing room and was now embracing the chicken—and Ilsa thought she might pass out.

"So tell me, Miss Hoffmann," said Wolfe, his face maroon with rage. "Do I need to worry about you?"

Fighting to stay conscious, she shook her head.

"I need to hear you say it," he said.

Ilsa regretted every single decision that had brought her to this place. "You don't need to worry about me," she said weakly. Her finger throbbed, and she was overcome with nausea.

"Good," Wolfe said. "Now, let's get you back to your hotel. You've got a big day tomorrow."

# 10

Diantha Marsh lived in a cozy Victorian cottage just north of the nearly completed Cathedral of the Madeleine, a Romanesque, sandstone marvel Diantha had enjoyed watching from her parlor window as it had risen from nothing to become the masterpiece it was.

Diantha ostensibly lived alone, as her marriage to Roger postdated the Church's First Manifesto and public renunciation of polygamy, and although church leaders continued performing plural marriages for years, those unions were conducted with discretion. Diantha had been given a house of her own, separate from Roger's first two wives to maintain the pretense that she was a woman alone with no connection to Roger—except that she lived across the street in a house nearly identical to his own.

Diantha had been sitting in the parlor of this home since sunset, watching the towers of the cathedral fade into darkness and mulling the situation with the journalist Francie Bream.

She'd agreed too impulsively to do these interviews, and no matter what she did now, Bream would run a story. Better then, perhaps, to trust the journalist, and give her ample reason to write something helpful. Though a nasty article could forever ruin any ambitions Diantha might have outside of Utah, a fair-minded profile in a major newspaper could do a lot for her.

She heard a key turn in the front door, and then Roger walked in, shoulders slumped, head bowed. He must not have seen her sitting there, because when she said his name, he gasped.

"You startled me," he said, and sat down next to her on the davenport.

"You look like you can barely keep your eyes open," she said.

"I met with Gilbert Snaith," he said.

"Why?" Diantha tamped down her panic at the mention of Snaith's name. She'd thought Roger knew nothing of Gilbert's offer and still hoped he didn't.

"Trying to secure funding for the new church," he said, "which I imagine you don't want to hear about."

Diantha let her body relax against the arm of the davenport. "No," she said. "I don't."

Roger smiled sadly at this. Over the course of the past several years, Diantha had gone from being an avid supporter of plural marriage to an uneasy skeptic, to a committed opponent of the practice, and she and Roger had had many heated arguments throughout this process, none more heated than when he announced he would be breaking away from the mainstream church in order to keep polygamy alive.

She looked at Roger now, wilted after a long day's work, and felt a modicum of appreciation for his acknowledgement of her feelings, small though it was.

"I need to speak to you about something," Diantha said.

Part of the reason she'd been sitting up in the parlor was that she wanted to let Roger in on her thought process. Because he wasn't such a bad man and she respected him, she didn't want to blindside him with whatever decision she made in the coming days.

"All right," he said, resting his hands on his knees.

"I'm thinking of leaving," she said.

He didn't react at first, and she wondered if he'd heard her.

"If you need some time away," said Roger at last, "I completely understand."

"No," she said. "I'm thinking of leaving for good. Of leaving *you*."

This kind of thing was far from unprecedented in polygamous marriages, and Roger nodded as if he'd been expecting it.

"Ah," he said, and turned away.

His eyes filled with tears, though, and Diantha felt a surge of affection for her husband, or not affection exactly, but a kind of tender protectiveness.

She knew many people had long thought of Roger as a bit of a fool, a good-natured bumbler whose heart was in the right place and who could be counted on to fall in line with the dictates of his stronger-willed fellows.

That had certainly been the dynamic when he was an Apostle. He'd been an odd fit in the Quorum, with a genius for neither ideology nor institutional politics, while the rest of his Brethren had possessed one or both in spades. During those years, Diantha wearied of the other men condescendingly describing Roger as being *so like Nathaniel of the New Testament, a man without guile.*

That was part of the reason everyone—church leadership, Diantha and the other wives, maybe even Roger himself—had been so surprised when Roger had refused to stop performing plural marriages, even after the Second Manifesto, when the Church abandoned polygamy in earnest. Roger had finally found an issue on which he was willing to take a stand, and the rest of the Quorum had reacted with their usual condescension. This was naivete plain and simple, or so they had thought.

The threat of excommunication had been meant as a wake-up call rather than an actual intended consequence, something to bring sweet, simple Roger back to his senses. But Roger hadn't backed down, and now, here he was.

But Diantha couldn't forget that while Roger possessed a certain sweetness, he was no innocent. He'd done much harm in his life through the perpetuation of polygamy and was about to do more.

Roger sniffed and wiped his eyes. "When?"

"If I go, I hope to be gone by Thanksgiving," she said.

Roger looked up at a painting of the Savior that hung opposite the davenport. He sighed and turned back to Diantha. "I realize when it comes to the doctrine of plural marriage, we don't see eye to eye," he began.

Diantha didn't have the energy right now to listen to Roger try and change her mind. She was about to stop him when he said something that surprised her.

"I wanted to wait until the new church was on more solid ground before bringing this up," he said, "but before you decide for certain whether to stay or go, I need you to know I've received several strong impressions. The Lord wants you to help guide this church, he wants the Sisters to have more influence in His Kingdom on Earth, and He wants you to lead them.

"And if I've understood you over the years, you object to the Church's practice of plural marriage because you believe it furthers the oppression of women in the world. Well, the newly revealed version of plural marriage doesn't have to do that."

Diantha laughed in both shock and indignation. "It's not that simple," she said. "*Any* system where a man can marry multiple women is inherently flawed."

"What if a woman could marry more than one man?" Roger said.

"Is that a hypothetical or a real possibility?" Really, no form of plural marriage held much appeal for Diantha, but if she really could guide Roger's new church toward more equitable practices, this would certainly be something worth considering.

"I've always believed," Roger said, "and still believe, that plural marriage is the most profound and beautiful doctrine the Lord revealed through the Prophet Joseph. I've also come to know through my years of service that the Lord rarely reveals His doctrine whole cloth to His Prophets. Instead, it is revealed over time. So, while I object to eliminating plural marriage, I do believe there's room for the Lord to reveal modifications to the version taught by Brother Joseph and his successors." He paused, looking at her. "In other words, yes, I believe a system in which a woman might marry multiple men is at least a possibility."

Diantha knew Roger well enough to know he wouldn't lie about something like this. If he was offering her a position of influence in his new church, he really meant it.

"I don't need an answer tonight," Roger said. "I'd like you to make this a matter of prayer, if it's of any interest."

Again, Diantha was so surprised, she didn't know what to say. With a groan of exertion, Roger stood from the davenport, wished her a good night, and left her with much to consider.

# 11

ADAM WOLFE STOOD OVER HIS KITCHEN SINK EATING A slice of bread and cheese. On days like these, he could get so preoccupied that he forgot to eat until arriving home for the night, when his stomach finally protested and his body felt weak. He prided himself on his stamina, and, more generally, on the simplicity of his needs.

With a wood-handled carving knife, he cut himself a second slice of bread from the loaf he'd purchased at Pound's Bakery the day before, and a second slice of cheese from a block of cheddar. They were in his mouth before the last of the first serving had made it down his gullet.

He reminded himself to slow down so he wouldn't choke.

He cut a third serving of bread and cheese, set down the carving knife, and headed for the bedroom, food in both hands. He was going to undress, take a bath, and call it a day. There was more work he could do, but tomorrow was an important day, and he needed to face it well-rested.

In the hallway, he passed the relics of several projects he'd abandoned over the preceding months, while he devoted his time to the needs of this new church: a small pile of boards intended for a kitchen stepstool; a dirt-caked shovel that had prepared the soil for a never-planted vegetable garden; an unhung, framed photograph of Adam and his late wife, Betsy.

Despite the painful memories it held, Adam liked his house, a modest bungalow on Third Avenue, just south of the cemetery. He felt the structure reflected his own solid simplicity.

In the bedroom, he kicked of his shoes and sat in the rocking chair Betsy had insisted on buying as soon as they were married for the purpose of rocking their future babies to sleep. Those babies never came, though, Betsy having developed first a visceral distaste for Adam that precluded any intimacy, and then an incurable case of tuberculosis.

Brushing the crumbs from his fingers, Adam swallowed the last of his bread and cheese. He took off his socks and flexed his toes, and removed his jacket, pants, shirt, and the temple garment he wore in spite of his recent excommunication. He sat back down in the rocking chair, naked and sleepy. He'd rest here for a moment before preparing his bath.

He wondered how effective the note he'd left for Francie Bream would be. Maybe he should have been keeping an eye on the train station this evening, watching to see if she left town.

It had seemed important to check in with Miss Hoffmann instead. He regretted losing his temper with the medium, but on the upside, she was unlikely to cross them now, knowing what he was capable of.

That still left him with the problem of the journalist.

Wolfe closed his eyes, remembering the route through the Hotel Royal to Bream's room. Perhaps he could return in the small hours of the morning, his face masked, his figure obscured by a loose overcoat. He could surprise Bream in her sleep, scooping her out of bed, stopping her mouth with a heavy rag to muffle any sound, and binding her to that severe wooden chair with several lengths of baling twine, the rough fibers pricking the bare skin of her arms.

A faint clatter somewhere in Adam's house jolted him from this vision.

He opened his eyes and called out. "Hello?"

Silence answered him. It was probably nothing, but Adam—thorough by nature—decided to investigate on the way to the bathroom.

"Hello?" he called out again in the living room, the dining room, the kitchen, all to no response.

"Hello?" he said again in the bathroom, but there was clearly no one there.

He opened the tap and began filling the simple bathtub. He watched the water flow and thought about all the wonderful changes Elder Marsh's reformed church would bring to his life: companionship, the opportunity to lead other men, communion with the Divine.

Many of Adam's contemporaries had rejoiced when the old church had finally put a stop to new plural marriages, a reaction which baffled Adam. These people said it was time for the Church to join the modern world and assimilate more fully with the rest of the country.

But for Adam, polygamy represented nothing less than a cure for loneliness, a condition afflicting not just himself, but so many in the world. It seemed absurd that anyone would want to *move past* it.

The bathtub was about half full, and Adam was still hungry.

In the kitchen, he found the loaf of bread and block of cheese right where he'd left them, but the carving knife was not there. Had he put it away without thinking?

As if in response to this silent question, Adam felt a sharp, sudden blow beside his left shoulder blade. He spun around, heard a metallic clatter, and saw the carving knife skitter across the floor, its blade drenched in a dark, viscous substance. It was blood—his blood?

Suddenly, he was in excruciating pain, hurting so, so badly.

As he stooped to pick up the knife—it seemed like the thing to do, though he wasn't sure why—he was having a hard time thinking in a straight line, and then he saw the journalist Francie Bream sprawled on the kitchen floor, watching him in terror.

Had he knocked her over when he'd spun around? He picked up the knife.

"No!" said Francie Bream. "No, no, no, no, no!"

She scuttled backward through the kitchen door, disappearing into the darkness of the dining room.

*Bream* had stuck the knife in him, he suddenly realized. She'd stabbed him. She'd tried to kill him. Adam dropped the knife and sank to his knees. His back was hurting so much. Could he breathe? Was he dying?

Brother Gordon Harris, a faithful Saint and his neighbor across the street, was a doctor. He'd know what to do. Adam just needed to stand up and walk over there. He thought he could if he really focused, and so he did, slowly, carefully, one leg at a time, and then he was back on his feet, a little wobbly, yes, but upright.

Adam felt a warm wetness all down his back and remembered that he was naked. He couldn't go outside without clothes. He'd need to stop by his bedroom first to get dressed. He was dizzy and hot and cold all at once—and scared, more scared with each passing moment. And he was tipping over again, but he caught himself against the counter and gingerly made for the kitchen door.

Bedroom, clothes, Brother Harris. He could do that.

He pushed off the counter and staggered through the kitchen door. Before he could celebrate this small victory, though, something hard and metallic and smelling of earth caught him full in the face and sent him sprawling onto his back.

He'd forgotten about the journalist. How could he have forgotten her? What was—

His self-reproach gave way to horror as the sharp point of a shovel came straight for his face, with Francie Bream wrapped around the long handle, bearing down with all her weight.

# 12

FRANCIE BREAM LEANED AGAINST THE DINING ROOM wall, her forehead damp with perspiration and her breathing fast and ragged. After the wet sounds of a skull being crushed, the room was frighteningly quiet.

The shovel lay at her feet, its blade smeared with clumps of hair and gore.

What she'd done felt unreal, although she knew she'd done it: Adam Wolfe was dead now. She stole a look at the jellied mess that had been his head, the bone fragments, the remains of a jaw spotted with acne that would never clear up, the bits of the brain that had once plotted her destruction.

Francie trembled with revulsion, both at the gory sight and at the fact that she'd been the one to create it. By the time she felt the vomit rising in her throat, it was too late to do anything but turn aside so the contents of her stomach landed not on Wolfe's naked, bloody corpse, but on the edge of the dining room rug. She wasn't sure why such a courtesy—if that's what it was—mattered at this point, and suspected it was more for her own sake than out of respect for the dead.

She hadn't come here tonight intending to kill him but given the opportunity to go back and face the same decision again, Francie felt nearly certain she would still murder Adam Wolfe.

It was important to call this what it was—murder—because no matter how necessary the act may have been, Francie couldn't afford to be anything but clear-headed about the moral implications of her actions. She'd done what she'd done and denying it would only confuse the ethics at play and impede her ability to navigate the treacherous waters of her current situation with integrity.

At the moment, she had more practical matters to attend to. She needed to keep Wolfe's murder secret until the séance tomorrow night, and the greatest obstacle would be Marsh, who no doubt expected his loyal aide at his side for tomorrow's crucial events. She could come up with a solution for this, if she had a bit of time to think.

As far as Wolfe's body, she could probably leave it right where it was; her surveillance during the previous weeks suggested that nobody ever came over to Adam Wolfe's house except for Adam Wolfe himself and, very rarely, Roger Marsh.

Still, it wouldn't hurt to, say, drag the corpse into the coal cellar on the off chance someone did stop by.

She moved all the dining room furniture off the area rug and then, grabbing it at one end, pulled as hard as she could. She'd hoped the rug would function as a sort of sled to ferry Wolfe's enormous body across the wood floor, but the rug—and Wolfe's body—wouldn't budge.

She leaned again against the wall to catch her breath.

She wondered how close Wolfe had come to discovering her secret. The threat he'd left for her seemed more like a clumsy swipe than a precise, knowing attack. She'd come here tonight looking for some indication of how much he knew, but she'd lingered too long at his writing desk, examining a troubling array of documents.

She'd heard the front door open and had then spent what had

felt like an eternity playing the world's least amusing game of hide-and-seek.

And then, of course, she'd killed him.

Francie looked again at his immovable body lying in the center of the bare area rug. Seeing his pale form like that, she felt remorse and horror and a kind of generalized numbness. She would have to take her chances and leave him in the middle of the dining room.

Her head was buzzing, and she realized she had sat down on the floor. With shaky legs, Francie got to her feet, turned her back on the body, and once again made for Wolfe's writing desk.

# 13

Despite the comfort of her hotel bed, Madame Ilsa slept uneasily. She'd taken some aspirin and splinted her broken finger upon returning from the Starshine—unable to afford, for many reasons, a doctor's visit. Her pinkie throbbed terribly and kept her in an unpleasant twilight state between wakefulness and sleep.

Her dreams, which seeped into her nocturnal reality, were all of bloody, vengeful Billy Lovelace, her ex-partner. He pursued her through tenements and fields and shops and deserts, sometimes crawling, sometimes staggering, sometimes running with an uncanny, jerking motion, his broken limbs flailing as they propelled his body forward.

Again and again and again, Billy's gruesome corpse caught up with her, his breath hot and putrid as he whispered, *Coward, coward.*

"I know," Ilsa would cry, pushing his body, rank with the stench of death, away.

But Billy held fast despite the rot that ate his limbs, and Ilsa screamed, waking herself up just enough to know she was dreaming, and then she'd fall back asleep only to be pursued by Billy anew.

# 14

And then, as if dreamed into existence, Billy Lovelace stepped off an early morning train at Salt Lake City's nearly completed Union Station, not dead or soaked in blood but an arresting sight all the same, his face possessing a cruel beauty enhanced by a network of scars, and if Madame Ilsa had been able to peer into her old partner's mind in that moment, her worst fears would have been confirmed, as Billy was in town for one reason and one reason alone: to seek justice for what Ilsa had done to him.

# 15

The life of a man with many wives is a complicated one, not least in terms of how he divides his time and his person among multiple spouses. From such negotiations in the domestic life of Roger Marsh, a whole slew of habits had developed and, over the years, taken on the weight of ritual.

One of these rituals was daily breakfast with his first two wives.

As per tradition, then, Roger found himself this Saturday morning at the table of the home shared by Adeline and Elizabeth Marsh. It was difficult for Roger not to define the women in contrast to each other: Adeline was tall, dark-haired (though graying now), quiet, and intense, where Elizabeth was short, blonde, talkative, and easygoing. He'd married Elizabeth only a year after marrying Adeline—decades ago now—and so they'd existed as a pair for nearly as long as he'd known them.

On the menu for this morning's breakfast were oatmeal with dates, scrambled eggs, and toast.

"Elizabeth and I enjoyed the rain yesterday," Adeline said.

Roger sat on one side of the table; his wives sat next to each other on the other side. "Yes, it was a refreshing storm," he said, absentmindedly filling his bowl with oatmeal.

"You have an eyelash," Elizabeth said to Adeline, and brushed the other woman's cheek.

"Thank you, dear," said Adeline.

Roger took a bite of oatmeal. Doubts he'd kept at bay for months had managed to breach his defenses, and he had awoken this morning ill at ease, profoundly uncertain about the viability and the provenance of his current endeavor.

He decided to stop by Adam Wolfe's house after breakfast, though they hadn't planned to meet today until noon. Adam had his shortcomings, among them a hot temper and a violent imagination, but he also had unwavering confidence in the rightness of the mission the Lord had entrusted to Roger, a confidence Roger badly needed to lean on right now.

"I wonder if it will rain again tonight," he said, but his wives didn't hear him. They were lost in a conversation about a woman who'd given birth on a train outside of Ogden. Adeline's hand rested on Elizabeth's as she spoke.

This had been the way with Adeline and Elizabeth for many years now; their relationship with each other seemed to matter more than their relationship with Roger. The women's bond had only been strengthened during Roger's six-month stint in Sugar House Prison for unlawful cohabitation back in the late eighties.

Ever since, they were especially content together and rarely seen apart. They even shared a bedroom, so strong was their friendship, and though he felt excluded at times, Roger supposed it was better that his wives enjoyed each other's company than to squabble and bicker from dawn to dusk as some plural wives were rumored to do.

He sprinkled another spoonful of sugar into his oatmeal and mixed it in. He took a bite and would prefer it sweeter still, but Adeline and Elizabeth were looking at him now, their conversation having apparently run its course, and Roger felt self-conscious about dipping into the sugar bowl again.

"The séance is tonight," he said. "I'm not sure if you're planning on coming."

Adeline shook her head.

"My back," she said simply. "I'm sure you understand."

"You could bring a cushion to sit on," he said and took another bite of his oatmeal.

"I'd rather not," Adeline said.

She rose from the table to retrieve a bottle of milk from the counter, trailing her fingers along Elizabeth's shoulders as she did so.

"Elizabeth?" Roger said hopefully.

"No," she said. "I'd rather stay here with Adeline."

"You're a very generous friend to her," he said.

"It's not generosity," said Elizabeth, looking at Adeline with unmistakable affection.

Roger smiled at Elizabeth's graciousness; Adeline took a long drink of milk.

"In any event," said Roger, "I'll take comfort in knowing you'll both be with me in spirit."

"You're always in our prayers," said Adeline.

She inclined her body toward Elizabeth, and Roger could tell his wives were about to embark on another private conversation.

"You know," he said, before they could abandon him again, "I was visited the other night by a revelation from the Lord."

Adeline nodded politely at this information.

"That's wonderful, Roger," said Elizabeth, buttering a slice of toast.

"A vision in dream form," he said, "in which I stood at the side of a dirt road. From a distance something approached, and as it neared, I saw that it was the Prophet Joseph Smith riding in a gilt coach pulled by twelve magnificent stallions. As he passed me, he removed his coat from around his shoulders and threw it, telling me to wear it in honor and good faith. And then the carriage was gone, and the vision ended."

"Hmm," Adeline said, taking Elizabeth's hand and gently squeezing it.

Roger paused. He'd been hoping for a big reaction, but his

wives seemed more absorbed by their breakfast than by the vision he'd just imparted.

"Yes," Roger continued. "It brought to my mind the story of the Prophet Elijah passing his sacred mantle to his disciple Elisha from a chariot of fire."

"Yes, I can see how you might make that connection," Elizabeth said mildly as she passed the plate of toast to Adeline. "Did you hear the Jorgensens got a new player piano last weekend?"

Though Adeline and Elizabeth had uttered not a word of criticism or discontent since his excommunication, Roger preferred Diantha's engaged opposition to this bland indifference.

"No," he said, and began shoveling oatmeal into his mouth with haste. This day was getting off to an inauspicious start. He needed some encouragement. He needed to talk with Adam Wolfe.

# 16

Between the nightmares, the throbbing pain of her broken finger, and the general impossibilities of the job before her, Madame Ilsa had only managed to sleep for a few, restless hours. Even so, she had woken up this morning with a clear idea of what she needed to do.

Her most pressing need was to find an assistant for the Summoning tonight. Visibly conjuring the spirit of Joseph Smith by herself would be impossible. An assistant, though, needed to be a person she trusted, a person with considerable experience dissembling in a professional context; someone who could be relied on to keep a cool head if the situation went awry.

Unfortunately, Ilsa trusted nobody in this town. The day before, this fact had made finding an accomplice seem impossible. But today she was willing to work with what she had. She would settle for two out of the three requirements and find a cool-headed dissembler. Thankfully, she already had someone in mind.

There were other challenges, of course: Ilsa knew next to nothing about the Mormons, and her clients expected a moving, speaking apparition intimately familiar with Mormon culture and history.

Her broken finger would also hinder many of the little filigrees she employed to make her Summonings memorable.

On the topic of her broken finger, she would also like to steer clear of Adam Wolfe today, as she didn't know whether he'd satisfied his appetite for violence last night, or if he still yearned to do her harm.

But she would take these challenges as they came.

Crossing the hotel room, her bare feet luxuriating against the carpeted floor, Madame Ilsa opened the larger of her two trunks to reveal a staggering jumble of curiosities: a brass trumpet, several wigs, a cardboard cutout of the face of Karl the Great, two lace tablecloths, a prop pistol loaded with blanks, fishing line, a set of spirit slates, a multitude of candles, a dark muslin shroud, several sets of historical clothing, plumber's putty, butcher paper, nails, screws, tacks, an electric lantern, a wax apple, and more.

Conducting a quick inventory of this eccentric hodgepodge, she found that, equipment-wise, she had everything she needed to succeed.

As she shaved and dressed, her nervous cheer began to bubble over. It was possible, though unlikely, that she could walk away from this job with a substantial sum of money, enough to give her breathing room to figure out how to change her current life trajectory.

On the way out the door, she checked her reflection in the mirror and, finding her face suitably enigmatic, set out to recruit Francie Bream to assist her with the Summoning.

# 17

Like most American cities of any significance, Salt Lake was as segregated as it was diverse, Japantown separate from the predominantly white Avenues neighborhood, which was separate from Chinatown, which was separate from Greektown, which was separate from the predominantly Black Franklin Avenue. On this particular Saturday morning, Greektown bustled with men leaving for their shifts on railroad crews, stopping by coffee shops to pick up the local Greek newspaper, and sitting to reminisce about home with their compatriots on the steps of the tenement buildings that had sprouted up south of the railroad depot over the past few years.

Billy Lovelace ascended a rickety staircase attached as an afterthought, it seemed, to one such tenement building, and he felt the cautious eyes of the neighborhood upon him. He tipped his hat to an older woman in a dusty wooden chair at the base of the staircase.

She had to be the landlady, as the neighborhood was almost exclusively populated by men, most lured from their homeland by exploitative labor agents telling tales of the comfort and easy riches in America.

The landlady looked away as Billy acknowledged her, either

made bashful by his electric presence or hoping to absolve herself of whatever mischief he was about to perpetrate.

Already, Billy had put in an hour's work finding this place, gladhanding suspicious locals for information about the whereabouts of Lars Arnasson, an old friend from vaudeville, he told them, which was the God's honest truth but still rang false somehow when Billy said it out loud.

He'd already chased a few red herrings and hoped this current lead was genuine.

He knocked on the door.

"Who's there?" asked someone from inside.

Billy smiled, recognizing the pugnacious tone of his old friend's voice. "Is that Lars Arnasson?"

"It may be," said Lars. "Who wants to know?"

Billy could picture him in there, clutching some makeshift weapon against the threats he had always seen lurking in any novel situation. "Lars, it's me," he said. "It's Billy Lovelace."

A heavy pause from inside the room.

"The hell it is," Lars said eventually. "Billy Lovelace is dead."

Billy was not displeased to hear that some people, apparently, believed him dead. Still, he needed to set his friend straight.

"Well, no, I'm not," said Billy.

The landlady watched from down below while paring her nails with a straight razor. Billy gave her a warm smile and a friendly wave, and she again looked away.

"Billy Lovelace is dead," Lars repeated. "Killed in Seattle about a year ago. Heard it from Chick Diaz, and he would know."

"And what I'm saying is that I am not dead," said Billy, "for I have risen."

"What?" said Lars.

"Come on," said Billy. "Just open the door."

Shortly, the door opened about six inches to reveal Lars Arnasson, big and blonde and shifty as ever, holding some kind of short-handled sledgehammer. When he saw Billy, he set it down and swung the door open wide.

"It is you," he said, looking more confused than pleased.

"I know," said Billy. "Now invite me in so we can talk."

It was a single room, bed against one wall and table against another, but at least Lars seemed to have the place to himself.

"You look terrible," said Lars after they'd sat down at the small, wooden table.

"Thank you, Lars," said Billy. "That really warms my heart."

"You do, though," said Lars. "What happened?"

Billy ran a hand down his scarred face and, glancing around the room, realized Lars was unlikely to offer him a cup of coffee or anything like it, as the room had no kitchen, or even a hot plate. "It's like Chick Diaz told you," he said. "I ran into some trouble in Seattle."

"And?" said Lars.

"And now here I am," said Billy. "And I need a favor."

Lars laughed without mirth. "Of course you need a favor," he said. "I remember when we were on vaudeville. You'd only give me the time of day when you needed something. 'How's my favorite baritone?' you'd say, and ask me for two bits, or tell me I needed to lie to some girl who'd be coming backstage after the show, or once, and this is not an exaggeration, you asked me for the literal shirt off my back right before you went on stage. And you never returned it!"

Billy watched a familiar flush of anger spread across his face.

"And the rest of the time, when you didn't need something from me," Lars said, "you acted like I didn't exist." He scoffed loudly then stared meaningfully at Billy.

"Can you help me or not?" Billy said, drawing a toothpick from his pocket and propping it on his lower lip.

Lars rose from his chair to pace the tiny room like a petulant tiger.

"Well?" Billy said after a minute.

"You still doing detective work?" Lars said.

"Yeah," said Billy.

"I might have a job for you."

Billy took a deep breath. "I take it you're about to suggest some kind of quid pro quo."

"Yep," said Lars.

"The favor I need is not worth that much," Billy said.

"We could pay," said Lars, as inept a negotiator as ever.

"We?" said Billy.

Lars sat back down at the table. "I'm with the IWW, Local 67," he said proudly.

"Industrial Workers of the World?" Billy said with a laugh. "You're a Wobbly?"

"Tell me your favor," Lars said, scowling now.

Billy could see no downside to showing his hand.

"I'm looking for a Spiritualist," Billy said. "Woman by the name of Madame Ilsa von Hoffmann. You might have met her on vaudeville. Before the medium act she was one of the Crimson Swans. Went by Mabel Fairfax."

Lars thought for a moment.

"Yeah, I think I remember her," he said. "She's supposed to be in Salt Lake?"

"That's the idea," said Billy.

Lars thought some more. "I can ask around," he said. "I know people who would know."

"It's urgent," said Billy.

"All right." Lars rose from the table and opened the door, gesturing for Billy to leave. "Be back here in an hour," he said, "and I'll have your information for you. If she's here in town, I can find out where and why."

Billy walked to the open door. He put on his hat. "And?"

"And, what?"

"What will I be doing in return for Local 67?" said Billy.

"You'll find out in an hour," said Lars.

# 18

THE AFTERNOON BEFORE, THE INTERVIEWS WITH Francie Bream had seemed so vital, but this morning Diantha Marsh could barely summon the interest to comprehend the journalist's questions. In fact, she could see from Bream's face that she'd yet again become distracted and had missed another question entirely.

"I'm so sorry," Diantha said. "Could you please repeat that?"

If Bream was annoyed, she hid it well. "Of course. What I said was, as I understand it, women in Utah gained the right to vote before many other women in the country."

"That's correct," said Diantha.

They sat in Diantha's parlor, where Roger had made his unexpected offer the previous evening. If she accepted a position of authority in the new church, Diantha wondered if she'd be able to steer the organization away from polygamy with time, and if that *were* possible, would the initial harm done to the women in new polygamous marriages be worth the eventual progress?

"Mrs. Marsh?" said Bream, and Diantha realized she'd yet again turned her attention away from the journalist.

Rather than ask Bream to repeat herself a third time, Diantha posed a question of her own regarding the ethics of her potential involvement with Roger's church. "Do you think, Miss Bream," she began, "someone could ever be justified in harming another person, if the harm was unavoidable in the pursuit of a larger good?"

To Diantha's surprise, Bream appeared disturbed by the question. Color drained from her face, and her jaw moved soundlessly up and down like a wind-up toy.

"Why are you asking me that?" Francie said after a moment.

Diantha couldn't imagine how she could have elicited such a shaken reaction from the hard-nosed journalist. "Why does the question upset you?" she asked in return.

But Bream had already composed herself, reassuming the mien of the unflappable journalist, though a remnant of unease lingered in her eyes. "I told you yesterday, Mrs. Marsh, that for these interviews to succeed, I need you to trust me. So far this morning, you've not only ignored my questions but tried to distract me with questions of your own," said Bream. "I need a decision from you right now. Are you ready to trust me and participate fully? And do keep in mind that if the answer is no, I will walk away immediately."

Today, these threats inspired only irritation in Diantha. Too many people were asking too much of her in too short a span of time. "You're trying to pressure me," she said. "And I don't like that."

Bream's demeanor turned chilly. "I'm sorry you feel that way," she said, "but I'm working under a very real deadline, and I don't have time to talk to someone who's only willing to provide fluff."

Diantha looked Bream hard in the eye. "What I've given you isn't fluff," she said, "but if you're not satisfied with these interviews, please do walk away."

Bream maintained her steely composure, though, again, something in her eyes suggested a deep unease. After several moments of tense silence, her face softened, and she gave a conciliatory bow of the head. "It seems you've called my bluff," she said.

"Yes," said Diantha. "I have."

Francie glanced down at her notepad and flipped through a few pages before looking back up at Diantha. "Perhaps we might discuss for a few minutes your husband's recent excommunication from Mormonism," she said.

"Yes, we may." Diantha settled back in her chair, wondering what could be inspiring such a haunted look in the depths of the journalist's eyes.

# 19

A PERSON COULD BE FORGIVEN FOR THINKING THAT Madame Ilsa's line of work had equipped her to deal with an angry ghost. Sadly for Ilsa, this was not the case. The spirits she communed with were, to put it bluntly, fake, and while she did work extensively with the recently bereaved, adjacency to mourning had not prepared her to confront her own powerful and complex grief over the death of Billy Lovelace.

Ilsa knew Billy was dead—she had watched him die—and yet, in every new city she visited, she saw his face everywhere. This morning in Salt Lake, for instance, she'd caught several glimpses of him, and each time, her stomach jolted with fear until, on second glance, Billy's face resolved into the face of a stranger: a streetcar conductor, a delivery boy, a greengrocer, or a bank clerk.

She was supposed to be searching for Francie Bream to recruit her as an accomplice in tonight's Summoning, but so far, the search had comprised nothing more than a distracted wandering of the streets of downtown Salt Lake where pseudo-Billys confronted her like vengeful specters everywhere she turned.

On the bright side, she hadn't seen that thug Adam Wolfe anywhere, but it was probably only a matter of time before he brutishly reinserted himself into her life.

In terms of finding Francie, Ilsa wondered if she might have more success if she just stayed put somewhere, say, the Wasatch Diner, where a midmorning coffee would revive her flagging spirits.

She found the diner fuller than expected and remembered it was Saturday. Still, the table she'd already come to think of as her own was still open. She sat down and, while sipping a passable cup of coffee, kept one eye on the door.

Many times, in her meetings with grieving widows and mourning parents, she'd heard well-intentioned acquaintances of the bereaved offer reassurances that time would one day heal their sorrow. While Ilsa had always vicariously resented the glibness of that truism, now she resented it directly. What vile nonsense! Time, if anything, had *heightened* her feelings about Billy Lovelace's death: sorrow, anger, and fear, but most of all, guilt over her role in eradicating from this life a man she'd known since she was not much more than a girl.

Ilsa had first met Billy when he was still a mediocre tenor on the small-time vaudeville circuit and she was still Mabel Fairfax, the ingénue half of Lammermoor and Fairfax.

At that time, it would have been a stretch to call them acquaintances; they were fellow professionals who politely encountered one another backstage and at the uniformly wretched dining establishments that served the vaudeville crowd. Given his unremarkable singing voice, Billy might have completely blurred into the chaotic background of performers in Ilsa's orbit, but his face possessed a kind of beauty that demanded careful consideration, as if the mind couldn't believe at first glance another human could be so stunning and needed to confirm again and again that, yes, this specimen was, aesthetically speaking, truly outstanding.

In a performance-based milieu like vaudeville, the sheer watchability of Billy's face guaranteed him both steady work and the resentment of his more talented but less beautiful colleagues. Resentment and, also, it must be noted, grudging adoration.

Mabel treasured her brief and sporadic interactions with Billy for the chance they gave to contemplate his face up close and luxuriate in the resulting inner glow. That glow was enough for Mabel, until the night when Billy kissed her long and hot and hard at the edge of a cornfield somewhere in Iowa. It was thrilling, like seeing the face of God, and it was also, Mabel had to remind herself, ultimately meaningless, as Billy had kissed many, many people without allowing those moments of ardor to blossom into something larger. And indeed, after that heady night, Billy was as polite to Mabel as ever, without any hint that their heady (to Mabel) rendezvous in the cornfield had ever happened.

Mabel was heartbroken for a few weeks, though she mentioned nothing of the incident to Lucy or the other Crimson Swans. Eventually, of course, she recovered, young, resilient thing that she was, and with time, it no longer pained her seeing Billy's face and knowing he would never be hers.

About a year after her rural tryst with Billy, Mabel attended her first séance. Up to this point, she had actively avoided the Spiritualist scene, not from lack of interest but because she knew she'd be disappointed by what she found. You see, Mabel had long felt an affinity with the dead, or maybe with death itself.

Though she *had* seen the ghost of a recently deceased neighbor when she was a child (his horse-trampled body glowing faintly as it slid through the air of Mabel's bedroom) she was not truly able to communicate with the dead. All the same, she'd always been compelled by the *trappings* of death: the solemn fellowship of graveyards, the drama of mourning wear, the pomp of funerals. Each created for Mabel an unexpectedly home-like atmosphere, an atmosphere she was loath to have perverted by some fraudulent spirit medium.

But then one weekend, another Crimson Swan, Alexandria Lake, invited her to a séance her open-minded aunt would be hosting, and curiosity finally got the better of Mabel.

This particular séance was held in Aunt Stella's slightly derelict manse in downtown Albany, with about a dozen people in attendance. Conducting the séance were two middle-aged sisters swathed in black who'd been tasked by Aunt Stella with contacting her long-dead husband regarding a missing pair of mother-of-pearl opera glasses.

Witnessing the sister's funereal magnetism, Mabel felt a grudging respect that turned to outright admiration as the séance progressed. She especially admired their deft use of a spirit typewriter through which Aunt Stella's dead husband informed the gathering that the glasses lay concealed within a disused stockpot on a high kitchen shelf.

A skeptical relative went to verify this information and returned shortly after with the opera glasses in hand and a look of astonishment on her face.

While Mabel still didn't believe the sisters had actually communicated with Aunt Stella's dead husband, what they *had* done was even more impressive. The mediums' weaving together of artifice and a genuine-seeming respect for the power of death spoke to something vital at the core of her being.

She left the séance in a daze, and by month's end, she'd quit her act with Lucy Lammermoor, re-christened herself Madame Ilsa von Hoffmann, and begun to develop an arsenal of techniques for communicating with the dead. Ilsa had a knack for cultivating intimacy, even with a large audience, and her stagecraft—sleight of hand, hidden mirrors, levitation—was impeccable. She also had a preternatural ability to speak the words of the spirits she channeled in a way that haunted listeners long after the séance had ended.

Within a few years, Madame Ilsa had developed the kind of reputation that meant lucrative private séances, and bigger and better lecture hall performances. At the time, Ilsa felt certain this trajectory could only continue, carrying her higher and higher, into the upper atmosphere of celebrity and power.

Unfortunately, that brief period of renown proved to be the summit of her professional success rather than its base. In retrospect, it was hard for Ilsa to put her finger on what exactly had precipitated her slow decline, but she'd lost the pulse of the moment, and by the time she realized it, she'd already descended to the grubby troughs of her profession.

During her time as a medium, Ilsa hadn't thought much about Billy Lovelace; in fact, she'd practically forgotten about him, but when she ran into him one day in 1905 (or maybe it was 1906) at a mortuary in Topeka, everything came rushing back.

She had been sitting in the lobby, waiting to speak to the mortician, when Billy emerged from the back offices, did a double take, and stopped to look at her.

The intervening time had only heightened Billy's stunning looks, to the extent that they literally took Ilsa's breath away. Billy seemed to sense this. He smiled and sat next to her, and Ilsa had to remind herself to exhale, then inhale, until her lungs resumed their automatic function.

"Mabel," he said, taking her by the hand. "It's good to see you."

"I go by Madame Ilsa now," she said, a tingle running up her arm from his gentle grip.

"I know," he said. "I saw an article about you in the newspaper a few years back, talking about what a success you'd become, and I said to myself, *That's Mabel Fairfax. Good for her.*"

The article had probably been written at the zenith of her career, now firmly in the past. Now she was reduced to bribing morticians for names of relatives with recently deceased loved ones, anyone who might be susceptible to her sales pitch.

"That's kind of you, Billy," Ilsa said. "What about you? Are you still on vaudeville?"

"It may come as a surprise to you," said Billy, with a smile that could melt gold, "but my singing career never panned out."

"I find that hard to believe," said Ilsa.

"Yes, well, I discovered my real talents lie elsewhere," he said. "These days, I suppose I'm what you might call a detective."

"With the police?" Ilsa couldn't square the Billy she'd known with a career in law enforcement.

"Definitely not," he said. "Not with the Pinkertons, either, or any other agency. I'm freelance. I like to describe myself as a Pinkerton man for folks who would never hire a Pinkerton man. Mostly, I look for people who are lost or track down hard-to-find information. Things like that."

"Honest work?" she said.

"Depends on the client," he said. "If they're poor or really need help, I'll treat them right, but if they're rich or rotten or both, I'm not above creating problems that need solving and then charging handsomely to make those problems go away."

"Like Robin Hood," she said.

"I wouldn't go that far," he said.

"I bet you're good," she said. "People always want you to like them. That must help."

"Doesn't hurt," said Billy. "I have to ask, because it's my job to be suspicious: Why are you trying to butter me up?"

Ilsa knew she might regret what came next, but she might equally regret letting the opportunity get away.

"I have a business proposition for you," she said.

Billy cocked his head, apprising her afresh. "Buy me dinner," he said, "and we can talk."

# 20

STEPPING OUT THE FRONT DOOR OF THE HOUSE HE shared with Elizabeth and Adeline, stomach roiling from too much breakfast and too many worries, Roger Marsh was stopped short by the sight of an envelope half tucked under the welcome mat. With a groan of exertion, he bent over and picked it up. He could see now it was addressed to him in Adam Wolfe's familiar hand.

The very sight of this envelope concerned Roger. It was more typical of Adam to stop by and talk in person when he had something on his mind. In fact, Roger wasn't sure Adam had *ever* left a written message like this one.

He tore it open and, leaning against the railing of the front porch, read the enclosed note:

*DEAR ROGER,*

*I received word from Karl Gustafsson that he's had a change of heart. Accordingly, I'm leaving on the five-a.m. train to Boise to secure his donation before his mind changes again. I'll wire you as soon as I have more news.*

*I'm sorry and disappointed that I'll miss tonight's momentous event, but I'm confident you have all well in hand.*

*Yours, &c.,*

*Adam*

ROGER DIDN'T LIKE THIS, didn't like this at all, though the news was ostensibly good. Karl Gustafsson was a distant relative who had made a small fortune in health foods. Earlier that year, Roger and Adam had spent a week in Boise trying to get Karl to donate to their fledgling religion, leaning heavily on his resentment of the mainstream Mormon Church, which had excommunicated him several years earlier for refusing to give them a discounted price on the imported fabrics he had trafficked in at the time.

They'd come close to convincing him, but in the end, Karl had gotten cold feet and concluded he'd rather save the money than spend it on a project that would spite his longstanding institutional nemesis.

"I've decided," he told the disappointed Roger and Adam, "the best revenge is a life well lived," and then he'd sent them on their way.

In the ensuing months, no significant financial backing had been secured for their enterprise, and right now, they badly needed money. This news about Gustafsson's change of heart should have thrilled Roger, but instead he felt acutely ill at ease.

It was true, as Adam had written in his note, that Roger *did* have things well in hand, which was to say, he knew God was fully behind their endeavors, although some unresolved details—for instance, how he would pay that medium they'd hired—worried Roger more than others.

But he wouldn't dwell on these worries, relying instead on the simple yet profound faith that had carried him this far in life.

If anything, Adam's absence and the manifold additional difficulties Roger faced today would magnify the Lord's role in the restoration of His True Church. This Roger believed, and it would fortify him to do what needed to be done.

He looked down again at the note Adam had left. Something about the message still bothered him. He would stop by Adam's house to ensure that nothing was amiss.

# 21

Given his line of work, Billy Lovelace hated nicknames. Sometimes they meant exactly what they suggested, sometimes the opposite, and sometimes nothing at all. For instance, a woman nicknamed Sweet Sally may have earned the name through a pleasant disposition, or just as plausibly, an exceptionally *un*pleasant one, or equally plausible still, by some triviality like dropping a jar of honey in the kitchen when she was twelve.

Billy often needed to evaluate a person in a short amount of time, and a nickname only muddied the water, suggesting insight while often offering none.

Take the case of Whiskey Joe Barnes, across from whom Billy was now sitting at the tiny wooden table in Lars Arnasson's tenement room. How had the famed (some might say notorious) labor organizer (one of the closest friends of Big Bill Haywood, so named because he was, in fact, a very large man) earned the alcoholic appellation? Was he a heavy drinker? A teetotaler? Neither? It was all quite frustrating.

On the other hand, much could be learned about a person by how they responded to a direct inquiry about a nickname.

"It's nice to meet you," Billy said after Lars introduced them. "Why the 'Whiskey'?"

Though only five or six years older than Billy, Whiskey Joe's skin was wind- and sun-weathered, and his hands were rough. He wasn't an especially big man physically, but he knew how to take up space.

Also, he'd scowled at the question about his nickname, which told Billy something.

"Because I never touch the stuff," Barnes said. "Lars tells me you're a detective."

"That's right," said Billy, not displeased by the man's directness.

Having breakfasted at a crummy little diner nearby, Billy had returned to Lars's apartment after the prescribed hour to receive the joyous news that, yes, Madame Ilsa was in town and staying at the Armitage Hotel at the expense of one Roger Marsh, who'd apparently hired her to conduct a séance in connection with some crackpot religious scheme. But then Whiskey Joe had arrived, and Billy had remembered, much to his chagrin, the deal he'd made with Lars.

"Are you any good at what you do?" Whiskey Joe asked.

"Yes," said Billy, uninterested in wasting the energy trying to convince Barnes one way or the other.

Whiskey Joe turned to Lars. "Is he?"

Lars hesitated.

"In my experience, Billy Lovelace is a real bastard," he responded, "but I believe he's very good at what he does."

"I don't care if a man is a bastard, or a son of a bitch, or even a shit-heel," said Whiskey Joe, addressing Billy now, "as long as he's on the side of the working man. Are you on the side of the working man, Mr. Lovelace?"

"I suppose so," Billy said.

"I would have appreciated more enthusiasm," said Whiskey Joe, "but I admire honesty in a man. Has Lars explained the situation we find ourselves in?"

"No," said Billy. "Have I told you my rates?"

"No," said Whiskey Joe.

Billy told them his rates, and Lars made a plosive *pah* sound with his lips.

"If that's going to be a problem," Billy said, "we can end this conversation right now."

"This is for a good cause," said Lars.

Billy stood from the table.

"No, no," said Whiskey Joe, waving for him to sit down. "A fair day's wage for a fair day's work. We'll pay the full rate."

"All right," said Billy, sitting back down. "Tell me what I can do for you."

Lars shook his head in disgust.

"The information we're about give you doesn't leave the room," said Whiskey Joe, all business now. "Do you understand?"

"I take my clients' privacy very seriously," said Billy, shifting more fully into his own professional persona. "Your secrets are safe with me."

Whiskey Joe considered him for a moment and then gave a nod of permission to Lars.

"All right," Lars began.

He explained that it started nine days ago at a Thursday night meeting at the Federation of Labor Building. They were meant to speak with the heads of the Carmen's Union about their dispute with E.H. Harriman, but before the meeting began, Gus Helton, a fellow member of IWW Local 67, rushed in and pulled Lars to the side.

Gus, who looked terrified, said that they needed to cancel their meeting: a spy was in their midst. As head of security, Lars was the right person to bring this matter to, and in Lars's experience, Gus Helton was as reliable and level-headed as anyone. But spy hunting was a messy, dangerous business.

Gus's information sounded solid, though. He had a couple of Wobbly pals in Denver who ran security for their local chapter, and they'd mailed him evidence of a highly placed turncoat in Local 67 hired by Gilbert Snaith, Utah's own Copper King.

Alarmed, Lars asked to see this evidence, and that's when Gus turned cagey. He made some vague excuses and promised to show Lars the documents he'd received as soon as he could. Then he left the meeting, and Lars hadn't seen him since.

His account complete, Lars drew a hand down his face.

"A spy hunt can tear an organization apart," he said. "And, you know, even though I thought I could trust Gus Helton, I'm starting to suspect that he's been bought, that the spy tip is a red herring meant to throw us into a disarray, but now Gus is having second thoughts about betraying us."

Whiskey Joe shook his head. "We don't want to waste our time chasing some half-assed hunch," he said, "but I suspect Helton got spooked because the evidence is real, and it proves there *is* a spy."

Billy didn't like the sound of either of these options, at least not as far as a potential job was concerned. Ascertaining whether or not there was a spy, and then identifying that spy, would be a labor of weeks or months. "Listen," he said. "I'm only in town for the weekend, and I hope you'll recognize that's not nearly enough time to catch a spy, if you even have one."

"We know that, Billy," Lars shot back.

"I think what my colleague means to say," said Whiskey Joe, "is that all we want, Mr. Lovelace, is for you to see if there's any sign Gus has been bought. Then, if we know for sure that he's acting in bad faith, the path forward is easy. We ignore his tip about a spy and remove him from the organization. On the other hand, if Gus hasn't been bought, then we'll need to make some tough decisions. But those decisions won't involve you, Mr. Lovelace."

To Billy, this was starting to sound more reasonable, like the kind of job he could knock out in an afternoon, which would leave him ample time to settle his score with Madame Ilsa.

"All right," he said. "Consider me hired."

# 22

Francie Bream's journalistic mind, normally a finely tuned machine, was currently a rattling contraption awash in paranoia. Her interview with Diantha Marsh had badly shaken her. What had Mrs. Marsh meant by that question: *Was it ever justifiable to do harm in the service of a greater good?*

Had it been a veiled accusation? Did Diantha know what Francie was up to, or worse, what she'd already done? She doubted the other woman would have been so collected if she *did* know, but still, even the remote possibility of discovery scared Francie.

To steady her nerves, Francie stopped in at a nondescript hotel bar a few blocks away from Diantha's house and ordered a Gibson, which she tossed back with alacrity.

"Another?" said the bartender, a tidy man in his late forties.

"That'll do me," said Francie, who needed to keep her wits about her.

She did, though, slide the little onions off their toothpick and pop them into her mouth, realizing as she chewed that she couldn't remember the last time she'd eaten something substantial.

The alcohol was already dulling the sharp edges of her anxiety, and she settled into an overstuffed chair in the hotel lobby to reflect on the progress she'd made in her current mission, an endeavor beginning two years earlier when Francie's mother, Dorothy Braddock Bream, was on her deathbed.

Francie had been working on an exposé of Pittsburgh hatmakers when she'd received a telegram in her mother's understated yet dramatic style. *Am dying*, the telegram read, *Come home to say goodbye*. And so, Francie handed off her story to another reporter and took a train to the small town in Missouri where she'd grown up.

When she arrived, she discovered her mother was, in fact, dying—pneumonia—and so began Francie's bedside vigil.

For the first few days, they shared happy memories from Francie's childhood and discussed what her mother wanted done with her home and possessions after she was gone. Dorothy Braddock Bream, beloved and feared schoolteacher, had always been a practical, levelheaded person, and so Francie was not surprised by the matter-of-fact attitude with which she approached death.

Late one evening, though, that stoicism melted away to reveal a woman so overcome with rage that Francie almost didn't recognize her.

"Mama, what is it?" Francie said, approaching her mother's bedside.

The older woman's skin had grown waxy, her hair wild, and her eyes bloodshot. She grabbed Francie by the wrist, and it was like being grasped by a corpse.

"There's something you need to know," said her mother in a rasp.

Her mother's tone made Francie want to plug her ears and run out of the room. Instead, she leaned closer. "I'm listening, Mama. Tell me whatever you need to."

Her mother closed her eyes. "It's a terrible thing, an ugly thing."

"Mama, what are you talking about?" Francie rested a hand on the woman's damp brow, hoping this was nothing more than a feverish delirium.

"I've never told this to anyone, not even your father, God rest his soul," said Francie's mother, opening her bloodshot eyes and looking directly at her, "and now you're the only one left. It will be your job to make things right."

Francie was feeling more frightened by the second. "I'm right here," she said, stroking her mother's face. "I'm listening."

"No!" said Dorothy, sitting bolt upright. "You're humoring me, but this is serious. This is life and death, Francie, a matter of blood. You have to promise that when I'm gone, you'll make this right."

Francie was frightened now in a way she hadn't been since she was a little girl. "What is it?"

"Promise me," her mother said. "You're my flesh and blood. Promise me."

Francie would have said anything to banish the look of utter desperation from her mother's eyes. "I promise," she said. "I'll fix this for you, Mama, whatever it is."

Her mother, still sitting upright, seemed fueled now by some otherworldly fire, all traces of her mortal illness temporarily at bay.

"Good," she said. "Now, listen."

Francie nodded her assent and leaned in even closer.

# 23

When I was sixteen years old (Francie's mother began), I found myself working as a prostitute in Ogden, Utah, servicing the men who serviced the trains that passed through town. I'd rather not get into the messy history of how I ended up in that line of work. Suffice it to say, it was the best means available to create a little security for myself in this world. The job was dangerous sometimes, but no more so than most jobs available to people like me.

Now, this next thing is difficult for me to say out loud, and what you need to realize, Francie, is that I was young and, in my own way, still very naïve, but during my time in Ogden, I was baptized a Mormon.

How it happened was this:

One of my regulars who worked the trains knew I liked to read and brought me books the passengers left behind. Most weren't interesting to me, but I read them to have something to read. And there *were* occasional gems, like a novel by Charles Dickens or Wilkie Collins.

One day, this client brought me a book which looked at first to be a disappointment. It was called *A Child's Catechism of the Doctrines of the Church of Jesus Christ of Latter-day Saints*. Not the most beguiling title, but as you know, I'll read anything, so I took a peek.

What I found at first was not promising, questions like, *Why should you obey your parents?* or *Why does God command us to be honest?* That kind of thing.

Up to that point in my life, I hadn't given God or religion much thought. I'd been beset by more urgent concerns as a child, and as an adult—although really, I was still a child at that point—I felt certain my chosen profession rendered me unwelcome in churches and repugnant to any god that might exist. So, I steered clear of religion.

Those first pages of the catechism did nothing to change that perception.

I was about to set the book aside when I came to a chapter called, "On the Knowledge of God," and what I read there stopped me short. The book asked, *How can you come to know God?* and went on to explain that people can know God through tradition, reason, and revelation. But the only true way to know God, it claimed, was through revelation. All you need to do is ask God with a sincere heart for knowledge of Him, and He will give it.

For some reason, this made me even angrier than the injunction to always obey your parents. This book was trying to tell me that encountering the Almighty required nothing more than a simple summons, like God was some kind of eternal bellhop. And so, almost out of spite, I knelt as I had seen other people do, clasped my hands and said a simple prayer:

*Dear God: I would like to know you. Thank you very much. Amen.*

Then I went to bed furious with myself for having tried something so foolish.

That night, though, I had a dream.

I was sitting in a train car moving through a snowy landscape, and even beneath a pile of buffalo robes, I felt the cold acutely. I rubbed my arms and stomped my feet, and suddenly I wasn't alone: across from me sat a being I'm not sure how to describe, except that this personage radiated power and love.

"Dorothy," the Being said to me. "The time has come for you to prepare to meet your Everlasting Creator. If you please, open your heart."

I did as the Being instructed, opening my heart, which in this dream was a straightforward, mechanical operation.

"Good," said the Being, and then the Being was gone.

For a brief moment, the chill of the wintry world outside the train overcame me, and I shivered with despair. I felt alone and more frightened than I've ever felt in my life.

But then, as if from within myself, a magnificent warmth filled the train car and a voice—sweet and clear and full—said, "Dorothy, be still and know that I am God."

I trusted the voice, and so I made myself still, and then I knew.

I woke up crying in my little room after that vision, and within a month, after reasoning that whatever institution had produced that little red book must be worth closer investigation, I was baptized a Mormon.

# 24

THE BIGGEST OBSTACLE TO MY FORMAL CONVERSION was, as you can probably guess, my line of work (Francie's mother continued), although even that was resolved without too much trouble when Sister Sarah Crawford— her husband was one of the wealthiest Mormons in Ogden—offered me a position as a maid in her household. I'd be earning less money than I had as a prostitute, but I wanted very badly at that point to be baptized, and so, I took the job.

There was one more complication: shortly after my baptism, I discovered I was pregnant. I'd been working until a few weeks before my baptism, so the baby's father could have been any one of the number of clients I'd serviced. It was a sticky situation, and in the past I might have gone to someone to take care of it for me, but I doubted that would align with the lifestyle my new church expected me to live, and I wanted to do things right and live in a way that was pleasing to the Being I'd encountered in my dream.

Ultimately, I came clean to the head maid, who told me she was sorry, but pregnancy entailed an automatic dismissal from service.

I had my bags packed and was about to cross town to ask for my old job back, when who should appear in my room but Sister

Sarah Crawford herself. She said she'd had a word with the head maid, explaining that my condition had come about in the days before I'd accepted the Restored Gospel in my life, and that being the case, a bit of compassion was in order.

Quite frankly, I was shocked, and with the benefit of hindsight, I should have thought more carefully about why Sister Crawford might be acting with such apparent generosity, because as I soon discovered, that generosity was not what it seemed. I can't be sure of her intentions, but I do wonder if some obscure part of her mind whispered to her that my condition was something that might ultimately benefit her.

You see, Sister Crawford was pregnant, too, a situation that became visible soon enough. She spent much of her time resting in various daybeds around the mansion, while I spent the entirety of my pregnancy hard at work polishing, dusting, mopping, and scrubbing. I was perpetually exhausted, but I survived.

When the time came, I gave birth without complications. The baby—it's hard to describe how I felt about the baby. Some mothers talk about being overwhelmed with love for their new infant, but for me, it was more a sense of duty, a recognition that this little creature couldn't fend for herself and needed me to keep her alive in this unwelcoming world.

I named her Edith. She was so small and vulnerable and alive, and I knew I would do whatever it took to protect her.

Well, a few days later, Sister Crawford gave birth to her child, also a daughter. It was a miracle baby, she said, her previous three babies having been stillborn. This had been a great trial to her faith, as she'd been promised as a girl in her patriarchal blessing that she would bear many children and they would be the great glory of her life. She'd been denied this blessing time and time again and had wondered what she'd done to displease the Lord. But now, her grief could come to an end. She had a child, and she was fulfilling her life's great purpose.

Sister Crawford told me this in the tiny room I shared with Edith, having made a habit of visiting me almost daily after the babies were born. I resented these visits, mainly because I had no real say whether they happened or not. She was my employer, and this was her house. The door to my room didn't even have a lock.

During one of those visits about a week after Edith was born, Sister Crawford walked into my room as I was putting Edith down to sleep. I was exhausted—I'd already started working again by that point—and asked Sister Crawford if we could skip the visit.

"I've brought you something," she said, ignoring my request.

Sister Crawford was an imposing woman. She seemed ancient to me at the time, though she couldn't have been older than thirty. She had a commanding physical presence—steely eyes and a poise that suggested you could no more disrupt her from her intended course than you could a charging grizzly.

That evening she had a wild look about her, hair wreathing her head like a crown of lightning, skin white like a corpse. She took another step into my room, and I saw she held a teacup in each hand.

"Chamomile tea," she said. "I find it calming."

I accepted the cup, reasoning that if I drank it quickly, she might leave me alone for the night. When I took a sip, though, I gagged on the bitter liquid.

"Is there something wrong?" said Sister Crawford.

"I don't mean to be ungrateful," I said, "but this tea doesn't taste right."

"It tastes how it's meant to taste, Dorothy," she said. "Now, drink it down."

I'd had chamomile tea before, and I knew full well it shouldn't taste like whatever wretched liquid filled that dainty teacup.

"Thank you very much, ma'am," I said, "but I'd rather not."

At that, Sister Crawford's eyes took on an eerie light, and I grew truly afraid.

"If you don't drink it," she said, her voice electric with malice, "I'll be quite offended."

Recognizing a veiled threat when I heard one, I nodded and raised the cup to my lips. The room was dimly lit, and turning my body, I managed to pour the liquid down the sleeve of my nightgown as I pretended to drink it.

Beaming at me now, Sister Crawford took the empty cup. She rose and kissed me on the forehead.

"Sleep well, my dear," she said. The wild look in her eye had transformed to one of manic triumph, but she left me alone.

I'd only had one sip of so-called tea, but whatever Sister Crawford put in it was strong enough to knock me out until the next day. I'm certain now that if I'd drunk the whole cup, it would have killed me. I woke up the next day at ten a.m., feeling completely wretched. My first thought, of course, was for Edith—she usually fed several times in the night—but I'd somehow slept through her cries.

I ran to her crib, and when I saw what was inside, my blood went cold. Edith was gone, replaced with a tiny corpse that had clearly been dead for at least a day. The dear, dead little baby looked nothing like my Edith. Her hair was wispy and blonde where Edith's was dark and thick, her nose narrow where Edith's was wide, and her body thin and sickly where Edith's was tending to plumpness.

I stifled a scream, but—horrified though I was, and still groggy from the drugged tea—it took me only a moment to surmise what had happened.

Sister Crawford's daughter may not have been stillborn, but she *had* been sickly, had died after only a few days of life, and Sister Crawford, in her monstrous grief, reasoned that one baby girl was as good as any other.

She'd tried to murder me, and she'd stolen my baby, replacing her with the tiny corpse of her own child.

The only question remaining was whether she'd been planning this from the moment she'd discovered I was pregnant.

# 25

Filled with terror and rage (Francie's mother continued), I bundled up the little corpse and stormed upstairs, a major transgression in itself. I burst through the door of Sister Crawford's chambers to find her cuddling my little Edith, my employer's features illuminated with joy, until she saw me, the servant she'd murdered the night before, standing on the threshold of her room with a dead baby in my arms.

Sister Crawford screamed, bringing half the household running, and you can probably imagine what happened next.

With regained composure, Sister Crawford responded to my accusations with pity, telling me and everyone else who'd come running into the room that I'd clearly been driven mad with grief on discovering my child had died in the night.

Her husband believed every word of it, either because he'd spent so little time with his own child that he truly failed to recognize her appearance had changed completely overnight, or because the truth was just too terrible to contemplate.

I don't think Brother Crawford had been in on the scheme before that moment, but when he saw me confront his wife, he quickly committed to her version of events. At one point, I threatened to go to the police—that's how desperate I was—and Brother Crawford countered with steel in his voice that I was clearly quite unwell and would likely benefit from a stay in the Territorial Insane Asylum.

I understood then that my life was still in danger.

The rest of the encounter is a bit hazy for me, but I must have continued to raise a stink, because Brother Crawford finally suggested a compromise: we should summon our bishop to seek the Lord's guidance on the matter.

This was not an uncommon recourse among Mormons, and while my preferred solution in this situation was for the Crawfords to immediately hand Edith back to me, I had faith at the time that our bishop had been called by God to mediate such matters and would see that justice prevailed.

The bishop in question was a young man by the name of Roger Marsh, and I do mean young. He was in his early twenties, only a few years older than I was, but he'd already gained a reputation as a discerning servant of the Lord with a bright future in Church leadership.

My primary impression of Bishop Marsh from church meetings was of a kind and gentle person, constitutionally averse to the kind of fire and brimstone approach to religion favored by then-Prophet Brigham Young. Which is to say, I trusted Bishop Marsh, as his general demeanor was not at odds with the God I had encountered in my revelatory dream.

He arrived at the Crawford mansion that very morning with two counselors in attendance and a look of concern on his youthful face. We all convened in the sunroom, where Sister Crawford had already arranged herself on a daybed with Edith in her arms. Brother Crawford sat at the edge of the daybed and held his wife's hand, while Marsh and his two counselors—I don't remember their names—squeezed together onto a davenport. I sat in a severe wooden chair.

"May we begin with a prayer?" said Bishop Marsh, looking with visible compassion to the Crawfords.

Marsh was already deferring to the wealthy couple. I felt sick to my stomach.

"Please," said Brother Crawford. "Would you offer it, Bishop?"

"Of course," said Marsh.

He lowered his head and, after a pause, began his prayer. He thanked God for the trust the Crawfords had placed in him and asked to be filled with the spirit of discernment to know God's will concerning the current situation.

I knew that if God had anything to do with it, I'd be walking away with my baby at the end of this meeting. I was also beginning to see that reality was much more complicated.

"Now," Marsh said when he opened his eyes. "What seems to be the problem?"

Before I could respond, Sister Crawford rehearsed her version of what had happened over the past day. She said I'd lost my baby, and grief had driven me mad. She said I'd accused her of stealing my baby and wouldn't be brought to my senses.

Bishop Marsh took in Sister Crawford's account impassively, while his two counselors reacted more theatrically; one shook his head in sorrow, while the other grasped at his heart.

"And you," said Bishop Marsh, turning to me. "What do you say?"

I told him exactly what had happened as Sister Crawford stared daggers the whole time.

"This shouldn't be up for debate," I concluded. "Look at the child: she has my hair, my nose, my face. The Crawfords look nothing like her."

"My mother had dark hair," Brother Crawford broke in. "And her chin—it's the classic Crawford chin."

"Hmm," was all Marsh said before lowering his head, lost in thought or prayer.

I noticed Marsh's counselors looking at me—examining me, really—and realized yet again what an impossible spot I was in. If I acted as distraught as I felt, I'd reinforce the Crawfords' allegation that I was a woman unhinged. And maintaining my composure could be seen as incongruous behavior for a woman at risk of losing her baby. Either I was lying or I was a different type of crazy —this is what I imagined them surmising from my calm demeanor.

I met one counselor's eyes, trying to communicate the truth through my gaze, and he immediately looked away.

Finally, Marsh turned to Brother Crawford. "Is there a room where my counselors and I could speak in private?" he said.

"Yes," said Brother Crawford. "Please follow me."

All the men left the room. I looked at Sister Crawford, who was gazing at Edith with all the tenderness of a new mother.

"Why are you doing this?" I said.

She stroked Edith's face, and my daughter stirred in her sleep. Sister Crawford looked up. "You poor thing," she said. "You poor, mad thing."

She looked so convinced when she said those words, and that's when I knew I was going to lose my baby forever. I can't describe how I felt, I can only say I hope you never feel something so wretched yourself.

I considered for a moment simply snatching Edith from Sister Crawford's arms, but how far could I get with no money, no reputation? The Crawfords would hound me until the day I died.

I was trapped. We were trapped. When the men came back some time later, I was already in mourning.

The bishop sat down on the davenport.

I only half listened as Bishop Marsh said in a gentle, ecclesiastical voice, "The Lord has made it known to me that this baby belongs with Brother and Sister Crawford."

I didn't respond, didn't even move, which might have been taken as a sign of agreement, or at least acquiescence, when in reality, I was swearing a vow before God to harbor eternal hatred for every person in that room, every person except my purloined daughter.

I stumbled out of the sunroom while Marsh was still speaking and went downstairs to my tiny bedroom, where I packed my meager possessions and my even more meager savings. I knew if I left then, the Crawfords wouldn't come after me. They'd be glad to be rid of me, in fact.

The real danger would come if I stayed, a living reminder of the terrible thing they'd done. Brother Crawford had already mentioned the Territorial Insane Asylum, and I suspected if I lingered, I'd end up an inmate at that horrible institution for the rest of my life.

I don't remember much about the weeks that followed. But I did decide that if truth was so malleable it could be used to snatch my daughter from me, I might as well mold it a little myself to improve my station in life. So, I reinvented myself as a schoolteacher, complete with forged letters of recommendation from previous employers, and found a position back east where eventually I met your father, settled down, and had you.

It's been a good life, and I've been happy enough, but I've never forgotten my little Edith, and what those people did to me. I heard, by chance, that Sarah Crawford died a few years after I left Ogden—complications from childbirth—and it's my dearest wish that if hell exists, she's suffering right now in its foulest pits along with her husband David, who apparently lost his entire fortune in the Panic of '93 and died by his own hand.

As for the rest of them...

# 26

A cough overtook Dorothy's body at this point, and Francie was glad for the interruption, and the chance to collect her thoughts before a response was expected. It was all so much to take in at once.

Francie handed her mother a glass of water, and she sat up, drinking it gratefully. Over the years, her mother had often alluded to a difficult past, so, in a way, the fact that she had worked as a prostitute surprised Francie less than this mystical religious experience.

For as long as Francie had known her, her mother had been religious in a way that was, if not perfunctory, then at least not very profound. She'd attended the local Methodist congregation with her husband and Francie but rarely spoke of churchy things outside of church.

And the Mormon angle—Francie had no idea what to do with that. She felt sick at everything she'd heard and wanted to lie down, close her eyes, and think of something else. But she willed herself to stay sitting as a few more coughs rattled her mother's body before her breathing evened out.

"You need to promise me, Francie," she said, "when I'm gone..."

More coughing interrupted her request, and Dorothy's fingers opened to reveal a square of yellowed cloth, which she pressed into Francie's hand.

"What is this?" Francie asked. "Did it belong to Edith? Was it a piece of her blanket, something like that?"

Still coughing, her mother nodded.

"You want me to find my sister," said Francie. "You want me to find Edith."

The coughing spell finally ended. Staring at Francie with incredulity, Dorothy took a handkerchief from her sleeve and dabbed at the spittle that had accumulated at the corner of her mouth.

"No," her mother said with a grimace. "You need to promise me that when I'm gone, you will find Roger Marsh and make him pay for what he did to me. You need to find him, Francie, and tell him who you are, and then you need to strike him dead."

# 27

Lieutenant Declan Mainwaring of the Salt Lake City Police reminded Gilbert Snaith of an indigestion-prone hunting dog his uncle had owned when Gilbert was a boy. The dog, when excited, would whine, run in a circle, and then, eyes bulging, vomit up the contents of its stomach with a human-sounding retch. His uncle had had to put the dog down, of course; it was useless on a hunt.

Currently, Gilbert and the lieutenant sat across from each other in wicker chairs in Snaith's sweltering greenhouse. Gilbert nursed a glass of fresh orange juice, while Lieutenant Mainwaring, sweating profusely, looked ready to burst with whatever inconvenient news had brought him here today. His discomfort brought Gilbert some small joy.

"This really can't wait, Mr. Snaith," said Lieutenant Mainwaring, squirming in his seat.

Gilbert took a sip of his orange juice. This was the last thing he wanted to be doing on a Saturday, but the demands of business never slept, and so, here he was. He wondered what Diantha Marsh was doing. Bathing, perhaps. Why not? Gilbert considered that possibility while Mainwaring's bodily agitation grew.

"All right, Lieutenant," Gilbert said finally. "What do you have for me?"

With visible relief, Mainwaring explained the potential problem with their undercover operative in IWW Local 67: Lars Arnasson and Whiskey Joe Barnes had hired an out-of-town detective to sniff around Gus Helton (the man they'd discussed in a previous meeting), and from what Mainwaring understood, this detective, this Billy Lovelace, was very good at what he did.

"And?" said Gilbert, wondering how Mainwaring had come to be such a clod, whether he'd been born that way or had developed his spectacular cloddishness with time and effort.

"And...what if Gus Helton really knows something?" said the lieutenant, looking confused.

Gilbert swirled his orange juice in its glass, returning his thoughts to Diantha and her bath. He imagined her rising from the bathtub holding a towel to her chest—a small towel—and the towel slipping...

"Mr. Snaith, sir?" said the Lieutenant.

"What?" Gilbert said, hoping his tone communicated his utter disgust with Mainwaring.

"What should be done about Gus Helton?"

"Why are you bothering me with this today?" Snaith countered. "I think you know exactly what needs to be done about Gus Helton."

Mainwaring shifted in his wicker chair, and a palm frond brushed against his face. Gilbert could practically hear the metal grinding in the gears of the lieutenant's sorry excuse for a brain.

"I think, sir," Mainwaring said, "Helton could be persuaded to stay quiet about whatever he knows if he were given the right sort of reminder."

Gilbert hated untidiness, hated taking chances, hated squeamishness in his underlings. "No warnings," he said. "Take care of this the right way, Lieutenant."

Mainwaring adjusted his collar. "You're sure about that?"

"Do I need to repeat myself?" Gilbert said.

Mainwaring sat up straighter.

"No, sir," he said.

Gilbert swallowed the last of his orange juice. "That will be all."

He ignored Mainwaring's clumsy formalities as he left the room and, with only a little effort, re-conjured his vision of Diantha Marsh rising from her bathwater like a Mormon Venus.

# 28

In the quiet of the Salt Lake City Cemetery, Roger Marsh stood before the stone obelisk that marked the grave of President John Taylor, the Prophet who'd extended the calling for Roger to serve as an Apostle of the Lord. The cemetery was the only hallowed space left in the city into which Roger was permitted entry, and over the previous months, he'd come here often to contemplate the weighty assignment God had bestowed upon him. Dissenting from his Brethren was the most difficult thing Roger had ever done, but he drew comfort from the memory of President Taylor, a man who braved prison on numerous occasions in defense of the sacred institution of Celestial Marriage.

Roger still hadn't made it to Adam Wolfe's house. He'd been waylaid en route by not one, but three potential attendees of tonight's séance who were getting cold feet: Edie Martin had concerns about the possible relationship between Spiritualism and witchcraft; Joel Woodruff wanted assurances that the tithing rate in the new church would not exceed ten percent; and H. William Atkins needed to know the Prophet Joseph wouldn't resent being summoned from the comfort of Paradise to their own fallen world.

Though Roger had talked them through their doubts, the pettiness of their concerns had dampened his own spirits considerably, and so he'd come to President Taylor's gravesite in an attempt to reconnect with the Spirit of the Lord.

Instead, he felt the weight of death around him, and a blanket of unwelcome doubt about the viability of tonight's séance. Roger drew a deep breath and shakily exhaled.

"Mr. Marsh?" said a man's voice, startling Roger from his melancholy contemplation.

A figure emerged from behind a Norway spruce, a Luciferian beauty of a man whose presence so alarmed Roger that he momentarily feared he was in the presence of the son of the morning himself.

"Who are you?" Roger demanded, but a tremor in his voice betrayed his fear.

"Billy Lovelace," said the man, drawing nearer. As he did, the spell was broken, and a network of facial scars suggested his mortality. "Your wife told me I might find you here."

"Which wife?" asked Roger, steadier now.

This Lovelace character laughed, not unkindly. "I'm sorry," he said. "Your question surprised me."

"It's quite all right," said Roger, though he was feeling nervous again, unsure what business this man could have with him.

"The woman was blonde, talkative, about your age?" offered Lovelace.

"Elizabeth," said Roger.

"Elizabeth then," said Lovelace. "A lovely woman."

"Yes," said Roger, looking around the empty cemetery and realizing that he and this Billy Lovelace were alone. "What do you want?"

Lovelace made a courtly gesture. "I'm a detective, Mr. Marsh, and I understand you've hired a certain Madame Ilsa von Hoffmann to conduct a séance for you?"

Roger wasn't going to give this stranger any information easily, and he held the other man's gaze, not responding.

"Well, in any event," Mr. Lovelace continued. "I regret to

inform you that Madame Ilsa, as she calls herself, is a complete fraud, no more able to communicate with the dead than I am."

Roger suddenly understood what was happening. Billy Lovelace may not have been the devil himself, but exactly as the Forces of Satan had tried to silence the prayer of a young Joseph Smith before his glorious vision of the Father and the Son, the Enemy had sent this detective to crush Roger's wavering resolve. Ironically, this recognition filled him with a rush of the confidence that had been eluding him all day.

"You say she's a fraud?" Roger said.

"I do," said Lovelace, "and I can prove it."

Roger felt a once-familiar surge of authority. "What if I told you I don't care?"

"Excuse me?" said Lovelace.

"I don't care if she is or isn't a fraud," Roger said.

He watched as Lovelace reevaluated him, calculating the possible implications of this statement.

"Are you saying you're in on the scam?" Lovelace said, sounding like he doubted it.

"Are you a religious man?" Roger asked him in response.

"Not especially," said Lovelace.

"Let me tell you something," said Roger. "One thing I've learned in my years of service to the Lord is that God's ways are not man's ways. Which is to say, at times, the machinations of our Father in Heaven will baffle you or me. Most often, this means He wants to teach us something in the process of bringing about His plans."

A gentle wind rustled the dying leaves of a nearby row of trees as Billy Lovelace appeared to consider this.

"I'm afraid I still don't follow," he said finally.

Roger beckoned to Lovelace, and the detective took a cautious step forward.

"The Lord showed me a vision," Roger said, "in which Madame Ilsa von Hoffman summons the immortal spirit of the Prophet Joseph Smith as a sign and token of the veracity of the enterprise the Father has called me to undertake. This visitation by the Prophet Joseph will fortify the faith of those who already believe and quiet the doubts of those who are wavering. So, whether or not Madame Ilsa is, as you say, a fraud, I know her to be the vessel God has chosen to carry out the Reformation of His True Church."

Lovelace took a step back and turned to look at the foothills to the east.

As he'd testified, Roger had felt the unmistakable presence of the Spirit, but he could already feel it ebbing away, its purpose served. Once again, he felt very alone.

Billy Lovelace turned back and looked at him intently, searching his face for something he couldn't seem to find. "Would you object if I attended the séance?" he said finally.

"Please do," said Roger, with a confidence he no longer felt. "Perhaps the Lord has put you in my path for a reason, and your heart will be changed by the experience."

"I wouldn't bet on it," Lovelace said quietly, checking his pocket watch.

Roger removed a pen and paper from his jacket and wrote down the time and location of the séance. He handed the paper to the detective. "Until tonight, Mr. Lovelace," he said.

# 29

Madame Ilsa's patience at the Wasatch Diner had not been rewarded. Her quarry, Francie Bream, never showed her face, and so Ilsa paid for her coffee and set out down the street to obtain a few necessary supplies from a hardware store she'd spotted earlier on an obscure side lane. She needed to make her purchases discreetly, and as she stood scanning the crowded street for any sign of Adam Wolfe or Roger Marsh, she saw yet another pseudo-Billy Lovelace strolling down the sidewalk.

This time, though, the man's face didn't dissolve into that of a stranger's upon second glance. Billy's face persisted no matter how hard Ilsa looked at it, and judging by the scars she could just make out, this was no ghost. Billy, somehow, had survived what had happened in Seattle.

Terror gripping her soul, Madame Ilsa slipped through the first open door she encountered—a milliner's shop—and watched Billy progress down the street through the shop's wide window.

She felt herself falling back into the past, to her chance encounter with Billy at that mortuary in Topeka several years earlier. Following a convivial dinner, the arrangement she and Billy had reached on that ill-fated day was this:

Billy would arrive in a large town or small city a couple of weeks ahead of Ilsa. During that time, he would attend séances held by the mediums currently working the area and debunk them one by one with inside information Ilsa had provided him with.

Then, once the ground was cleared, Ilsa would arrive. She would hold a Summoning, Billy would attend, and the locals would watch with bated breath for the detective to debunk yet another medium. Only this time—could it really be?—Billy would discover no trickery in the proceedings.

"Obviously, I'm not comfortable calling this medium genuine," Billy would say of Madame Ilsa, "but I will say, I can't for the life of me figure out how she's pulling it off."

It would become high drama from there, the town's bigwigs climbing all over each other to hire both Ilsa and Billy—the former to communicate with the dead, the latter to finally prove it was all hogwash—for increasingly exorbitant fees.

Inevitably, Ilsa would be called away at the height of the fervor to perform a Summoning for an anonymous, high-profile client in another city, and with Ilsa gone, Billy had no one else to debunk and would soon move on.

It was a crackerjack routine, and Ilsa was earning nearly as much as she had at the height of her fame. Billy seemed happy with his earnings, too, and they probably could have kept this up for years if it hadn't been for Seattle.

Billy had already cleared the other mediums out of the city, and Ilsa had performed her first Summoning, which Billy, much to his false consternation, had been unable to debunk. It had played especially well in Seattle, for whatever reason, and Ilsa was feeling good about the weeks (and dollars) to come.

Then one evening, she was stopped in the lobby of her hotel by a well-dressed couple around her age who said they'd like to buy her dinner. Ilsa declined, as she did all such offers, but the man pulled his coat aside and rested his hand on the Colt .45 tucked into his belt.

"We must insist," he said.

They led her to a diner a few blocks from the hotel and took a table far from the other patrons.

"You see," said the woman, "we have a history with your friend Billy Lovelace, and when he showed up in town a couple of weeks ago, we hired a Pinkerton man to confirm this was the same Lovelace we knew."

"As part of his investigation," said the man, "our Pinkerton agent uncovered the little scheme you and Lovelace have going."

"We have no quarrel with you," the woman hastily added. "That is, as long as you're willing to lend us a hand."

The couple paused, apparently ready now for a response from Ilsa.

"I don't even know your names," she said.

"I am Cecily Standish," said the woman, "and this is my brother, Anton LeFleur."

Ilsa responded with a neutral nod.

"But back to the matter at hand," said Cecily. "Are you going to help us, or are you going to ruin your life?"

Ilsa did not want to ruin her life, and she did not want to assist this threatening brother-sister duo.

"What are you hoping I'll do for you?" Ilsa said.

Cecily Standish fixed her with a commanding stare.

"Tomorrow morning, both you and Billy Lovelace will receive invitations to a private dinner in our home," Cecily said. "I know you typically decline such invitations, but this time, you will convince Billy to accept."

"And what happens at this dinner?"

"We teach Mr. Lovelace a lesson," said Anton.

"What does that mean, exactly?" said Ilsa.

"That's our business," said Cecily.

"Are you going to hurt him?"

"Not permanently," Anton said with a chuckle.

Later, Ilsa was unsure why she agreed to the duo's terms. She knew something was off about them, and she and Billy were a clever pair. If she had brought her partner into her confidence right away, they could have plotted a means of avoiding the worst consequences of the siblings' ire.

She wondered if part of the reason she had so readily acquiesced was a buried suspicion that, knowing Billy as she did, he probably deserved whatever reckoning he would face in the hands of Standish and LeFleur. Billy had a long history of maintaining relationships only insofar as they directly benefited him and tossing people aside once they ceased to have utility.

Ilsa had little doubt that something of this nature had been the case with this disgruntled brother-sister pair. She even, upon later reflection, wondered if she had delivered Billy to his fate to preempt his inevitable wearying and ultimate abandonment of Ilsa and their business arrangement.

Whatever her hidden motivations, she had, relying on the trust they'd built over the years working together, convinced him to accept the invitation and accompanied him to the steps of Mrs. Standish's mansion. The whole thing felt so unreal—like a game or an amateur theatrical production—and Ilsa had trouble at the time conceiving any concrete consequences for her actions.

Of course, they did have consequences, terrible ones.

Midway through dinner, which had proceeded stiffly though not suspiciously, Cecily Standish lowered her fork and caught Billy's eye.

"Do you truly not remember me, Mr. Lovelace?" she said.

Billy looked at her, his face a mask of befuddled affability, though Ilsa could discern traces of incipient alarm around his eyes.

"Have I had the pleasure of meeting you before tonight?" he said.

Anton LeFleur pushed back his chair and stood up. "You've had the pleasure of a lot more than that," he said, hefting a silver-topped walking stick he'd leaned against the wall at the beginning of the meal.

"Oh," Billy said, keeping his tone light. "I'm embarrassed to say I don't remember our previous meeting."

"Salem, Oregon," Cecily said. "Eighteen-ninety-five."

Billy smiled and put on a thinking face as Anton LeFleur walked around the head of the table toward Billy. Ilsa wanted to call out to Billy, to warn him to leave, but her voice caught in her throat.

"Her name at the time was Cecily LeFleur," said Anton, "and she was engaged to be married to Victor Harris, the richest man in Salem."

Fleeting amusement creased the corners of Billy's eyes.

"I keep forgetting that you two are brother and sister," he said.

"What's that supposed to mean?" Anton said.

"Nothing," Billy said, collecting himself. "Only that I'm forgetful, as you've already seen by my failure to remember your lovely sister."

"I think you do remember me," said Cecily, her voice turning hard. "You seduced me when you were passing through Salem with your mediocre singing group. You bent my will with your pretty words and warm embraces. I was a foolish girl, foolish enough to believe your whispered endearments. And even if you don't remember the promises you made to me that weekend, you surely must remember the moment my fiancé, Mr. Harris, caught us in—what shall I say?—a delicate position. He broke off the engagement, which, in addition to breaking my heart, was a serious setback in my material circumstances.

"You see, Anton and I have always been poor, and marrying Mr. Harris would have brought a level of security to my life that was difficult to imagine. But you ruined that, Mr. Lovelace. You ruined me."

While Ilsa was not unsympathetic to the tale, she was also surprised that Cecily seemed to believe Billy would remember her. Unlike Ilsa, she apparently had no idea that the scenario she had just described was one of a multitude in Billy's life. He wasn't feigning ignorance this evening, Ilsa didn't think. There had been so many women like Cecily in his youth that she had no chance of being remembered.

"You seem to have done all right for yourself," Billy said,

looking around at the elegant trappings of the mansion's dining room.

Anton LeFleur stepped closer to Billy's chair. "We had to leave the city to escape the stain on my sister's reputation," Anton said. "And it was only with great effort and good luck that Cecily was able to secure a relationship with Mr. Charles Standish."

"Ah," said Billy. "Dear, departed Mr. Standish, who left poor Cecily his entire fortune, I assume?"

Billy should have been placating these people, not antagonizing them. Ilsa didn't understand how he couldn't see that, but this dinner seemed to have chafed against some sensitive spot of her colleague's soul.

"I loved my husband," Cecily said, "you good-for-nothing piece of filth."

"I'm certain you did," said Billy, his voice dripping with irony. He winked at Anton who, without further warning, raised his silver-topped stick and swung it like a baseball bat into the side of Billy's face.

Spewing blood from his mouth, Billy fell sideways from his chair. He was still conscious somehow and attempted to pull himself upright while Anton wound up for another swing.

"Anton, stop!" Ilsa yelled, rising from her seat. "You said you weren't going to hurt him!"

Billy turned his blood-smeared face to look at her. "You knew?"

Before Ilsa could answer, Anton brought the cane down hard on the top of Billy's head, and he dropped to the floor, unconscious. Ilsa expected this to be enough for Anton, but instead of stopping, he hammered the prone body on the floor again and again until it seemed there was not a bone unbroken.

Ilsa could no longer see the rise and fall of Billy's chest, and a deep chill passed through her body. Anton paused, wiping his sweating brow. Ilsa heard someone screaming, *Stop, stop, stop*, and then realized it was her, that she'd been screaming throughout the whole, terrible assault.

Cecily Standish stepped around her brother to look at the corpse of Billy Lovelace. She rested a hand on her brother's arm and squeezed it tenderly. "Thank you," she murmured.

Then, as if they'd forgotten about Ilsa's presence completely, brother and sister looked at her in surprise. Ilsa tried to say something but could only manage a gibbering string of nonsense.

Anon LeFleur leveled his bloody walking stick in her direction. "Get out," he said, "and don't tell anyone about this, or you'll be next."

Ilsa had no doubt that LeFleur would make good on this threat, and so, without a word, she turned and ran out of the house, with a picture of Billy's pulpy corpse seared into her vision forever.

Her partner was dead, and she was to blame. She could have stopped it. She could have saved him at so many points before it was too late.

Now, standing in the milliner's shop in Salt Lake City, Ilsa waited until Billy—very much alive—was well out of sight, and, overcome with guilt and fear, she leaned against the window for support. A shopgirl approached to ask if she was all right.

"No, I'm not," said Madame Ilsa, bringing herself upright and looking into the worried face of the young employee. "But there's nothing you can do to help me."

# 30

In spite of her mother's deathbed request, Francie Bream did not immediately commence a campaign of vengeance against Roger Marsh. She was an up-and-coming journalist, after all, not some dime-novel vigilante. The story had upset her, certainly. How could it not have? But the past was the past, and Francie had her own future to consider. She couldn't afford to dwell on distant injustices, even if they had touched the life of someone so close to her.

That was the response she *wanted* to have, but the reality was more complicated. Her mother's tale, rather than spurring her to revenge, had fostered over time a feeling of intense shame. Though her family had been far from wealthy, they'd always been steady, respected members of the community, certainly *not* the kind of people who had babies stolen from them, people who had to concoct false identities to escape captivity in some wretched insane asylum. This new reality rocked Francie's fundamental sense of who she was, and her first priority was to ensure that this awful family secret died with her.

That all changed a year-and-a-half later, on the last day of a gut-wrenching month of work. She'd had a string of tough stories—a landlord evicting a whole tenement of struggling workers, a textile factory dumping poisonous dyes in the river, a city councilman selling out his constituents for a fat payday from the city's titans of industry—each one of which could be boiled down to the headline, *Powerful Person Hurts Less-Powerful People, Faces No Consequences.*

The incident that pushed her over the edge, though, was the trial of a local finance man by the name of Matthew Stockwater, who had, in plain view of nine witnesses, beaten to death a shoeshine boy, age nine, who'd allegedly scratched Stockwater's shoe and refused him a refund. Stockwater repeatedly struck the boy across the face, lifted his small body into the air, and threw him across the sidewalk. The boy's head had hit the curb, killing him on impact. Stockwater's conviction had looked like a sure thing, until his expensive lawyers got the whole case thrown out on a technicality.

"He killed that boy, nine people saw him do it, and nothing's going to happen to him," said Francie. "You should have seen the smile on his face when he walked out of the courtroom this morning. Sheer delight. Just beaming. Beaming, Margaret. It made me sick."

Having just filed her story on the trial, Francie now sat in a Pittsburgh diner favored by the newspaper's staff, bending the ear of her friend and colleague Margaret Amador.

"It's a terrible thing," said Margaret. "It really is."

Francie sawed away at the overcooked porkchop on her plate.

"And it keeps happening, you know?" she continued. "These people like Stockwater literally get away with murder, and all we can do is write pointless coverage that ultimately changes nothing."

Margaret gave her an incredulous look. "Francie, I know it's hard to see something like this happen," she said, "but I would say —most people would say—we're living in a *golden age* of newspapers right now. The press has influence. *Nothing changes?* I strongly disagree. What I mean is, for good or ill, look at Hearst and the war in Cuba. Look at Upton Sinclair and the meat industry. Look at Ida Tarbell and Standard Oil. Look at Ida B. Wells and—"

"No, I know," said Francie. "I know, I know, I know. But we're up against a hydra here, Margaret. For every injustice addressed because of muckrakers like us, three new problems grow up in its place. It's exhausting—hopeless, is what it is."

Margaret set down her coffee cup. "It's discouraging sometimes," she said. "I agree with you about that. But if you look at the big picture, people like us *are* making a difference. Fighting the powers that be is a big job, but it's not *hopeless*. And anyway, what else is there to do?"

Francie shook her head, her mouth full of pork. She swallowed and pointed her fork at Margaret. "We talk a lot about writing to our readers," she said, "about really considering our audience."

"We do," Margaret said.

Francie set down her fork. "I've been thinking about this question: How do you write to your reader if your reader is someone like Matthew Stockwater?" Francie said. "Which is to say, if I wanted to get through to Stockwater, for instance, how would I do it?"

Margaret pursed her lips. "That's a difficult question."

"Is it, though?" said Francie. "Or is it completely straightforward? What I mean is, people like Stockwater communicate through violence and coercion and intimidation. That's their *language*, Margaret, and maybe that's the only way to get through to them."

"By committing acts of violence? That's a grim vision of the world, Francie."

"Yes, but what if it's the only way to change things?" Francie said. "Violence inspires fear, and fear is powerful. It's like...it's like an emotional salt intensifying the flavor of the messages, inspiring people to action, maybe more than anything else."

Margaret gave her a long, hard look. "These are some troubling thoughts you're voicing."

"No, listen to me," Francie said. "I'm completely serious right now. Say, for instance, someone killed Stockwater in retaliation for what he did to that child. I'm not saying someone *should* do that, but *if* they did, think about how it might discourage other men like him from abusing their power."

"Just like when Czolgosz killed McKinley, and it brought about a Socialist utopia in the US of A," Margaret said.

Her mentor was being deliberately obtuse.

"This would be different," Francie said.

"How?" said Margaret.

Francie shook her head and was quiet for a long time.

"Listen," Margaret said finally, breaking the silence. "We could talk hypotheticals all night, but like I said, I think journalism *is* achieving something. Not as much or as fast as we all would like, but we're making progress. Real progress."

Francie pretended to agree with that, and the two colleagues finished up their meal with a stream of benign chit-chat.

The Stockwater incident continued to disturb Francie, though, and she didn't sleep that night or the next one. She replayed her conversation with Margaret again and again. Why couldn't her friend see the way people in power slipped through the fingers of justice again and again and again?

It was time to try a different approach to stop those people, and where better to start than with the wrongs suffered by Francie's own family, wrongs that had caused her so much shame?

A week later, she was on a train to Ogden, Utah, where her mother's first child had been stolen decades earlier. Francie wasn't going to *kill* anybody, of course, but she planned to investigate her mother's claims, see where they led her, and use whatever means available to make things right.

# 31

Having failed, despite their best efforts, to eradicate prostitution in Salt Lake, the municipal government had opted instead to contain it—quite literally—within an enormous, walled compound that filled the block between Fifth and Sixth West, and First and Second South.

This veritable city within a city contained nearly a hundred ten-foot-by-ten-foot chambers, built in stable-like rows in which prostitutes could ply their trade, as well as a dance hall, three restaurants, two cigar shops, several saloons, and one opium den. The Stockade (as it had come to be known) was all but complete on the day Madame Ilsa passed through the compound's sole entrance into the office of Rose Montague, the woman the city had contracted with to manage the Stockade's affairs.

Ilsa's sighting of Billy had initially incapacitated her, but she had quickly rebounded, recognizing that if she hoped to survive the day, she needed to act.

"What can I do for you?" asked Miss Montague, a woman around Ilsa's age who seemed eminently comfortable being in charge.

Rose had invited Ilsa into her tastefully decorated office as if she'd been expecting her, and the two women now sat across from each other in matching straight-backed chairs.

"I'd like to hire one of your young women for an unusual task," said Madame Ilsa.

"How unusual?" Rose asked matter-of-factly.

"I'd prefer to keep the details between me and the young woman," said Ilsa, "but in broad terms, I need someone to find information for me. I've learned from experience that few people know a city better than its prostitutes. I'm looking for someone who's been working locally for a while and can think on her feet."

Miss Montague regarded Ilsa for a moment and then reached over and pressed a hidden button on the side of her writing table. Almost immediately, the office door opened, and a mountain of a man stepped through.

"Big Ernie," Rose said. "Please tell Lillian Paree I need to speak with her."

"Yes, ma'am," he said before closing the door.

Rose Montague folded her hands in her lap. "So, Miss von Hoffmann," she said, "what line of work are you in?"

"Spiritualism," said Ilsa.

"Ah," said Miss Montague. "You talk to the dead. I have a cousin who could do that, until she had her first baby, and then I guess the dead lost interest. Now she knits."

"Probably for the best," said Ilsa.

Miss Montague shrugged. "Much money in talking to the dead?"

"Not for me," said Ilsa. "At least, not these days."

"Shame."

There was a knock at the door.

"Come in," said Miss Montague.

A tired-looking woman—maybe twenty years old—entered the office.

"Lillian Paree," said Miss Montague, "meet Madame Ilsa von Hoffmann. Madam von Hoffmann, meet Lillian Paree."

"Pleasure," said Lillian Paree with a quasi-curtsey.

"Likewise," said Ilsa.

"Miss von Hoffmann has a job offer for you," said Miss Montague. "Why don't you explain."

"As I said before," said Ilsa, "I'd prefer to discuss this in private with Miss Paree."

"Sorry," said Rose Montague, "but that's not an option. It's my job to know how my girls occupy their time, so I'll be sitting in on this conversation."

It wasn't ideal, but Rose seemed discreet enough, and what else could Ilsa do?

"I understand," she said.

"Now," said Miss Montague. "About this job."

"Yes," said Ilsa, turning to Lillian Paree, who remained standing.

Ilsa explained as succinctly as possible the situation with Billy Lovelace, who was in town to do Ilsa harm but also seemed preoccupied with other business. What Ilsa wanted was for Lillian to ask around town to find out who Billy had been talking to, what he'd been talking about, and what his plans might be.

"Is that something you think you could handle?" Ilsa asked Lillian.

"Absolutely," said Lillian, who seemed eager for a break in the monotony of her usual work. She turned to Miss Montague. "That okay with you, boss?"

Rose Montague nodded. "As long as the price is right."

Before the meeting, Ilsa had pawned a crystal scrying dish, a brass trumpet, a beloved emerald ring, and two of her best wigs. She held what she hoped was enough to secure Lillian's services. If Ilsa could obtain an inkling of what Billy was up to, it might still be possible to outmaneuver him.

"I'm willing to pay a fair price," Ilsa said, and she and Rose negotiated a fee that, while at the upper end of Ilsa's budget, was still manageable.

The women shook hands all around.

"Be back here at four o'clock," Rose Montague said to Ilsa, "and I'm sure Lillian will have more information than you'll know what to do with."

# 32

STILL FEELING BEFUDDLED BY HIS ENCOUNTER IN THE cemetery with Ilsa's strange employer, Billy Lovelace struggled to keep his mind on the other matter requiring his attention, his investigation of IWW Local 67's own Gus Helton. Billy thought he should start by meeting the man himself, as it might help him refocus on his assignment from Lars and Whiskey Joe and give him a sense of the man he was meant to be evaluating.

As Billy neared the billiards parlor where Gus Helton was said to spend his Saturdays, he could tell something was very wrong.

A small crowd clustered near the entrance of Big Dipper Billiards, their faces animated with shock, sadness, disbelief, and in some cases, morbid glee. This was trouble if Billy had ever seen it, and as he shouldered his way through the mass of gawkers, his fears were confirmed. A man broadly matching Helton's description—short, thin, dark hair—lay dead at the edge of the sidewalk.

Blood pooled beneath the body, and the head was turned in a way that heads were not meant to turn. The face, though bloody and partially crushed, looked like a kind one to Billy, and young—much too young.

This was not the first dead person Billy had ever seen, but it was the first one he'd encountered since his own near-death experience, and he felt an eerie kinship with this mass of blood and broken bones that used to be a living man.

"Is that Gus Helton?" Billy asked someone.

"Sure is," said the man, lifting the brim of his hat. "You a friend of his?"

"Nope," said Billy, and the man looked at him with suspicion.

Billy didn't care. He'd planned on this job being quick and easy. Whiskey Joe and Lars hadn't even asked him to *prove* anything. A situation like this, what you needed to do was sniff around the guy's financial situation, see if he's spending or saving more money than a profession like his would allow.

Now, though, Gus Helton was conveniently dead right when Billy needed to talk with him. He didn't believe for a second the death was accidental—he'd long ago stopped believing in coincidences—which, in a way, was confirmation enough that something was amiss in the Local 67.

The smart move would be to go straight to Lars and Whiskey Joe with this new information and then walk away from the whole mess. He was about to do just that, in fact, let caution prevail for once, when two cops showed up to clear away the small crowd.

The other onlookers scattered at first sight of the officers, not so quickly as to seem like they were avoiding the police, but not so slowly that the police might get a chance to talk to them.

"Come on," the older of the two cops shouted to the few stragglers. "Clear the area."

"You heard Lieutenant Mainwaring," said the younger cop. "Clear out!"

The two cops—Mainwaring, apparently, and the younger guy —waved their hands at those departing with lazy authority.

And then it was only Billy standing there—Billy, the bloody corpse of Gus Helton, and the two cops.

"You deaf?" demanded Lieutenant Mainwaring, brandishing his nightstick at Billy.

The younger cop circled the gory body on the sidewalk, jotting down his observations, presumably, in a little notebook.

"Who do you think threw him from the roof?" Billy asked Mainwaring, nodding at Helton's body.

"He jumped," said Mainwaring. "Now get out of here."

Billy brought a hand to his face and stroked his chin thoughtfully. "In my experience," he said, in no hurry now to go anywhere, "a suicide's always going to choose a much higher building. Doesn't want to take his chances. This building here—" He jerked his thumb at Big Dipper Billiards, "—is only three stories tall."

"So what?" Mainwaring narrowed his pale blue eyes at Billy.

"So, you might die from that fall, or you might not," Billy said. "Bad bet for a suicide."

Both men looked at the corpse on the sidewalk.

"Well, it seems to have done the trick," said Mainwaring. "Now clear out of here, or are you hoping for a trip down to the station?"

"What I suspect," said Billy, ignoring Mainwaring's threat, "is that Mr. Helton was dead before he hit the ground, that a couple of thugs, maybe even a couple of cops, beat him to death on that rooftop and threw him over the side. What do you think, Lieutenant? That theory hold any water for you?"

Mainwaring's jaw had clenched, and his eyes bulged at Billy.

"Hey!" The lieutenant called to his partner, who was still jotting down notes like there was actually a mystery to solve. "Get over here!"

The younger cop nodded and trotted in their direction. Billy knew what was coming, but he held his ground.

"I was telling your partner," Billy said, "this death was no—"

Before he could finish his sentence, the younger cop grabbed him from behind, and Mainwaring swung his nightstick hard into Billy's gut. The pain was horrible, and then after a moment, it was even worse, making Billy wish he could crawl out of his own body until the feeling passed. Instead, he could only double over in the younger cop's arms.

"All right," Mainwaring said, and the younger cop dropped Billy to the sidewalk.

Billy tried to speak, but no words would come, only breathy sounds of pain. Mainwaring leaned down, reached into Billy's jacket and pulled out his wallet. He found Billy's license, read it with a sneer, and threw wallet and license to the ground.

"If I were you, Mr. Lovelace," said Lieutenant Mainwaring, "I'd catch the next train out of Salt Lake and never look back."

Billy moaned in response, and Mainwaring kicked him in the gut, rekindling the agony in Billy's torso, and then the younger cop dragged him into a nearby alleyway and dumped him onto a pile of garbage.

Billy lay there with his eyes closed, planning his next move and trying not to weep out loud. As soon as he recovered his breath, he rose cautiously and walked to the nearest telegraph office, where he sent a wire to a trusted associate in Albuquerque informing him of the broad details of the Gus Helton case and where to point a finger if anything were to happen to him.

In Billy's experience, such insurance policies paid off more often than not. But if he were being cautious, he'd do as Mainwaring had suggested and get out of town.

He wasn't going to do that, though, partly because he intended to finish his business with Ilsa, and partly because he didn't like being told what to do.

Someone didn't want Billy poking around the Helton case, and so he meant to find out who that someone was.

# 33

Back in her room at the Hotel Royal, Francie set down her purse and removed the gun she kept within it, a Smith & Wesson .38 double action revolver that had been weighing heavily on her, body and soul, all morning. She set the gun atop her suitcase and pushed her purse to the floor.

She needed to find Madame Ilsa von Hoffmann and insinuate herself into tonight's séance, but she also needed some sleep—a lot of sleep, actually—but only had time for a little. She set her alarm clock to ring in half an hour and slid between the scratchy bed sheets.

When her alarm went off, Francie felt like she hadn't slept at all. She got out of bed, put her gun back in her purse, and set out for the Wasatch Diner. She didn't feel hungry, but she also couldn't remember the last time she'd eaten and couldn't afford to lose her strength at some inopportune future moment.

Rather than catch a streetcar, Francie decided to use her nervous energy to walk to the diner. Walking helped her process her thoughts, and right now she needed clarity. She'd woken from her brief sleep with a vivid memory of the first person she killed.

Francie came across Amos Boylan's name in the archives of the *Ogden Standard Examiner* soon after her arrival in Northern

Utah. It was a brief item from thirty-some-odd years before about the reorganization of the bishopric of the Ogden Fourth Ward, a newsworthy development in the heavily Mormon town. The twenty-two-year-old Roger Marsh was called as Bishop, with Amos Boylan his First Counselor, and Thomas Christianson Second Counselor.

Further research revealed that Christianson had since died, but Amos Boylan was alive, though in his eighties.

Francie had been in Ogden for several weeks at that point, having left her job at the *Pittsburgh Gazette* to devote herself to investigating her mother's story. She'd holed up in a tiny, rented room on the wrong side of town and, after ingratiating herself with the staffs of the local newspapers and libraries, spent all her waking hours combing the city's archives to learn about Roger Marsh, the Crawfords, and Mormonism.

The broad details of her mother's story had checked out, but now here was a chance to talk to someone who'd been present on that fateful day when Francie's half-sister was stolen.

It was time to get out into the field and investigate firsthand, and so Francie procured some working-class garb, adopted the alias Maggie Green, and found a part-time cleaning job with a family—the Perrys—who moved in the same social circles as the Boylans.

Ruth Boylan—Amos's daughter-in-law—was a frequent guest of Jane Perry's, and through strategic eavesdropping, Francie was able to glean over the course of a few weeks the following information about Amos Boylan:

Most of the older men in Ogden, whether through official Church positions or mere cultural deference, were revered patriarchs. Amos Boylan, on the other hand, was primarily a cause of discomfort to his family. His physical health was perfect. At eighty-six years old, he was as strong as a mule. But his mind was gone.

Francie pitied the man—her time undercover in an insane asylum as a rookie reporter had engendered an immediate and profound sympathy for anyone who had lost their wits—and at first, discounted him as a potential resource. A subsequent conversation between Ruth Boylan and Jane Perry, though, changed her view of Amos.

"He can't remember what he was doing five minutes before," said Ruth Boylan, "but ask him about something that happened fifty years ago, and he'll describe it like it was yesterday, down to the smallest detail."

"My mother was the same before she passed," said Jane Perry, a troubled look on her face. "How strange that must be."

Ruth nodded and turned to face Francie.

"Can we help you, Maggie?" she said.

Francie hadn't realized she'd paused her scrubbing of the floor.

"No, ma'am," she said, and returned to her task with alacrity.

That night Francie began working out the details of an audacious plan. She would approach this task, as was her custom, with both cunning and flair. Over the next week, she gathered her materials, including several yards of white muslin, a jar of phosphorus, and an imperious-looking ledger. Her plan would require stealth, finesse, and a bit of luck, but she felt increasingly certain she could make it work.

Amos Boylan slept alone in a corner room on the ground floor of the sizeable home, while the rest of the family quartered upstairs, far from the elderly patriarch. Francie had figured out the layout through a series of questions posed to the Perrys' chronically incurious housekeeper, Mrs. Wilson, and so it was with some confidence that Francie picked the lock of the rear door late one Thursday night and crept through a series of rooms and hallways to another closed door.

She tested the knob and found it unlocked, and then, to aid her stealthy passage, applied a thin coating of grease to the hinges. Pushing the door open noiselessly, she stepped into the bedroom and closed the door behind her.

Francie looked around the darkened room and, sure enough, there was Amos in a narrow bed pushed against a wall. She breathed a sigh of relief.

Opening her knapsack, she removed a glowing muslin robe,

which she shimmied into before applying phosphorus to her face and hands. She then tucked the massive ledger beneath her arm and approached the bed.

"Brother Amos," she intoned in a voice she hoped was both resonant and quiet enough to not carry outside of the room.

The old man stirred in his sleep, his papery eyelids fluttering, but he didn't wake.

"Brother Amos," she said again, and this time he opened his eyes. They were pale and blue and filled with confusion. For a moment, Francie worried her plans would be scuttled by the old man's disorientation, but then he seemed to fully take her in, and he nodded, as if he'd been expecting a visit from a glowing, otherworldly being.

He sat up in bed and spoke in a surprisingly clear and confident voice. "To what do I owe the privilege of this visit?"

Francie was about to speak when Amos held up his hand to stop her.

"First," he said. "I need to determine whether you're a true messenger of the Father, or an emissary of the great Deceiver."

He extended his hand toward her.

She wasn't sure what kind of test this might be, but she took a chance and shook his hand.

He nodded and looked at her with increased respect. "A resurrected being."

"That is correct," she said, following his lead. "I am Moroni, favored angel of God, who delivered the plates of gold to the Prophet Joseph Smith."

This was the extent of her research; anything further would require improvisation.

"Moroni," said Amos. "Of course."

Francie was touched by the man's childlike response to an angelic visitor, but then she remembered her cause and rededicated herself to her purpose.

"Brother Amos," she said, "the Lord has elected you to a special purpose."

Amos nodded, still apparently unsurprised by any of this.

"He has selected you to bear witness to a deed performed by Roger Marsh when he was still a young Bishop, a judgment in the case of two women who each claimed an infant as her own. Do you recall the event to which I refer?"

"Yes, of course," Amos said without hesitation. "It was one of Bishop Marsh's finest moments."

Both appalled and thrilled, Francie nodded and, opening the glowing ledger (to which she'd also applied a coating of phosphorus), she sat down in the simple chair next to the bed.

"Now," she said, "the Lord requires an accounting of the events that day."

"I'm happy to provide one," Amos said.

Francie uncapped a pen, and Amos began to speak.

# 34

To start with (Amos Boylan said), I'd like to testify that Bishop Marsh was one of the most inspired men I've ever had the privilege of serving with, and this was clear to everyone who knew him. The members of his ward often called on him to discern the Lord's will in tricky situations, and every time, he did so with grace and humility.

It made sense for Brother Crawford to come to Bishop Marsh then, when that young prostitute claimed Sister Crawford had stolen her baby. And as the bishop explained to me and Brother Christianson, this was a situation that would require every ounce of wisdom the Lord saw fit to bestow upon us.

I remember Sister Crawford's earnest testimony, as well as the pitiable ravings of that young prostitute. It was a heart-rending scene, it really was, and with heavy hearts we—Bishop Marsh, Brother Christianson, and I—adjourned to seek the Lord's will.

Before we prayed, we discussed our first impressions of the situation and asked ourselves if any clear evidence pointed one way or the other. Bishop Marsh mentioned that the living baby *did* more closely resemble the young prostitute, and it did trouble him that all of Sister Crawford's previous babies *had* been stillborn, or died soon after birth, as one of these babies had.

"Are you suggesting that Sister Crawford is lying?" said Brother Christianson.

Young Bishop Marsh pursed his lips.

"What I'm saying," he said, "is that if we look at the evidence—"

"If we look at the evidence," Brother Christianson interrupted, "we have a young woman who debased her virtue for money accusing a faithful sister of lying. Quite frankly, I don't believe a word out of that mendacious trollop's mouth."

This characterization seemed to trouble Bishop Marsh.

"Even still," he said. "I believe we must petition the Lord for enlightenment as to which of these women gave birth to the baby who still lives."

"I think that would be a waste of the Lord's time," said Brother Christianson. "We know exactly who birthed that baby: Sister Sarah Crawford."

Though Bishop Marsh was not a quick-tempered man, I could see his anger rising, and so, before tempers could flare, I intervened with an insight I'd been saving for the right moment. "There's another way we might think through this dilemma," I said. "Yes, the most obvious question is, *Who gave birth to this baby?* But what if instead, we asked: *Who* should *be this baby's mother?*"

Brother Christianson looked skeptical, but Bishop Marsh's eyes lit up.

"Please, Brother Boylan," he said, "explain what you mean."

I felt a warm glow of approval, whether from God or Bishop Marsh, I'm not sure.

"I like to believe that in this life there are no accidents," I began, "that the Father's will shapes events in ways we can't anticipate or even understand. And with that in mind, when I look at this situation, I have to wonder how God's hand might be involved.

"Look at the two women laying claim to this child. First, a young woman who's wasted her youth in adultery, who, yes, has repented and is seeking to follow the straight and narrow path but has little experience in doing so. I have to ask myself what kind of life this young woman could provide this fresh and innocent child.

"And then we have Sister Crawford, about whom I don't need to say much, other than we all know her to be one of the elect, a choice daughter of our Heavenly Father whose only blemish has been an inability to bear thriving children.

"I think of the life this child might have with Brother and Sister Crawford, and I can't help but smile. As for the question of who gave birth to this baby, I don't know the answer. I do know, however, whom this baby *should* belong to."

I couldn't tell at first what Bishop Marsh thought, as he'd lowered his head in profound contemplation. When he looked up, his eyes were wet with tears.

"Well said, Brother Boylan," he said. "Well said."

We knelt on the thick rug, the three of us, and we presented our solution to the Lord.

"Our Father in Heaven," Bishop Marsh prayed. "We thank Thee for this opportunity to act as Thy representatives on this earth and ask for Thy guidance in resolving the situation of this baby, this spirit fresh from Thy throne. We believe the child should remain with Brother and Sister Crawford, as they have much to offer. If this is in accordance with Thy will, please send us confirmation through Thy Spirit, we humbly ask Thee, in the name of Thy Beloved Son, Jesus Christ, Amen."

We continued to kneel after Bishop Marsh completed his prayer, and then, as we had been blessed to experience on a few previous occasions, the three of us felt the honey-sweet presence of the Holy Ghost warming our hearts, confirming that the path we had selected was the right one. It was a powerful feeling, and we couldn't speak for quite some time.

Finally, we rose and returned to the Crawfords' sunroom, where we informed those present of the Lord's decision. Brother and Sister Crawford were immediately overcome with joy, falling to their knees and cradling that precious child between them. The other woman, the prostitute, stood there sullenly, her reaction as strong a confirmation to me as anything that we had made the correct decision, acting rightly in the eyes of the Lord.

# 35

AMOS PAUSED, LOOKING THOUGHTFUL, AND FRANCIE wondered if he was about to express some regret or ambivalence for the outcome of that terrible day. Francie, for her part, was shaking with rage, her hands so unsteady she had to hug the ledger to her chest.

Though she'd never exactly doubted her mother, Francie now had confirmation through Amos Boylan's testimony, and the reality of it settled into her bones like a winter frost.

With a look of unmistakable self-satisfaction, Amos smiled at her. "And that, Brother Moroni, is my account of Bishop Marsh and the Crawford baby."

Francie felt like her fury might lift her from the chair like a mighty angel of destruction. She set down her pen.

"Very good," she said to the old man, closing the ledger. "The Lord is pleased with the service you provided."

Again, Amos nodded. Francie rose from the wooden chair and then hesitated. She looked at the old man sitting up in his bed with that same look of certainty and satisfaction she'd seen on the face of the child-killer Matthew Stockwater when he'd exited the courthouse a free man, and on the faces of so many other powerful, destructive men she'd encountered in her life, and she was overcome in that moment not with more anger, but with a crystal-clear sense of purpose.

"Lie down," she said to Amos Boylan.

He obeyed.

"Now," she said, "take that pillow and place it over your face."

He hesitated for a moment but complied.

"Remain still," she said.

Francie leaned the full weight of her body on the pillow, surprised at how simple it was to cross this line, to transition from being someone who never would dream of killing another human being to a person currently smothering an old man with a pillow.

Amos didn't go easily. As Francie pressed the pillow harder into his face, he flailed his long limbs, tangling them in his bedding until the sheets held him like a roped calf, and although Amos was strong for a man in his eighties, he was still a man in his eighties, and Francie was a robust woman in prime health, and before long, the squirming stopped, and the old man was still. She waited for one minute—counting the seconds—then two minutes, and then she removed the pillow.

Amos Boylan was dead, with a look of wide-eyed horror on his wrinkled face.

Francie propped the pillow under his head and untangled him from the sheets as best she could. Next, she removed her costume, returned it to her knapsack, and snuck out of the house the way she'd come.

Slipping into the darkness outside, Francie felt like a different person, baptized by the act she'd committed. She was prepared now, she knew, for the mission ahead of her. She felt frightened and determined all at once as she sensed the vengeful spirit of her mother at her side, urging her on to complete the work she'd just begun. Francie didn't sleep for the rest of that night, nor the night after that.

As Francie had hoped, Amos's family assumed he'd died in his sleep and didn't give the cause of his death a second thought. Out of an abundance of caution, she stayed in town for another month, not wanting anyone to link her departure with the death of Amos Boylan. During that month, she surreptitiously continued her research, and in the process learned something that only heightened her desire to bring Roger Marsh to justice.

When the month was up in early October, she caught a train to Salt Lake City.

# 36

The hiring of Lillian Paree had put Madame Ilsa far behind schedule, although the notion of a schedule in such a dire situation was laughable. Still, Ilsa liked to maintain some illusion of control, and at the moment, that illusion was the only thing keeping her from falling apart. So she constructed a new timeline in her head that would allow her to achieve everything she needed to before the Summoning.

First, she would need to eat a quick lunch at the Wasatch Diner, which she was rapidly approaching on foot, and then she would find Francie Bream and ask her to assist with tonight's job.

Ilsa opened the door of the diner and was met with the aroma of competently prepared food. Her spirits lifted a fraction, and the sight of Francie Bream sitting alone in a booth lifted her spirits further.

Finally, a piece of luck!

After ordering her food, Ilsa approached the table and was delighted to see Francie waving her over, although that delight was immediately replaced with a reflexive distrust cultivated over years of professional experience.

Why was Francie Bream excited to see her?

"Madame Ilsa," Francie said as she sat down. "I'm afraid we

got off on the wrong foot yesterday. I don't think I communicated very well how deeply I regret that article I wrote for the *Standard Examiner*. You must forgive me."

Ilsa looked carefully at the journalist. She needed the woman's help but couldn't appear too eager. "What can I do for you, Miss Bream?"

Francie glanced around the diner and then leaned confidentially across the table. "I'd like to help you with the séance you're doing tonight for Roger Marsh."

Ilsa had no idea how Francie knew so much about what was happening tonight, but she didn't care.

"Listen," said Francie, "Marsh is expecting something spectacular tonight, and we both know you could use my help."

Ilsa hadn't expected a hard sell from Francie—this was proving suspiciously easy— but since she already distrusted the journalist, this new development altered Ilsa's calculus not at all. Still, for form's sake, she hesitated.

Francie pointed to Ilsa's hand. "What happened to your finger?"

"Adam Wolfe happened to my finger," Ilsa said. "Do you know him?"

"I've seen him around," said Francie. "Marsh's stooge, right?"

"Yes," said Ilsa. "I'd keep my distance if I were you."

"Thanks for the tip," said Francie. "And tonight? Will I help you with the séance?"

Ilsa looked at the journalist, whose eyes held a new hint of desperation.

"Be at my suite at the Armitage Hotel in one hour," Ilsa said at last, "and we can get to work."

# 37

Billy suspected that any useful information once contained in Gus Helton's apartment had already been harvested by whichever parties had broken his neck and thrown him from the roof of the billiards parlor. Still, it was possible they'd missed something and so, in the name of due diligence, Billy climbed the stairs of Gus's drafty building to the third floor.

Number 304 was the address Billy had been given, but when he stopped outside, he heard voices coming from inside. He put his ear to the flimsy door and caught the voice of his newfound nemesis, Lieutenant Mainwaring.

"...has to be here somewhere," the policeman said.

So, they hadn't found whatever they'd been looking for in Helton's apartment, which was good news for Billy. He hoped they wouldn't find it during this current search.

"Keep looking," Mainwaring barked.

If Billy could only come up with a way to get the cops out of there. As he ran through a litany of impractical schemes, the door across the hall opened and a woman about ten years his senior stuck out her head. She'd clearly seen Billy listening at Helton's door, but before he could make an excuse, she put a finger to her lips and beckoned him over.

This seemed promising.

He walked across the hall and followed the woman into her apartment.

"Police in there again?" she asked in a low voice after closing the door.

"Sounds like it," Billy said. "Were they here earlier?"

The woman gave a tight nod.

"They hauled poor Gussie off a little before lunchtime," she said.

"You knew him?" Billy said.

"*Knew* him?" the woman said, cringing.

"Yes," said Billy. "He's dead. I'm sorry."

The woman looked saddened by this but not surprised. She seemed like the kind of person who'd had at least her share of pain in life. A perpetual wince creased the skin around her eyes, and her shoulders stooped from a combination, Billy supposed, of disappointment and the kind of work that requires a person to hunch their body for hours on end.

"I'm Billy Lovelace, by the way," he said.

"Minnie," said the woman. "And I didn't know Gussie well. Just enough to say hello when we passed in the hall, have an occasional chat, you know? He seemed like a good egg, which was why..." And then she stopped and bit her lip.

"Why, what?" Billy prompted.

Minnie seemed to think this over, and then she reached into an inner pocket of her worn overcoat—it was as chilly in her apartment as it was tidy—and removed something small which she pressed into Billy's hand.

It was a key on a cheap metal fob that read, *Wasatch Springs Bath House #99*.

"What is this?" said Billy.

Minnie glanced at her door and then moved closer to Billy.

"Day before yesterday," she began in a near whisper, "I get a knock at my door as I'm about to turn in, and when I see it's

Gussie Helton, I know something's wrong. He knows when I go to sleep and wouldn't disturb me if he didn't have to.

"When I ask what's going on, though, he shakes his head, looks scared half to death, and says it's better for me not to know. But he hands me this key and says if anything happens to him, I need to give it to someone I trust, someone who can get things done.

"I ask him again what's wrong, but he won't say, even though he's shaking like a leaf. He asks me to promise I'll take care of this key for him, and normally I'd say no to something like that—I've learned it doesn't pay to get involved in other people's problems—but like I said, Gussie seemed like such a good egg and I heard myself saying the words, promising to take care of it for him."

Minnie gestured at the key now in Billy's hand.

"And now my part is done," she said. "Please don't mention me to anyone. I wash my hands of this business, whatever it is."

"Of course," said Billy, considering the key. "But what made you trust me?"

"I don't trust you," Minnie said. "I just want that thing out of my house."

She walked to the door and placed her hand on the knob.

"One more question," Billy said. "Wasatch Bath House?"

"There's a trolley stop in front," Minnie said. "Take the red line going north."

"Thank you," he said quietly as she practically shoved him out the door.

He could still hear Mainwaring and his partner inside Helton's apartment as he passed.

Walking down the stairs, Billy wished the pair all the ill luck in the world.

# 38

Autumn had arrived in Liberty Park, painting its leafy canopy in a palette of reds, yellows, and golds, and on this Saturday afternoon, it seemed that half the city had turned out to take in the arboreal splendor. The park teemed with people walking arm-in-arm, which rendered the semi-illicit meeting of Diantha Marsh and Gilbert Snaith practically invisible.

They'd contrived to accidentally run into each other to discuss Gilbert's proposition, but at the moment, they merely strolled the grounds of the park together like old friends or lovers.

Diantha enjoyed the feel of her arm in Gilbert's, his body young and firm and strong (at least compared to her husband's). What she did not enjoy, however, was Gilbert's conversation. He'd been explaining to her the ways in which automobiles were superior to streetcars but inferior to horses, or something along those lines. She couldn't say for sure; she'd ceased listening after Gilbert had plowed through her attempts to participate in the conversation not once, not twice, but three times.

The thing that Gilbert didn't seem to understand, that Roger didn't understand, that *no one* understood was Diantha had big ideas, too; in fact, her dreams and plans and fantasies and theories were equally thrilling, just as consuming as those of any man in her life, and yet they remained relegated to the stuffy closets of her mind.

"You must admit," Gilbert said, "you'll never think about horses in the same way again, isn't that right?"

"I suppose I won't," she said vaguely and hoped he'd change the subject.

"Well," said Gilbert, lowering his voice. "As pleasant as this chat has been, should we discuss the business at hand?"

She wished now he would keep talking about automobiles and horses.

"Yes," she said. "We should."

"Good. Now, I don't want to rush you," he said in a way that suggested that this was exactly what he would do, "but I want to emphasize again how eagerly I've been waiting for your response to my proposal."

He reached over and took Diantha's hand in his, a gesture impossible to misinterpret as mere friendliness.

"Gilbert," she said, withdrawing her hand. "We need to talk about the conditions attached to your proposal."

He stopped walking and looked at her with unconvincing alarm. "There are no strings—"

"Don't," she interrupted. "If you want me to consider this offer, I need to know if you're hoping for any sort of relationship with me outside the running of the charity."

For a moment, Gilbert's face retained its expression of affront, as if he intended to commit more fully to his faux innocence. But then his countenance shifted to one of resignation.

"Yes," he said simply. "I love you, Diantha, and if you accepted my offer, I certainly wouldn't *force* any kind of relationship, but if you were amenable, I'd like to marry you."

Diantha was glad, at least, to have Gilbert's intentions out in the open, and she considered the three compromised options before her:

First, Roger's surprise offer of a leadership role in his new church, which would also require Diantha to stomach more polygamy—at least at first—and also, presumably, some continuing relationship with Roger.

Second, Gilbert Snaith's offer to support her financially while she ran a charitable organization that would further many of her long-held ambitions, with drawbacks, namely an obligation to marry Gilbert, who was not an unattractive man nor especially unpleasant to be around, though he was, in general, ethically repugnant to her.

Third was an alliance with the Dowlands, which was to say, the mainstream Mormon Church. This would likely mean some financial support if she walked away from her marriage with Roger, though that support would not be extravagant and would lump her in with the destitute widows sustained by resources from the bishop's storehouse.

Since she wasn't sure at this point if an alliance with the Dowlands was feasible, she needed to settle the question before she could give a definitive answer to either Roger or Gilbert Snaith.

"Well?" said Gilbert, once again taking her hand.

"Well, what?" Diantha said.

"Will you marry me?" Gilbert said.

In spite of herself, Diantha laughed and then stopped abruptly when Gilbert's face twisted with hurt and resentment. She turned conciliatory on a dime, stroking his hand and peering up at him through lowered lashes.

"Gilbert, darling, your patience means the world to me," she said.

His face softened, and he gently squeezed her hand.

"I'll have an answer for you by this evening," she said, beaming at him. "I promise."

# 39

On the dressing table in front of her, Madam Ilsa von Hoffmann placed a deck of cards, a length of rope, and a pair of handcuffs. She looked into the mirror and saw her own angular face looking solemn and mysterious and, behind her, the relative luxury of the hotel suite. She needed to see how much her broken pinkie would inhibit any finger work she'd need to do tonight. Splinted as it was to her ring finger, it was certainly unwieldy.

She also needed to prepare herself, physically and mentally, for a tricky afternoon with Francie Bream, and the finicky attention required by sleight of hand seemed as good a means as any.

Ilsa picked up the deck of cards and ran through a levitating shuffle, a boatman's cut, a top shift, a double top shift, and a palm change. So far, so good. She had to focus, but she could still execute each manipulation with her broken pinkie.

She moved on to the rope next, practicing a series of trick knots which proved more difficult than the cards but still manageable.

Finally, she picked up the handcuffs, made them disappear and reappear in her hands, and disappear and reappear again, only this time manacling her wrists. And then she disappeared them from her wrists and gave her reflection a modest bow.

Feeling, if not good then less bad, Madame Ilsa glanced through the notes she'd made for tonight's Summoning, and she sat down on the edge of her bed and allowed herself to think about what she'd done to Billy Lovelace.

Until she'd delivered a friend and colleague into the hands of bloodthirsty vigilantes, Ilsa had considered herself a more-or-less good person. Some might point out that her career, by its nature, trafficked in deception, but within those admittedly compromised parameters, Madame Ilsa had scruples. She only plied her trade with the wealthy or near-wealthy, for instance, and she eschewed violence and blackmail. Outside of her work, she was honest and loyal to her friends, which meant that even by her own idiosyncratic standards, her role in Billy's apparent death had been unconscionable.

She'd spent the ensuing months punishing herself for her crime, allowing her work to grow shoddy, and slipping from the modest tier of professional viability she'd occupied before Billy's death.

Her low point had come when Lucy Lammermoor invited her to join her and the Crimson Swans on their bound-to-be-ill-fated farm commune, but Ilsa was rewarded for holding to her principles when, not long after turning down Lucy's offer, she received a letter with a train ticket enclosed from one Adam Wolfe offering her a job in Salt Lake City with a paycheck big enough to revitalize her floundering career.

It had seemed like good fortune at the time, but now, sitting in the hotel suite financed by Roger Marsh, Ilsa wasn't sure whether to laugh or cry at her previous eagerness about this trainwreck of a situation.

# 40

Billy Lovelace disembarked from the trolley car in front of a simple building nestled against a scrubby foothill. Painted on the front were the words *Bath House*, and he caught a whiff of sulfur from the adjacent hot springs.

Really, he didn't have the time to pursue the killers of Gus Helton, but he hadn't felt this invigorated by a case since before his near death.

When Billy entered the bathhouse, he was greeted by an attendant at a counter, a young man chewing an unlit cigar.

"Towel and dressing room?" asked the attendant.

"Yep," said Billy and placed a coin on the counter.

The attendant handed him a folded towel and a key identical —except for the number—to the one Minnie had given him back at Helton's apartment building.

"Dressing rooms that way," the attendant said with a jerk of his thumb.

"Thanks," said Billy.

The changing area was crowded with Saturday bathers, and so Billy went about his task as casually as he could without drawing attention.

Each wooden dressing room door had a small metal plate with

an etched number. None of those numbers, however, matched the *99* on the key from Minnie. They stopped at fifty, which also ruled out the possibility that the *99* was actually *66*. A dead end.

Billy returned to the counter out front.

"I couldn't find the dressing room that goes with this key," he said, handing it to the cigar-chewing attendant.

The attendant glanced at the metal fob and did a double take. Solemnly, he took the cigar from his mouth and set it on the counter. "Gus is dead," he said, a statement not a question.

"I'm sorry," Billy said.

The attendant's face fell. "I thought Gus was being..." he began. "I didn't think..." He put his hand on his cheek and looked away.

Though Billy wanted this man to have his moment to mourn an obvious loss, he also needed to know what the key meant.

The attendant turned and walked back through a door behind the counter, presumably to hide his grief, but when he emerged a moment later, he held a folded manila envelope, which he handed over.

"What is this?" Billy said.

"Stop waving it around," he said, and Billy tucked it into a coat pocket. "I don't know what's in there. Gus gave it to me a couple of days ago and told me not to look inside. He said he was in trouble, and I should only give it to the person who came here with that key."

"What else did he say?" Billy said, but just then a trio of laughing men entered the bathhouse and lined up behind him.

"You need to go," the attendant said in a low voice, and Billy obliged.

# 41

When Francie Bream arrived at Madame Ilsa's suite at the arranged time, the medium dispensed with any pleasantries, sitting Francie immediately down in the parlor and explaining what Roger Marsh wanted tonight: a visit from the ghost of Joseph Smith giving his blessing to Marsh's new religious offshoot. As she listened, Francie worked very hard not to grin at her good fortune. She couldn't have wished for a better setting in which to assassinate Marsh.

"The key to creating a convincing full-figure apparition," Madame Ilsa was saying, "is getting the voice right. That does a lot more to convince people than you might expect."

The two were now assembling the Joseph Smith costume Francie would wear for the Summoning. Francie sorted through Ilsa's supply of outdated men's clothing while Ilsa trimmed and styled a light brown wig sitting atop a mannequin head on the dressing table.

"Is that so?" said Francie.

"Yes," said Ilsa. "I've seen mediums who can rig up the body of a ghost with the best of them but botch the whole illusion when their apparition sounds like a constipated schoolmarm."

"I'm not sure what that would sound like," Francie said, laying out a long coat on the bed next to the trousers she'd selected.

"Not like a ghost, I can tell you that much," Ilsa said. "Now, show me how you would speak as a dead man."

Francie dropped her voice as low as she could. "I would speak like this."

Ilsa looked up from styling the wig. "That's too low," she said. "You sound like someone pretending to be a man. Try a little lower than your natural speaking voice."

"Like this?" said Francie, adjusting accordingly.

"That's fine," said Ilsa. "Now make it ghostly."

"Like this?" said Francie, stretching the words and giving them a mournful quaver.

"That sounded ridiculous," said Ilsa, "Just try to sound, I don't know—perhaps *tired*, but also *powerful*."

"That makes no sense," said Francie.

Ilsa set down her comb and scissors and turned around. "Like this." She straightened her back. "Who summons me from the realm of the spirits?"

She sounded both very tired and very powerful.

"All right," said Francie, duly impressed. "Like this?"

She sat up as straight as she could. "Brothers and Sisters," she intoned, "I have longed to see your faces for lo these many years."

"Better," said Ilsa, with a shrug, "but you're still giving it too much of a quaver,"

"Not bad, though?" said Francie.

Ilsa cocked her head. "I'd say we've got a lot of work to do before nine o'clock." She picked up the comb and scissors and bent once more over the light brown wig.

Francie watched the medium at work and realized she was starting to like Madame Ilsa, which was an unfortunate development, given the extent to which Francie's plans for tonight would irrevocably damage the other woman's career.

# 42

DIANTHA MARSH DIDN'T HAVE THE PATIENCE TO pretend this meeting with the Dowlands was anything other than what it was, a strategic transaction between people who used to be friends. Right now, what she needed from Elder Hyrum Dowland was a significant token of good faith, a solid indication that if she betrayed Roger, she would find community in the mainstream Mormon Church.

They had convened again in the Dowlands' parlor, and neither Elder nor Sister Dowland looked happy to be here.

"Did you present my proposal in the temple this morning?" Diantha asked, getting right down to business.

"I did," said Hyrum, "and I think you'll be happy with the result." He crossed his long legs while Vilate, seated in the armchair next to his, watched Diantha with an unreadable expression.

"I certainly hope so," Diantha said carefully. "What did the Brethren decide?"

Hyrum raised a bony finger. "First, I believe you were going to tell me what, exactly, Roger was getting up to tonight."

Diantha looked to Vilate, who stared grimly at her hands.

"I need to know what you and the Brethren decided before I

can give you any more information," Diantha said to Hyrum, her heart sinking already.

Hyrum shook his head. Vilate still wouldn't look at Diantha.

"You should know as well as anyone, Diantha, what happens in the House of the Lord is sacred, which is to say, it's not to be discussed outside the temple," said Hyrum.

Diantha felt something break inside her. "Enough, Hyrum," she snapped. "Just tell me what happened."

Hyrum and Vilate both looked at her in alarm. Diantha didn't care.

"All right," Hyrum said at last. "I presented your proposal to the Brethren to discuss the merits and potential drawbacks of moving forward with it, and then we went to the Lord in prayer."

"And?"' said Diantha.

"We all felt it is not the Lord's will to alter the role of women in the Church at this time," he said.

Diantha was not exactly surprised by this news, but she was angrier than she might have anticipated. "I thought you said I'd be happy about the results."

"Yes," said Hyrum. "I assumed you'd be happy to learn the will of the Lord on this matter."

Diantha laughed, a single, sharp syllable of pain. She should have seen this coming. "And that's it?" she said, though she already knew the answer.

"I'm sure you wouldn't have us attempt to constrain the Spirit," said Hyrum.

"Of course not," Diantha said bitterly.

Hyrum uncrossed and then re-crossed his legs.

"I don't think you understand, Sister Marsh, the crossroads at which the Church finds itself right now," he said. "Surely, you recall how the rest of the country looked at us during those years the Church practiced plural marriage. They compared us to Mohammedans, to Orientals, to savages and barbarians, but now that we've given it up—as the Lord has instructed us—all that can change.

"This is our chance to show the rest of the country that we're as civilized, as worthy, as white as they are, which places me and the rest of the Brethren in a truly delicate position, Diantha. I want you to attempt to understand that. We cannot—I repeat, *cannot*—afford any form of radicalism at this time, be it polygamy, an upending of the traditional roles of the sexes, or racial intermingling. None of it."

Eminently tired of men like Hyrum Dowland, Diantha was ready to play her last remaining card. "*You* need to understand, Hyrum," she began, "with this approach, you won't obtain the information you want about when and where Roger's holding his séance."

Hyrum Dowland only smiled. "He's holding the séance tonight at nine, at an old dressmaker's shop downtown."

And there it was.

Hyrum had secured another source of information all along, either someone on the inside, or just as likely, someone observing carefully as Roger and his crew of amateurs attempted to carry out their clandestine preparations. Diantha had been nothing but a fallback source, and this whole charade had been—what?—some kind of loyalty test, she supposed.

It was all so humiliating.

"You clearly don't need me then," Diantha said, rising from her seat. "I'll show myself out."

Neither Hyrum nor Vilate protested.

"I'll see you at nine o'clock," Hyrum said, unruffled by her show of temper. "Unless you manage to convince Roger not to show up tonight, that doing so will only humiliate him and his misguided followers. I hope you can manage it."

# 43

At a sticky table in the Antelope Bar and Café, Billy Lovelace sat with a steak and a beer and considered what he'd found in the manila envelope obtained at the Wasatch Springs Bathhouse: compelling evidence confirming a highly placed spy in IWW Local 67 reported directly to Copper King Gilbert Snaith, and this spy was none other than Whiskey Joe Barnes himself.

Billy didn't like this one bit, but the evidence Gus Helton had assembled—a stolen employee dossier for an undercover operative of the P.L.B. Detective Bureau of Denver, heavily annotated after the theft to demonstrate that this Agent 84 and Whiskey Joe Barnes were one and the same man—was hard to argue with.

Add to the paper trail Gus Helton's murder and Lieutenant Mainwaring's ongoing efforts to secure some lost object (presumably this very file), and Billy was hard-pressed to argue Helton hadn't hit the nail on the head.

The question now was what to do with this information, and as far as Billy could see, there was no good way to play it.

He took a long drink of beer and glanced around the mostly empty saloon. Given the quality of his steak—tough, charred, oversalted—Billy wasn't shocked the place was deserted. The only other occupant, a very old man in a filthy overcoat that appeared to date from the Mormons' first arrival in the Salt Lake Valley, raised his drink to Billy.

Billy nodded in return. He sawed off another piece of steak and placed it in his mouth.

He couldn't take the file to the police, as they were in on it. Furthermore, Barnes and Snaith's arrangement was likely legal enough (murder aside), and anyway, Billy would never collaborate with the police if he could help it.

He also doubted Lars Arnasson would be receptive to Gus Helton's conclusions. Lars was already convinced the whole thing was a wild goose chase fabricated by their enemies, and once a person jumped onto that train of thought, there was no coming back. Billy could imagine Lars arguing the file proved nothing, that Helton's murder and the search for the document were all staged to sell the lie that the organization had been infiltrated. While that was certainly possible, Billy didn't think it was likely.

Approaching Whiskey Joe himself was off the table, as Billy had no leverage to force the man to change his traitorous course and would only endanger himself by showing Barnes his hand.

He supposed he could confront Gilbert Snaith. In the past, Billy had found that rattling the cages of those at the top sometimes got things done, but he'd be putting his own life at risk by letting Snaith know he knew about the spy.

No, Billy didn't like any of this, not at all.

"You all right, son?" asked the old man at the nearby table.

"What?" he said, startled.

The old man pointed at Billy's hand. "You look like you're about to stab someone with that steak knife."

Billy looked down. It did, in fact, look like he was about to stab someone with his steak knife. His knuckles were white, and the knife blade shook in his grip. "No," he said, setting it down. "I'm fine, thanks."

As the old man looked away, Billy recognized that over the course of his ruminations, he had become very, very angry. It was dangerous, he knew, to overly sympathize with a dead man, but in light of his own near-death experience, it was hard not to see himself in that battered corpse on the sidewalk in front of the billiards parlor.

*Someone* needed to do right by Gus Helton, and if Billy didn't, who would?

He finished his beer and his steak and left the Antelope Bar and Café knowing he was about to do something rash.

# 44

Roger Marsh still hadn't made it to Adam Wolfe's house. Following his cemetery encounter with that ominous detective, Roger had tried to convince himself that Mr. Lovelace's claims about Madame Ilsa changed absolutely nothing for him, but in truth, his uncertainty had grown with each passing minute after the detective's departure.

If Roger could only see Madame Ilsa again in the flesh, perhaps the Lord would reconfirm that this woman had been divinely appointed to assist in the marvelous work at hand. Which was how he found himself in the lobby of the Armitage Hotel, waiting like a nervous suitor while a bellhop summoned Madame Ilsa.

When the medium arrived, she did not look happy to see him. Her dark clothing was disheveled, there were lines beneath her eyes, and her finger, he noticed, was in a splint.

"Have I interrupted something?" Roger meant it solicitously but realized as soon as he spoke it sounded like a rebuke.

"If I may speak freely," Ilsa said. "Yes, you have. I have a special routine of spiritual exercises I undertake before a Summoning, and you've caught me in the middle of one. What do you need, Mr. Marsh?"

Roger wished he had Adam Wolfe with him right now. Adam

always knew how to deal with prickly characters like Madame Ilsa, but Roger inevitably felt completely at sea in situations like this one.

He could, he supposed, simply tell her the reason he was here.

"I was approached by a private detective this afternoon," Roger began, "who said he can prove that you are a fraud."

Ilsa looked at him stonily.

"I told him I have the utmost faith in you," Roger continued.

Nothing changed in Ilsa's face. "If that's all," she said, "I'm going to return to my room to continue my preparations for tonight."

She turned to go. Why did Adam have to leave Roger alone today of all days?

"Wait," said Roger.

"Yes?" she said, only half turning around.

"Do I have any cause for concern with you?" he said.

Ilsa looked truly affronted at this question.

"I find your hesitancy troubling," she said, "and I'll need a show of good faith from you to continue my work here. Half my fee before the Summoning happens."

Roger could see he was at risk of being outmaneuvered on his own territory, and though Ilsa's request terrified him, he knew exactly how to respond to it.

"Those aren't the terms we agreed to," he said. "You'll receive the full amount when the séance is over."

Ilsa glowered impressively.

"Well, I'm changing the terms," she said. "If you want the séance to happen, I need half the money now."

Roger wished even more acutely that Adam were here to handle this; Roger just couldn't convey menace in the same way he could, couldn't convince people that he might actually harm them.

"No," he said as firmly as he could, "we'll stick to our original terms."

"Then I regret to inform you that the Summoning tonight

won't be happening," said Madame Ilsa. "You see, I'm beginning to suspect there is no money."

"Trust me," said Roger. "We have your money."

Technically speaking, this was only partly true.

He had some of her money, and when he'd envisioned this whole scenario—literally, when he'd received a divine vision of it—the funds hadn't been a problem. He'd thought that, following the séance in which Joseph Smith appeared to Marsh and the other faithful few in attendance, people would open their purses to the cause, perhaps even without Marsh having to ask. And one of these people, or a few in collaboration, would provide Madame Ilsa with her required fee.

For the moment, though, that money was purely notional.

"Forgive me if I'd like a little more proof than your word," said Madame Ilsa, jolting Roger back to the present. "I need half of my money now, or I'm leaving town."

Emboldened by desperation and, perhaps, a desire to test the Lord and the veracity of the vision he'd received, Roger stood his ground. "Then leave town," he said. "But I'm not paying your train fare if you do."

Judging by the look on Madame Ilsa's face, this move had won Roger the upper hand, at least for the moment. "I suspect, Madame Ilsa, you're completely broke," he said, channeling Adam Wolfe as best he could, "and you need me more than I need you."

After a long moment of silence, Madame Ilsa said: "But I'll need to *see* the money before I start the Summoning, do you understand? That's completely non-negotiable. When you show up, if you're not carrying a bag full of money, then I'm leaving this godforsaken city behind me forever, even if I have to beg for train fare on a street corner."

"Agreed," said Roger. It was in the Lord's hands now, a sentiment which, in the past might have brought him great comfort.

# 45

THIS SATURDAY WAS NOT GOING HOW GILBERT SNAITH had hoped. First, that out-of-town detective had started sniffing around his prize spy, and then Diantha Marsh had hesitated to accept his marriage proposal, and now he was trapped by the Alta Club's greatest eugenics enthusiast, Rutherford Andrews, the other man having ambushed him at his table in the club's stately dining room, ignoring Gilbert's subtle hints that he'd prefer to be left alone.

"Skull measurements can only tell you so much, Snaith," Rutherford said, spittle flying from his bearded face, his affronted tone suggesting Gilbert had disagreed with him when, in fact, he hadn't spoken in minutes. "If you want to understand a man's character, you must—and I can't emphasize this enough—you *must* examine his toes."

Rutherford slammed his hand down on the table for emphasis, and as the eugenicist showed no signs of abating any time in the near future, Gilbert returned his attention to the twin frustrations of his Saturday.

First, Diantha: Her request at the park for more time had surprised Gilbert, and he couldn't suppress a hint of irritation at her hesitancy. His offer was so clearly superior to Diantha's current situation. Realistically speaking, what was there to think about? Had he completely misread this woman who'd so taken his fancy? Was she slow-witted, or perhaps more entangled in the sinister tentacles of the Mormon Church than he'd suspected?

"If you familiarize yourself with the literature on the ratio of the length of the big toe to the length of the second toe, and I mean *really* familiarize yourself," Rutherford was saying, almost shouting, actually, "you will be shocked at what you find."

"Ah," said Gilbert.

He supposed this judgment of Diantha was unworthy of him. Some people found change difficult, even a change for the better. Being a gentleman, Gilbert would extend his patience a little further while Diantha gradually came to her senses.

"And the pinkie toes of the criminal classes, Snaith—you would blanche at the knuckle placement," Rutherford said. "Absolutely revolting."

Gilbert raised his eyebrows obligingly at Rutherford's claim.

He wished Diantha was the only problem he had to deal with today, but there was also that Billy Lovelace investigating the IWW spy situation. It would be difficult for the detective to prove anything, let alone oust Gilbert's treasured spy, but this was a matter of honor.

Gilbert hated to be challenged, hated the prospect, however remote, of losing something. He'd worked so hard to arrive at his station in life, and he wasn't about to allow some cheap sleuth to think he could rattle him in any way.

Lieutenant Mainwaring had given repeated assurances that he would take care of everything, but the man was an ignoramus, and Gilbert doubted the incompetent officer would contain this situation to satisfaction.

With a sigh, he began to listen again to his Alta Club tablemate. Rutherford had procured a pen and paper from one of the waiters and was now sketching a diagram of variously shaped toenails and their relation to a person's propensity for thievery.

Perhaps Gilbert's most pressing task, actually, was removing himself from the stupefying clutches of Rutherford Andrews.

# 46

Madame Ilsa left her conversation with Roger Marsh feeling more annoyed than anything else. What had he really wanted from her? He'd seemed genuinely troubled by what Billy had told him but also completely committed to moving forward with the Summoning. It was all very strange—and also frustrating that she hadn't been able to wheedle any money out of him. Getting her hands on half her fee would have made a big difference, though she'd never entertained an expectation that Marsh would oblige her.

Also, the interaction had raised some important questions. Such as, what was Billy up to, aside from trying to discredit her? And where was Adam Wolfe? This seemed like the type of meeting he existed to attend, to serve as a threat while Marsh did whatever Marsh had been doing.

Ilsa shook her head and walked into her suite to find the parlor empty. "Hello?"

"I'm trying on the costume," came Francie Bream's voice from the bedroom.

Preparations for the Summoning were going better than anticipated. Francie was a quick study, sharp and knowledgeable about the Mormons.

Ilsa sat down on the divan.

"What did Marsh want?" Francie called.

It was then that Ilsa noticed the journalist's purse at the other end of the divan. Francie had kept the bag close to her all afternoon, and Ilsa was surprised to see it unattended.

As she explained to Francie what had transpired in the lobby, Ilsa opened the purse and, beneath a handkerchief and a bag of saltwater taffy, found a Smith & Wesson .38 revolver.

While Ilsa generally didn't make it her business what a woman traveling alone might carry for her protection, this was a gun meant for killing, not for scaring off muggers and rakes, and Francie's involvement in tonight's Summoning made the possession of such weaponry very much her concern.

She considered asking Francie outright why she had the gun, but her instincts told her it would be better to feign ignorance. "Anyway," she said, as if she weren't holding a loaded pistol in her hand, "I told him I'll need to see the money before I start the Summoning."

"That seems fair," said Francie. "How do I look?"

Realizing Francie was about to step out from the bedroom, Ilsa panicked and, rather than return the gun to the purse, she hid it behind her back.

The truth was, with the wig and the trousers and the long coat, Francie made a passable Joseph Smith. Ilsa looked over at the costumed journalist and tried not to think about the gun in her hands.

"I think this might work," Ilsa said. "Give me your spirit voice, please."

For some reason, this seemed to amuse Francie. "All right," she said. "*They say honey is sweet, and so do I. I can also taste the spirit of eternal life.* Etcetera."

Francie's Joseph Smith voice was still a bit forced, but it was definitely improving. "It's better than it was," Ilsa said. She had to think of a way to get Francie back into the bedroom so she could return the gun to its hiding place.

"Careful," said Francie. "All that praise may go to my head."

"Do you want me to flatter you, or do you want this to work?"

"Both." Francie moved toward the divan and her now-much-lighter purse.

Necessity forced Ilsa's hand, and with more urgency than the spoken sentiment required, she said, "Those black trousers—I worry they might melt too much into the darkness. Would you try on those gray ones you were looking at earlier?"

"I thought you said those were too light," Francie said, pausing midway to her purse.

"I changed my mind," Ilsa said. "Try on the gray ones."

"Yes ma'am," said Francie, raising her eyebrows.

She picked up the gray pants, and as soon as she was out of the room, Ilsa crossed the parlor, gun in hand, to her trunk of stage props. She began searching for something she hoped she hadn't gotten rid of.

"What are you doing?" Francie called out.

"I'm looking for a lighting device I may want to use," Ilsa said.

She rummaged through her props, and just when she thought she wouldn't find it, her fingers landed on precisely the thing she was looking for: a box of blanks for her stage gun, .38 caliber, which she hadn't used in ages.

Working as quietly and as quickly as she could, she removed the live rounds from the Smith & Wesson and inserted the blanks.

Francie's reasons for participating in the séance remained murky to Ilsa; the only thing for certain was the reporter had an ulterior motive, and until Ilsa could discern what that was, she was not—for her own safety, and for the sake of the Summoning—going to let Francie walk around with a loaded .38.

"Just one last button," Francie called out.

Ilsa scurried back to the divan and returned the gun to the purse just as Francie emerged again from the bedroom.

"Well?" Francie said, doing a turn.

"Yes," said Ilsa, breathing a little bit easier. "I think I do prefer these gray ones."

# 47

Billy Lovelace hated the dining room of the Alta Club the moment he saw it. In fact, he hated the whole club, hated *all* clubs like this one for the way they swaddled their members in lavish and exclusive comfort like the malevolent babies they were.

Billy had broken into the club via a basement window, having tailed Snaith from his mansion. A combination of sweet-talking and bribery of a club attendant had directed Billy to the dining room, and now he hailed a waiter and told him that a Mr. Gilbert Snaith was expecting him.

"Just over there," the waiter said, indicating a table where two men sat in conversation.

"And Mr. Snaith?" Billy said.

"The one without the beard," said the waiter, shooting him a suspicious glance before scuttling off to a needy table.

Billy knew his current actions were both unnecessary and reckless. Confronting Snaith wouldn't net him any new information about the murder of Gus Helton and might get him killed. During his walk from the Antelope Saloon, he'd tried to talk himself out of what he was about to do, to no avail. Something about Helton's murder had unleashed a powerful torrent of emotion.

Approaching Snaith's table, Billy noted that the Copper King was a vigorous-looking man in his forties wearing an expensive suit and an expression of desperate boredom in response to his bearded companion's monologue. As Billy pulled out a chair and sat down, Snaith's eyes lit up with relief, and then disbelief, and then fury.

"Good afternoon, gentlemen," Billy said.

The bearded man was saying something about bunions and continued speaking for several seconds before Billy's arrival seemed to register and he sputtered to a stop.

"Who on earth are you?" he demanded, correctly ascertaining that Billy Lovelace was not the type of person generally admitted to the Alta Club.

Billy turned to Gilbert. "Aren't you going to introduce me to your friend, Mr. Snaith?"

"I don't believe I've had the pleasure," Snaith responded, visibly working to maintain his composure.

"I think you know who I am," Billy said.

Gilbert Snaith clenched and unclenched his hand while the bearded man looked in alarm from Snaith to Lovelace.

"You must be Billy Lovelace," Snaith said.

"I am," said Billy.

Snaith's eyes glinted. "You may not be for long."

"Are you going to have Lieutenant Mainwaring throw me off a building?"

Snaith took a long drink of brandy and set down his empty glass. He seemed annoyed, yes, and maybe a *little* angry, but not as rattled as Billy had hoped he'd be.

"You," said the bearded man to Billy, like he was addressing a stray dog. "Get out of here."

Both Billy and Gilbert Snaith ignored him.

"I know Whiskey Joe is your spy," Billy said.

"Good for you." Snaith rose from his chair. "Now, if you'll excuse me."

Snaith's indifference was making Billy feel like nothing more than a pesky child, and he jumped up to face the multi-millionaire. "I can prove it," Billy said.

"To whom?" Snaith growled, leaning in closer, almost daring the detective to strike him.

Billy resented having his bluff called so quickly and decisively. As he'd previously reasoned to himself, the police were in Snaith's pocket, and Lars was unlikely to trust Helton's intelligence.

At that moment, the bearded man hurled a teacup at Billy's head. The cup bounced off, fell to the floor, and shattered.

Gilbert looked from the shattered cup to Billy's surprised expression and roared with laughter. "You're an embarrassment, Mr. Lovelace," he said, once his guffaws had subsided. "If you ever speak to me again, I can promise you'll regret it as much as Gus Helton would regret *his* shenanigans right now if he weren't dead."

At that, Billy sprang forward, or tried to, because just then two burly waiters grabbed him from behind, having been alerted, apparently, through the gestural vernacular of the wealthy, that Billy was a nuisance who required removal.

Billy struggled mightily, but the men held him tight as Gilbert Snaith stormed past him and out of the dining room. The burly waiters dragged Billy to the club's rear entrance and threw him out the door onto a moist heap of garbage.

# 48

SITTING IN GILBERT SNAITH'S IMMACULATELY appointed parlor, Roger Marsh felt disconcertingly like a schoolboy waiting outside the principal's office for a paddling. Roger had come by Snaith's house unannounced, and though the butler had shown him to the parlor, he'd also hinted strongly that Roger might be happier coming back at another time. Roger had ignored the hint and said he'd be happy to wait.

He needed money, and he needed it fast. Not a lot of money, relative to Gilbert Snaith's fortune, just enough to pay Madame Ilsa tonight for her services. He didn't relish the process of begging, hat in hand, and was considering leaving when Snaith strode into the room, visibly agitated. When he saw Roger, though, he offered an almost convincing smile.

"Roger," Gilbert began, "I haven't had a chance to speak with my accountant yet—"

"No, of course," said Roger. "I wasn't expecting that you had."

"Ah," said Snaith, whose eyes suggested his mind was somewhere far from here.

"I've come at a bad time," said Roger.

Snaith drew himself up into a ramrod posture. "Of course

not," he said. "Everything is perfectly fine. And you, Roger? How are the preparations for your event coming along?"

Roger recognized the question was posed out of politeness at best, but still, the fact of someone inquiring after his well-being broke down his defenses.

"It's going well," Roger began stiffly, and then shook his head. "It's not, actually. Or it could turn out well, but I don't know how."

His voice was ragged, and he wasn't addressing Snaith so much as the universe, or God, or whomever might lend a sympathetic ear.

"I don't know what's going to happen tonight," Roger said, almost in a trance. "I have a sense of foreboding, like my life is hanging by a thread. Or worse, that my soul is hanging by a thread, but I don't know if that's because I'm moving forward with my plans, or because I'm tempted to hesitate. I just don't know. But the consequences feel enormous."

It was both liberating and alarming to say this out loud, and Roger felt a sublime lightness in his body that he hadn't felt in weeks.

Then Gilbert Snaith cleared his throat, and the lightness within Roger gave way to a humiliating weight as he suddenly remembered himself, remembered where he was and the purpose of his visit.

Snaith looked at him with contempt.

"But I should get to the point," Roger said.

Snaith shook his head. "No, you shouldn't."

"What?" said Roger.

"You make me sick," Snaith said, flinging his hands outward. "Here you are, a prince of this city, married to three women, one of whom is young, beautiful, and vivacious, and yet you dither over God and His blessings. You know, I used to admire you, in a way. Not you specifically, understand, but the Mormon Apostles with their brazen, sanctimonious rascality."

Speechless, Roger felt in danger of being crushed by the force of the other man's emotion.

"I'm of the belief, Roger," Snaith continued, eyes aflame, "if you want something, you should take it, you should enjoy it, and you should make no apologies. You Mormons have things all turned around. You're bucking social approval to do what you want, but you're not *enjoying* it, and that's what I find perverse."

Roger's skin was hot with indignation.

Snaith pressed on. "And you're the worst of them all, the most pathetic little handwringer I've ever met. It's no wonder Diantha's leaving you. I can't for the life of me imagine *any* woman wanting to be with you, let alone three."

Roger wasn't sure he'd heard that last part correctly. "What's this about Diantha?"

"She's leaving you." Snaith grinned—or rather, snarled. "She's written several letters, telling me how much she admires me, and today when we were strolling hand in hand through Liberty Park, she said what a relief it was to be touched by a young and virile man. For *years*, she's been aching for that kind of touch, she said."

Roger had been grappling for some time with the possibility that Diantha could leave him, but it had never occurred to him that she might leave him for another man. His eyes felt hot, and he hugged himself around his middle.

"I'd bring you a drink to brace your nerves," Snaith said, "but you don't drink, do you?"

Roger was only dimly aware of Snaith's leering presence. He felt as if someone had injected a decoction of pure sadness into his veins. He *loved* Diantha, loved her enough to be willing to grant her a separation, if that's what she wanted. But the thought of her living with Gilbert Snaith was devastating.

"You've been bested, Elder Marsh," Gilbert was saying. "How does it feel?"

Roger rallied the little dignity still at his command and stood up. "I'll no longer require your funding for the enterprise I mentioned yesterday," he said, voice barely audible. "Please consider our meeting on Monday cancelled."

Walking out of the parlor, his perceptions of his marriage to Diantha completely upended, Roger thought he heard Gilbert chuckling throatily behind him.

# 49

Back in the Stockade office of Rose Montague, Madame Ilsa waited for the return of Lillian Paree, hoping the young prostitute had been able to ascertain what exactly Billy Lovelace was up to in Salt Lake.

Though she wouldn't go so far as to say she felt hopeful, Ilsa was, at the very least, not displeased with what she and Francie Bream had accomplished back at her suite. With a little luck, the Summoning tonight could work, and if she could find a way to manage the Billy situation, she might leave Salt Lake in one piece, with more money in her pocket than she'd had in quite some time.

Of course, Ilsa was no fool. At any point, this whole situation could turn belly up, and so, before coming here to the Stockade, she'd hidden an escape bag within a secluded row of shrubbery at the Salt Lake City Cemetery.

Now, sitting in the office of the Stockade's formidable manager, Ilsa glanced at the clock on Rose Montague's desk.

"It's not four o'clock yet," Montague noted defensively. "We did agree on four o'clock."

"I'm not worried," Ilsa said, and then, as the clock tolled four, Big Ernie opened the door and escorted in a beaming Lillian Paree.

Lillian nodded at the two women already in the room, and Rose Montague gestured for her to take a seat.

"Well, what do you have to show for yourself?" Montague asked as her young employee sat down in a straight-backed chair.

All business, Lillian reached into her tattered handbag and removed a much-folded scrap of butcher paper covered in cramped handwriting.

"It is now my pleasure to present to you fine ladies the discoveries I made whilst investigating Mr. Billy Lovelace, as hired by Madame Ilsa von Hoffmann to do," she said with a theatrical formality that drew an admonishing glance from Rose Montague.

"All right," said Lillian, tilting her head in apology to her employer. "Here's what I found out."

She explained that Whiskey Joe Barnes and Lars Arnasson, two local labor bigwigs, had hired Billy Lovelace to find out if Utah millionaire Gilbert Snaith had planted an undercover operative in IWW Local 67. Gus Helton, a member of Local 67, was thrown off the top of a building later that day, and Lovelace tangled with the local cops on the scene. A little later, Lovelace was thrown out of the Alta Club, where he'd confronted Snaith himself, and that brought things up to the present moment, more or less.

Oh, and also, Billy was looking for Madame Ilsa, but no one knew exactly what for.

Lillian refolded her scrap of butcher paper and returned it to her bag.

"My goodness," Ilsa said. "That was very thorough. How did you find all that out?"

"You mean, how do you know I didn't just make it up?" Lillian said.

"Well, yes," said Madame Ilsa.

Lillian said that she'd gathered her information by a few different methods: she'd spent some time tailing Billy Lovelace himself and asking around town about the detective, and then to tie it all together, she'd consulted her fellow prostitutes, who were real treasure troves of information gleaned from loose-lipped clients.

Madame Ilsa looked to Rose Montague, who gave a nod of confirmation.

"My girls know more about the goings-on of this city than any other single group of people," Rose said proudly.

Ilsa turned back to Lillian. "Color me impressed," she said. "You did some real top-notch work today."

Lillian smiled proudly and turned her gaze demurely to Madame Ilsa's purse.

"Of course," said Ilsa. "The rest of your fee. You've certainly earned it."

"All in a day's work, ma'am," said Lillian.

As Ilsa counted out the bills, she said, "This Lars Arnasson—is he tall, blond, big mole on his cheek?"

"That's right," said Lillian. "One of the girls told me he used to be a singer."

"On vaudeville?" Ilsa said.

"I think so," Lilian said.

Ilsa stood and began to pace the office, forgetting for a moment the presence of the two other women.

"What's wrong, ma'am?" Lillian looked at her with concern. "Are you frightened?"

"No," said Ilsa, and she wasn't. She was pacing not from fear but excitement. She had a plan now—a good one—to outfox Billy Lovelace.

# 50

In a more respectable part of town, Francie Bream—having first tailed Madame Ilsa to the city cemetery where she observed the medium stuffing a carpetbag inside a row of bushes—arrived at the home of Diantha Marsh for a final interview, the interview in which she would change Diantha's life forever.

During her weeks of research in the various archives of Ogden, Utah, Francie had made an astonishing discovery. Eighteen years after awarding the wrong baby to Sarah and Frank Crawford, Roger Marsh had turned around and married her, making young Diantha Crawford his third wife.

The discovery had horrified and thrilled Francie—horrified because this man wouldn't leave her family alone and thrilled because she'd found her mother's long-lost first child. Diantha Marsh was not just any victim of polygamy: she was Francie Bream's half-sister.

Diantha needed to know this, and Francie was the one who needed to tell her. And yet, unsure how Diantha would take the news, Francie was as nervous as she'd been in some time.

Steeling herself, she knocked on the front door.

When Diantha answered, she looked almost happy to see her. "Please," she said, "come in."

Francie barely had time to settle into a chair before Diantha turned the tables on her. "I wonder if I could ask your advice," Diantha said. "I know we don't know each other well, but that's part of the appeal."

"Oh," said Francie, her mental agenda disrupted. "Yes, I suppose...yes."

Diantha was tapping her toe against the rug in a muffled drumbeat. "I've reached a point in my life where I can no longer live as I've been living," she said. "That much is clear, but where I go from here is not."

"All right," Francie said.

"The main issue is how to support myself," Diantha continued, "because if I leave Roger, his financial situation isn't what it was, and I know I'd only get limited support. I have received an offer from a local millionaire, but I'm afraid I'd have to marry him to accept his money. That prospect doesn't appeal to me."

As a woman who'd supported herself professionally her entire adult life, Francie didn't think Diantha's situation sounded so impossible. "If you left Roger," she said, "don't you think he'd let you keep this house?"

"I suppose he would," Diantha said.

"And if you already have a home," Francie continued, "I'm certain you could find sufficient work to pay for your necessities, and then some."

Diantha appeared to consider this.

Francie said, "Would you worry about Roger, or maybe the Mormons, harassing you if you stayed in Salt Lake City?"

Diantha shook her head. "No, I wouldn't."

"It seems to me you have a starting point, at least," Francie said. "Leave Roger, find a job, and then take some time to think about what to do next. No need to marry millionaires, unless you want to."

Diantha drummed her fingers against the arm of her chair. "I suppose you're right," she said, unconvincingly.

Francie's journalistic instincts told her she wasn't getting the full picture. "But it's more than material circumstances, isn't it?" she said.

Diantha sighed and looked away. "I already feel like I've lost the best fifteen years of my life," she said, "and so what I do next needs to really *matter*. I need to make it count. Roger married me when I was only eighteen years old; he was in his forties, with two wives already. He's always treated me with kindness and respect—not every woman is so lucky, I'm well aware—but I still can't help but feel like he stole something, like he robbed my life of so many wonderful possibilities.

"I was still a girl when I married him, and the whole thing seemed so exciting and romantic at the time. This was after President Woodruff issued the manifesto stating the Church would no longer perform plural marriages, but those in the know understood this wasn't the case. The practice would continue, but more secretively than before. I felt like I was part of something clandestine and brave, something important.

"Instead, I'm just another wife, an appendage to my illustrious husband, who's not even illustrious anymore; he's a disgrace for hanging onto something all his peers have recognized is no longer politic to support. I want to—I don't know—do something or be something in my own right, something that makes up for all the years I spent as this semi-anonymous woman in Roger Marsh's shadow. I want to make important decisions, too, the same way men make important decisions. I'd like to speak for God every once in a while, the way Roger and his friends speak for Him. Is that so much to ask?"

Diantha smiled as she concluded this speech, and Francie smiled back. All this made perfect sense, though Francie wondered if learning of her true parentage would embolden or further discourage Diantha. There was only one way to find out.

"This may seem like a tangent," said Francie, "but what do you know about your parents?"

Diantha looked confused. "What do you mean, what do I know about my parents?"

"I should be more specific," Francie said. "What do you know about your parents' connection to Roger Marsh?"

"Oh, that," Diantha said with relief. "Yes, he was their bishop when he lived in Ogden. One of those funny little coincidences."

"That's it?"

Diantha eyed her warily. "What do you *think* you know?"

Francie took a deep breath. "It has to do with your true identity," she said. "Would you like me to tell you?"

Diantha hesitated over this for some time. "Tell me," she said, finally.

After a short pause, Francie recounted the story her mother had told on her deathbed. She explained how she'd been able to corroborate the story through archival research and eyewitness testimony from people in Ogden.

What Francie omitted from her account, for now, anyway, was the fact that the woman who told the story was her own mother and that she and Diantha were sisters.

When Francie was finished, Diantha closed her eyes and said nothing for a long while.

"And Roger was the one who made the decision," she said finally.

"That's correct," Francie said.

She let out a long, slow breath. "I don't intend to rely on your word for this."

"Nor should you," said Francie. "Ask Roger if you'd like. Or ask around in Ogden. I'd be happy to share my sources."

Diantha pressed her lips into a thin line and stared at some imagined point far beyond her parlor wall.

Francie wondered if Diantha had heard her, if she'd made a serious mistake. "If you'd like," she said, "I can leave you to consider."

Without looking at her, Diantha said, "I think that would be for the best."

# 51

Billy Lovelace sat collecting his thoughts on a park bench on the grounds of the Mormon Temple. His body ached from the punishment it had already undergone today; between being beaten by Mainwaring and thrown from the back door of the Alta Club, it was a wonder he wasn't hurting more than he did.

A couple of years ago, this level of pain would hardly have bothered him, but since nearly dying at the hands of Anton LeFleur, Billy had developed a more solicitous relationship with his body. He understood in a way he hadn't before that his physical form required care and tending, understood further that he could be killed just as easily as the next person.

It was astonishing, really, that he wasn't dead. But after being horribly beaten by that coward LeFleur, he'd awoken some hours later in a rustic shack that stank of fish.

His rescuer turned out to be a confoundingly decent fisherman who'd seen a body thrown onto the beach from the back of a carriage, and upon closer inspection, discovered a faint pulse. He'd carried Billy to his nearby shack and called a trusted doctor to tend to the near-dead man.

Billy wasn't sure how long he'd spent recovering in that tiny wooden dwelling. The fisherman was unfailingly generous and vehemently refused all offers of compensation for the care he'd provided.

When Billy was well enough, he left the fisherman, thanking him as profusely as he knew how, and embarked on his meticulous campaign for revenge. He would find LeFleur and Standish and von Hoffmann, and he would kill each one where they stood.

Unfortunately, the trail to LeFleur and Standish led, after many zigs and zags, to Roumania, a locale too distant for Billy to follow. He didn't intend to bankrupt himself in pursuit of revenge, and he figured that having forced the pair to flee the country would have to be victory enough.

Madame Ilsa proved even more elusive, and after a few months, Billy, being the practical man that he was, reached two important decisions: first, he would subordinate his search for the medium to his career as a detective-for-hire, and second, when he found Ilsa, he wouldn't kill her. She hadn't *directly* tried to kill him, after all; destroying her career would be justice enough.

Now, on the cusp of enacting that tempered revenge, Billy felt proud of his restraint and perseverance, and, looking up at the Mormon temple, he reminded himself why he had come to Salt Lake: to settle his score with Ilsa.

He would set aside the Helton case, at least until tomorrow morning, and tonight he would attain the objective he'd been working toward for so long now.

# 52

Roger felt grubby and mean rummaging through Diantha's things without her permission, but he felt worse leaving Gilbert Snaith's insidious claims uninvestigated. If Diantha really were in love with Snaith, as the Copper King had claimed, she would have saved the letters he'd sent her, and if she'd saved Snaith's letters, they had to be somewhere in her house.

Roger had already searched every room but the bedroom and found nothing, though he knew the bedroom would be the most likely place to hide such letters. Roger didn't *want* to find them, couldn't bear the thought of Diantha in love with that smooth-talking multi-millionaire.

There was no more avoiding it. He would search her bedroom.

He looked between the pages of the books on her nightstand, behind the framed paintings on the walls, beneath the mattress of her bed, and came up with nothing. He began to hope he would continue to find nothing, but then, between the covers of a hollowed-out copy of *The Pilgrim's Progress* sitting atop Diantha's writing desk, he found a bundle of papers.

With a heavy heart, Roger sat on the edge of the bed and unfolded and read one of the letters, and then another, and then another. They were not as damning as Snaith had insinuated—his professions of love existed almost entirely between the lines of what was actually written—but their presence, and the fact that Diantha had kept them hidden, suggested that Snaith's claims were not entirely baseless.

Roger sank to the floor, overcome with sweet affection for his soon-to-be-former wife. When he had tendered that contested baby to Frank and Sarah Crawford all those years ago, he'd had no idea he was also laying in store a vibrant young wife to brighten the glum and arid years of his own middle age. Wasn't that often the way with the Lord, though, concealing miracles within miracles, treasures within treasures?

The second time Roger met Diantha Crawford, he was forty years old, and following his six-month incarceration in Sugar House Prison, he'd been dwelling, metaphorically speaking, in the slough of despond. Though he served as an Apostle of the Resurrected Lord Jesus Christ, his life and its events felt flat and empty of meaning.

He woke each morning, prayed, attended the requisite meetings, and conducted the necessary business, all with a vacuity that enervated his soul. Part of it, he believed at the time, was his failure to sire any children, and because he'd tried with two separate women, he suspected the issue (or rather the lack of issue) lay with him.

His malaise was more free-floating than that, less tied to any one circumstance and more suffused throughout his being like the chilly water droplets of a dense fog. And then one spring day at a picnic on the lawn at Temple Square, he saw Diantha, and the choking fog lifted.

She was seventeen that day, a month out from her next birthday, and had just slipped off her shoes to run through the cool April grass, exclaiming how delightful it felt before one of the chaperoning adults admonished her for the small impropriety. She was a picture of life and vitality, Roger thought at that moment, with her cheeks flushed, her skin fresh and new, her smile still endearingly childlike.

He knew immediately he had to marry her, that if anything could bring a long-absent zest back into his life, it was this young woman.

During his ensuing courtship of Diantha Crawford, Roger was entirely scrupulous, obtaining all the requisite permissions from his fellow church leaders, his two current wives, and the girl's father. Those considerable hurdles cleared, Roger was thrilled and delighted when young Diantha accepted his suit.

They were married that summer.

Over the years, it was true, their relationship had known its share of difficulties, but on the whole, Diantha had brought so much joy to this second half of his life, so much liveliness and spark.

Now, he was about to lose her to that smug millionaire, Gilbert Snaith. Despondent, Roger rose to his feet and returned the letters to their hiding place in the book. He couldn't let this great personal loss distract him, though. He had a vital task to accomplish tonight, and the Lord, if not Diantha, would be with him.

# 53

After checking at a couple of diners, a tenement building, three separate bars, a billiards parlor, and a smoke shop, Madame Ilsa finally found Lars Arnasson—formerly Tom Whippoorwill, of the Four Songbirds—enjoying a bit of dinner theater at the Cocoanut Club where, onstage, a spirited troupe performed a burlesque parody of Ibsen's *A Doll's House* with skimpily costumed women in the male roles and even more skimpily costumed women in the female ones.

Arnasson occupied one of the club's small, round tables by himself, and when Ilsa sat down, he shot her half a glance before looking resolutely away.

"Feeling nostalgic for your time treading the boards, Tom?" she said.

He flinched. "You must have me mistaken for someone else. Name's Lars. Lars Arnasson."

"Used to be Tom Whippoorwill," she said, "at least on vaudeville."

He still refused to look at her. "You're very confused," he said.

Onstage, the actress playing Nora Helmer sang an innuendo-laden ditty about her unsatisfying marriage. The rest of the crowd laughed, but Lars looked like he was passing a kidney stone.

"Don't pretend like you don't recognize me, *Lars*," she said. "I already know you're the one who gave me away to Billy."

This was a bluff, and the first in a long line of falsehoods and semi-falsehoods about to leave her mouth.

"I'm not angry," she said.

Lars finally turned to look her in the face. "He told me he wasn't going to hurt you."

Ilsa doubted this very much. "And he hasn't," she said. "So why are you acting so skittish?"

The musical number ended, and the crowd applauded.

Lars looked skeptically at Ilsa. "Aren't you the reason he almost died?"

"It's more complicated than that," she said. "But yes, I was there when it happened. Billy and I had words about that earlier today, but we've mended fences."

All untrue, but Lars didn't seem to disbelieve it outright.

"When he told me he needed to find you, it seemed pretty urgent," Lars said. "More urgent than a mending fences kind of conversation, that's for sure."

This part was going to be tricky.

Ilsa tried to sound casual. "He's working out a new scam that needs two people to run, and he's convinced I'm the only person who could do it," she said with a toss of her hand. "Which is neither here nor there. I wanted to find you, Lars, because you're a local, or close enough, and I need your insight. I'm working on some banter for a Summoning I'm performing tonight, and I need to know how certain references may play with the Salt Lake City Mormon crowd."

Lars looked confused. "Slow down a minute," he said. "You said Billy's working on a new scam?"

"That's right," said Ilsa.

"Billy's a detective now," Lars said. "He doesn't do that kind of thing anymore."

Ilsa laughed long and loud, and then said, "Is that what he told you?"

"I've heard it from other people too. He's a detective now." Lars sounded less sure of this assertion the second time.

"That's what he tells people," said Ilsa. "But you know his routine when he and I worked together, right? I'd get hired as a medium, and Lovelace would try to debunk me. Only he wouldn't be able to, so we'd both get paid. We never got caught, until we did. Or he did, anyway."

Lars gave her a skeptical look, but Ilsa could tell his heart wasn't in it.

"I'm telling you the truth, Lars," she said. "Billy and I were *partners*. Who would know better than me?"

As he took this in, the crowd cheered at the entrance of a bare-legged actress in a false beard playing the part of Dr. Rank.

"What's the scam?" said Lars. "The new one he wants you for."

"I don't want to talk about Billy right now," she said. "I want to talk about my Summoning."

Lars shook his head. "First tell me what the scam is."

Ilsa made a show of great reluctance. "I didn't even get all the specifics, because I'm not interested," she said. "All I remember is something to do with labor unions."

"What kind of scheme with labor unions?" Lars said through clenched teeth.

"Lars, I don't remember the details," she said. "Can we please change the subject?"

"Tell me all the details you remember," said Lars.

Ilsa saw anger and fear in his eyes. She'd hooked him. "All right," Ilsa said. "If you're going to make such a fuss about it, here's what I remember. It's something with—he realized a while back that every union believes they have a spy, and so Billy capitalizes on that belief by—I'm not sure how exactly, this is where things got convoluted for me—but the crux of it is, from a distance, he plants information about a spy and then shows up in town to find this nonexistent spy, for a fee. That's all I can remember. Honestly."

Another musical number began onstage. Lars ran his tongue along his teeth while his fingers tapped on the table. "I can't believe him," he said. "Well, I *can* believe, but still. This is low, even for Billy Lovelace, that son of a bitch."

"What do you mean?" she asked innocently.

"I have to go," Lars said. "Right now."

"Wait," said Ilsa, as Lars bolted from the Cocoanut Club. "We need to talk about my Summoning."

# 54

Still shaky from Francie Bream's sensational claims about her parentage, Diantha Marsh pounded on the front door of Gilbert Snaith's stunning mansion. She needed some resolution in her life right now, and so when the butler answered the door, she shoved past the man and tore through the house until she found Gilbert in his oak and marble library listening to a recording of Enrico Caruso on his Edison phonograph. He wore a paisley dressing gown and an expression of surprise as she breathlessly strode into the room.

"I'm not going to marry you, Gilbert," she said. "It doesn't matter how much money you have."

Just then, the butler caught up to her. "I'm very sorry, sir," he said, poking his head in the door. "Would you like me to show Mrs. Marsh out?"

"Leave us alone please, Bernham," Gilbert said, and the butler retreated with a discreet nod.

Gilbert rose and gestured for Diantha to sit.

"No, thank you," she said. "Did you hear what I said?"

Barely suppressing a smile, Gilbert nodded. "You said you won't marry me. May I ask why?"

Diantha hadn't thought this far ahead, or about how she would answer that question.

"Because I don't want to," she said, having decided after a moment's reflection that this was the truest response.

Gilbert snorted. "You sound like a petulant child."

"Excuse me?"

"*I don't want to,*" he mimicked in a high, whiny voice.

This show of pettiness stunned Diantha, rooting her in place.

"I didn't think you were so naïve," Gilbert continued. "You stand to gain much more than money if you marry me. Have you really taken into account, Diantha, the damage your reputation will incur if you stay with Roger? Honestly, the damage it has *already* incurred.

"In terms of your political work, the Gentiles—as you amusingly call them—take you even less seriously than they did when you were the polygamous wife of a Mormon. Now you're the polygamous wife of a man too reactionary even for the Mormons. In their eyes, you're an odder specimen than you were before."

Gilbert was building up steam and didn't seem to notice or care that Diantha's face had hardened into an expression of deep resentment.

"And in terms of the Mormon community," he went on, "you're an outcast there, too. Your husband was excommunicated, which I don't think I need to remind you of, but considering the way you're talking, maybe I do."

"So, what?" said Diantha, finding her voice again. "I should give up and marry you because I'm all washed up either way?"

"No," said Gilbert. "What I'm saying is, I hope you'll agree to marry me, first because you love me, or at least find me agreeable, and second, because I could do so much to further your cause.

"I have money, Diantha. I have *so much* money, and as someone who hasn't always had it—I grew up poor, you may recall—I understand the difference that kind of money can make. For instance: everything I said about your reputation—guess what? I'm rich enough that reputation doesn't matter.

"You want to further your pet political causes? My money will get you into the room with people who can make those kinds of dreams a reality. I'm talking about senators, I'm talking about governors, I'm talking about kings and queens, and other rich men like me who could be persuaded to throw some money after a worthy cause if the right person was convincing enough. And I think you're that person, Diantha. You have talent, and that talent is being wasted on the Mormons."

She knew Gilbert wasn't wrong about what his money could do. But he was trying to purchase her right now, as he might purchase a fine rug or a costly jewel that caught his fancy.

"I might also restate," said Gilbert, misreading her silence, "Roger has two other wives, and I'm not sure why he's entitled to someone as enchanting as you, Diantha. He is, if I may be blunt, a fool."

It was then that Diantha noticed the stack of dime novels on a shelf of the open phonograph cabinet. Struck with curiosity—Gilbert had never seemed much of a reader—and needing time to think, she walked to the cabinet and picked up a handful of the cheaply bound books.

When Gilbert saw what she was doing, he lunged forward with an uncharacteristically panicked, "No!"

By the time he reached her, though, the books were already in her hands, and he stopped short of grabbing her by the arm. "Those are nothing," he said. "Don't think they mean something, because they don't."

Diantha shuffled through the thin volumes, taking in their elaborate, often florid titles: *The Bradys and Mr. Mormon, or Secret Work in Salt Lake City*; and *Old Cap. Collier in Salt Lake City, or "Piping" the Mormon Conspirators;* and *Frank Merriwell Among the Mormons, or The Lost Tribe of Israel*. The colorful covers featured men and women in modern garb encountering outlandishly attired Mormons wearing either severe, outdated clothing or hooded robes, standing against picturesque mountain backdrops or inside underground caverns.

"You should put those down," said Gilbert, sounding genuinely nervous.

Diantha flipped open to a random page and read a description of a band of vicious Danite Avengers, murder in their eyes, closing in on a brave and desperate federal agent sent to stop their rampage of death. She flipped to another page and read a geographical description of the Salt Lake Valley constructed more, it seemed, from wishful thinking and guesswork than from direct observation or maps.

"I don't really read them," Gilbert was saying.

Another passage described the rescue from polygamists of a virginal, raven-haired beauty by an intrepid adventurer. In the arms of her savior, the young woman trembled with gratitude, her flesh soft and warm in his strong arms.

Diantha laughed and then read aloud from the novel: "'Hold me closer,' Rachel said, and Dick Powers obliged, his mind recoiling at how close this unspoiled beauty had come to ruination at the lecherous hands of old Apostle Hawthorn. Powers caressed the alabaster skin of her face, and Rachel responded with an appreciative whimper.'"

"Give me that," said Gilbert, snatching the book from her hands and sending the rest of the novels spilling to the floor.

"Is that what you've been hoping to get from me?" said Diantha. "An appreciative whimper? A kiss from my yielding and grateful lips?"

Gilbert's face had flushed to a deep and dangerous red. "I rescind my offer of marriage," he said. "I rescind every part of my offer."

"It's too late for that," she said. "I already turned it down."

Gilbert was practically quivering with rage, but after a series of deep breaths, his face regained its equanimity, his body its easy posture. Diantha was impressed by his sudden self-control, if nothing else.

"You've made your position quite clear," Gilbert said evenly, "and it's now incumbent on me to accept your decision with graciousness."

"I appreciate that very much, Mr. Snaith," said Diantha, and then, indicating the heap of dime novels on the marble floor: "I'm sorry some of your books were damaged in our little fracas."

Gilbert refused to look at the books, instead giving her a curt bow of the head, and wishing her a good evening.

# 55

On the second floor of an ostentatious Romanesque building in downtown Salt Lake, Madame Ilsa fit the last piece of tonight's puzzle into place.

The Summoning would be held here, in an open and echoey space previously occupied by an upscale dressmaker who'd left behind—some months ago, by the looks of it—nothing but a pair of broken dress forms in a cobwebbed corner and a slew of fabric scraps strewn about the dusty floor.

More to Madame Ilsa's interest was a barely visible, waist-high door in a far wall that opened onto a long, dark crawlspace.

"We can hide you in here," Ilsa said to Francie Bream, who was slowly walking the perimeter of the room.

"A crawlspace," she said approvingly. "This venue is perfect, isn't it?"

Ilsa looked around the old dressmaker's shop. "Well," she said, "I don't like the big windows, there's only one exit, and the echo is a bit of a double-edged sword, but yes, the crawlspace is good."

Francie looked amused by this assessment, but then her expression turned somber. "We're actually going to try and pull this off, aren't we?"

"Yes, we are," said Ilsa, wondering again what Miss Bream's

game was. "Why don't you change into your costume so we can get you situated."

Francie glanced at the crawlspace. "Situated, how?"

"I have some dark canvas we can hang as a false wall in case anyone shines a light in there," Ilsa said. "You'll wait behind it."

"Clever." Gathering the pieces of her Joseph Smith costume, Francie stepped into the stairwell to change, closing the door behind her.

Madame Ilsa took this opportunity to oil the hinges of every door in the room and to conceal a few tools and an apparatus of her own design within the abandoned dress forms.

When Francie Bream re-entered the space in her boots, trousers, overcoat, and wig, she made a compelling Joseph Smith. If Ilsa squinted (the illusion would be flawless in the dark), she could believe that a nineteenth-century American prophet stood before her, and, on top of that, Francie *did* have real stage presence; Ilsa didn't want to look away.

"You look excellent," she said.

"Thank you," said Francie with a manly bow.

"Here," said Ilsa, handing the journalist a tub of makeup. "Face lightener. You'll put it on just before you come out."

"Right." Francie slipped the tub into a coat pocket. "Into the crawlspace with me?"

Ilsa looked the journalist up and down and felt the pang of some melancholic emotion she couldn't quite name. "You know," she began, and Francie looked at her with concern.

Ilsa paused and then continued. "Even in the beginning, I could never really hear the voices of the dead, but back then, I wasn't a fraud. Not exactly. What I was doing, I did because I liked it and was good at it, but also because I thought it could help people. I really did. I believed if people could speak with their loved ones one last time, maybe it would be easier to let them go."

Francie looked uneasy and a little confused.

"But it's been a long time since I've believed that." Ilsa paused. "For years and years now, it's been a long series of empty, cynical gestures. In other words, Miss Bream, I'm a charlatan, maybe even a feckless one, which is to say, your assessment of me back in the *Dubuque Standard-Examiner* stung me badly because it was correct. If I'm being very honest with you, it was an astute review, and I think you should know that."

"Well," said Francie, shifting her weight from one foot to the other. "Well."

Ilsa dabbed at her eyes, careful not to smudge her makeup. "Well, indeed," she said. "Now. Let's wall you up inside that crawlspace."

# 56

BILLY PLANNED TO SO THOROUGHLY HUMILIATE Madame Ilsa at her séance tonight that she would never work again. To do so, he needed to first familiarize himself with the venue, which was why he now walked casually down the sidewalk across the street from the three-storied, Romanesque monstrosity where his source had told him the séance would be held.

A moment earlier, Billy had thought he'd seen movement through one of the second-floor windows, and he was about to cross the street to investigate when a figure approached.

"I thought I might find you here," said Lars Arnasson.

Whatever this was about, it wasn't good.

"Our meeting's not until tomorrow morning, Lars," Billy said, trying to look past the tall, blond man at the building behind him.

"Good to see you too, Billy," said Lars, staying right in his space. "Whiskey Joe wants an update."

"Which I'll give him tomorrow morning." Billy didn't have time right now to mollycoddle a nervous client. Really, he never had time to mollycoddle a nervous client, but especially not now.

"Joe wants to be sure you're making progress," said Lars.

"I am," said Billy, and tried to push past him.

Lars grabbed Billy's arm with a surprisingly firm grip.

"Hey," said Billy, twisting free with some effort.

"A few minutes, that's all," said Lars.

The quickest way to resolve this, Billy decided, would be to give Lars what he wanted. "I can fill you in, but it has to be fast," he said, calculating which details to share with Lars and how he might construe them. "I've been asking around about—"

"Not here," interrupted Lars. "We need to go someplace private to talk."

"Are you kidding?" Billy watched as two hulking figures stepped from the shadow of a nearby building to stand just behind Lars, and that's when Billy knew he was really in trouble.

"Let's talk over here," said Lars, gesturing toward a dark alleyway.

"That looks like an alleyway, Lars," Billy said. "I'm not going into a dark alleyway."

The two giants closed in.

"Fine," he said. "We'll talk in the alleyway."

And then Billy ran in a desperate bid for freedom that was curtailed within a few steps as many strong hands grabbed and dragged him between the buildings.

One of those same hands held a pungent rag to Billy's nose, and then he was out.

# 57

When she got back home from the Snaith Mansion, Diantha was not altogether surprised to find her husband in her sitting room. As they greeted each other, Diantha noted that Roger looked terrible: clothes rumpled, hair askew, face mushy with sorrow.

"You know," said Roger, as Diantha removed her coat and laid it across the back of a chair, "if you chose not to attend the séance tonight, I wouldn't be hurt."

Diantha smoothed the fabric of her coat and looked at her melancholy husband. She wondered what this was really about, although she had a decent guess. "Do you think that's why I'm going?" she said. "Because I don't want to hurt your feelings?"

Roger stared past her, and for the first time ever, he looked old to her. It was a shock to feel the passage of time like that, almost a physical sensation, something swift and cruel coursing around her. Her breath caught in her throat, and she sat down in the armchair, leaning her head back against her woolen overcoat. She closed her eyes for some time, and when she opened them again, she saw that Roger was crying.

"I found the letters from Gilbert Snaith," he said, and then: "How could you?"

She was surprised by his response to this discovery. "Says the man with three wives," she replied, and laughed at the terrible absurdity of it.

"That's different," Roger said fiercely.

Diantha was so, so tired of the hypocrisy of it all. "How is it different, Roger?" she said. "Explain that to me, please."

He looked affronted that she would even ask. "Because there was no lying when I did it," he said. "Because I received the blessing of each of my existing wives before I entered into a new marriage."

He said this like it was the most obvious thing in the world, and Diantha remembered why they had agreed not to discuss polygamy.

"So, if I had asked for your blessing," Diantha said, "you would have given it?"

"No," he said. "That's not how it works. Women don't need—"

"Don't you dare tell me what women need," she said.

"It's not me telling you," Roger said. "It's the Lord."

"And don't hide behind God right now, either."

Oozing self-righteous forbearance, Roger shrugged his shoulders. "We'll just have to agree to disagree," he said. "Although, on one point, I have to ask: Is your conscience truly clear when it comes to this business with Gilbert Snaith?"

She didn't owe him an answer but gave one anyway. "Nothing happened with Gilbert."

"Really?" he said. "Nothing in the least bit inappropriate?"

This was taking on the tone of a worthiness interview.

"No, Roger. Nothing," she said. "But, you know, I was speaking with Francie Bream earlier today—the journalist who's been interviewing me—and she had an interesting story to tell. Would you like to hear it?"

"I assume it's relevant somehow," Roger said.

"Very relevant," Diantha said.

In truth, she had no desire to repeat the story, because if she did, Roger might confirm it, and she still didn't know how she felt about the possible strange and far-reaching implications.

"Go ahead," said Roger.

Before she could change her mind, Diantha repeated to Roger the story she'd been told of the two mothers and the contested baby. She watched his face as she spoke, and his demeanor changed from annoyance to concern to fear as the tale unfolded. By the time she finished, Roger looked so thoroughly harrowed that she knew it had to be true.

"It happened, didn't it?" she said. "Just like Miss Bream said."

"In terms of the general details, yes, that's what happened," Roger said, "but Miss Bream has misunderstood the essential substance of the incident."

Diantha could see Roger clinging to this nascent argument like a drowning sailor grasping at a bit of flotsam. She wondered—through her shock and pain at the confirmation of the story—where Roger could possibly be going with this.

"Please," Diantha said. "Illuminate the situation for me."

"What Miss Bream's version of events doesn't take into account," Roger began, watching her carefully as he spoke, "are the principles of stewardship and divine revelation, the idea that God will reveal His will for His children through those He has called to be servants. In this particular situation, I was that servant, the mouthpiece for the will of the Lord. Would you say that's a fair characterization?"

Diantha didn't want to play this game right now. "Do you honestly believe in your heart of hearts," she said, "that Sarah Crawford was the one who gave birth to me?"

Roger furrowed his eyebrows. "For me, that was never the question."

"Excuse me?" Diantha leaned forward in her chair. "I believe that was *very much* the question for the two women who claimed to be her mother. My mother, I should say."

"That's not the question I felt impressed to take to the Lord," Roger said. "What I asked in my prayer was which woman should be given the baby, not which woman had given birth to her."

"Given birth to me," Diantha said. "To reiterate, we're talking about *me* right now. And can you truly not see how irresponsible it was of you to make that decision?"

"I wasn't the one making it," Roger said. "The Lord was."

"You're not infallible, Roger," she said. "Receiving revelation is a messy, imprecise process. I think we both know that."

"I never said I was infallible," Roger replied. "I only said I was the one He had called to act as His voice in this situation."

"You have to acknowledge that if you're not infallible, it's possible you got things wrong in this instance, no matter which question you were asking," Diantha said.

Roger nodded slowly. "Mistakes may happen from time to time," he said. "To be clear, I'm not saying mistakes were made in this specific situation. We're all only human, and what's more human than making mistakes?"

"There are mistakes, and there are *mistakes*," Diantha said. "You stole somebody's baby, Roger. That's more than a mistake."

"Once again, that's not an accurate portrayal of the circumstances," Roger said. "The Lord made His will known to me, and I simply carried it out. Understand, Diantha, that God's ways are not man's ways, and it's not always for us to understand His revelations. But even I, an imperfect servant, can see the wisdom in the decision the Lord handed down that day. Just think how blessed your life has been and how different life might have looked if you'd been raised by that misguided courtesan who claimed to be your mother."

"From what I understand," Diantha said, "that *misguided courtesan* made quite a good life for herself."

If this information bothered Roger, he didn't show it.

"Well, as I said, it's not for us to comprehend the will of the Lord, only to obey it," he said.

They were going in circles now, and Diantha was dizzy with rage. "Enough," she said. "Enough."

She was so tired of being on the outside of things, of lacking the power of men like Roger.

"I can't believe you never said a word to me about any of this the whole time we were married," Diantha said.

"It didn't seem right to share something with you that your parents never did."

"You mean the people claiming to be my parents?"

Roger looked away in annoyance.

"I hope it goes without saying," Diantha said, "that our marriage is over."

"I surmised as much," Roger said.

"Since it was never legal in the first place, I suppose we can, just between the two of us, declare it finished," Diantha said.

"Yes, it's finished," he said. "And now you're free to marry Gilbert Snaith."

"I'm not going to marry Gilbert Snaith," she said.

He turned to look at her again. "Why not?"

"Because I don't want to," Diantha said. She took some pleasure in Roger's evident confusion. "What I would like, though," she said, "is for you to sign over the deed for this house to me. I think it's the least you can do."

Roger considered this for a moment and said, "Yes, I believe that's fair."

Diantha thought of the various options before her, and then she did something that surprised both of them.

"Is this séance tonight going to work?" she asked.

"What?" he said. "What do you mean?"

"Will it convince people to join your church?"

Diantha could tell there were many things Roger wanted to say but instead, he took his time considering a concise and measured response.

"Yes, I believe it will," he said finally.

Diantha nodded. "I may not be your wife anymore," she said, "but if the offer's still on the table, I will lead this new church with you."

Roger looked at her like he'd never seen her before. Diantha herself couldn't quite believe what she'd said.

"Well?" she asked.

Roger kneaded his hands against each other and was quiet for a long moment. "All right," he said cautiously.

"Shall we shake on it?" she said.

He nodded, and they did.

# 58

Billy Lovelace woke up tied to a wooden chair in some disused barn illuminated by a single, flickering lantern. Before him stood Whiskey Joe, Lars, and one of the giants who had wrestled him into the dark alley. Shadows played across their faces, giving them a strange, mutable appearance. On a dilapidated workbench nearby sat an assortment of rusty farm implements: sickles and shears and rakes, among other potential horrors.

"He's awake," said the giant.

"Good," said Lars, in a way that suggested this would not be good for Billy at all.

Billy felt sick with fear. To say he regretted his reckless confrontation with Gilbert Snaith that afternoon would only begin to capture the resentment he now harbored toward his earlier self.

At the time, his behavior had felt downright swashbuckling, maybe even a little brave, but now that he was tied to a chair in an old barn with three men who all wanted to harm him, he felt much differently. His poor, vulnerable body couldn't take much more violence today, or ever, really. Billy didn't want to die in some anonymous barn in Utah. He needed to start acting very, very sensibly.

"We know you're the one who sent the file to Gus Helton," Lars said, with the kind of melodramatic indignation only a failed vaudevillian could muster, "and now you're charging us to ferret out the spy you invented."

This was interesting.

Billy wondered who'd authored the tale—Snaith himself, or maybe Whiskey Joe? It was a pretty good one, plausible enough and difficult to disprove, but Billy noted this with more fear than admiration. Any missteps, and he could die here tonight.

Lars had murder in his eyes. Whiskey Joe, on the other hand, regarded him coolly, and Billy decided to appeal to him.

"There are a lot of things I could say right now," Billy began, "but I'll cut to the chase: Whiskey Joe, I'd like to speak to you in private about Agent 84."

Whiskey Joe narrowed his eyes. After a moment, the labor legend produced a toothpick from an inner pocket of his jacket and propped it on his lip. Billy, Lars, and the giant watched him with bated breath.

"Lars, Patrick—leave us alone for a minute, would you?" Whiskey Joe said.

Lars and the giant hesitated.

"Go on," said Whiskey Joe. "If I need you, I'll give a shout."

Lars and the giant exchanged a glance and then left.

"All right," said Whiskey Joe once the other men were gone. "What is it you think you know?"

Billy watched Whiskey Joe's body for signs of impending violence.

"You're the undercover operative," Billy said. "Gilbert Snaith hired you through the P.L.B. Detective Bureau and keeps you on retainer. You've been feeding him information for a few years now."

"That so?" Whiskey Joe responded.

"It is," Billy said. "I have the agency's file to prove it."

The toothpick bobbed from one side of Whiskey Joe's mouth

to the other. "If that were true," he said, "it would make a lot of sense to kill you right now."

Whiskey Joe wandered over to the table of farm tools and picked up a rusty pruning saw.

"You should know," Billy said, "I've wired the case details to a colleague of mine. If anything happens to me, he'll come looking for you."

Whiskey Joe swung the rusty saw from side to side, and it whistled through the air. "And what? He'll bring this whole operation to its knees?" He tested the edge of the blade with his thumb.

"He could cause you a lot of trouble," Billy said, but the words sounded weak as they left his mouth.

Whiskey Joe walked over slowly from the table of farm tools to the chair. He looked at Billy. Billy looked at him. Whiskey Joe walked around behind the chair and pushed the blade of the saw against Billy's neck, the rusty teeth sharp against his skin. Billy swallowed hard.

"You don't strike me as an idealist," said Whiskey Joe.

He wasn't wrong, necessarily, but Billy resented the observation.

"I like to think of myself as a pragmatist," Billy said.

"However you put it," Whiskey Joe said, "I don't believe you want to cause any more trouble than you already have. Is that a fair assessment, would you say?"

It was less that Billy didn't want to cause trouble and more that he didn't want to die, but he wasn't about to split hairs with someone holding a blade to his all-too-tender throat.

"Yes, it is," said Billy.

"Let's say, for the sake of argument, I decide to let you walk out of this barn alive," said Whiskey Joe, adjusting his grip on the pruning saw. "Can I assume you understand what would happen if you were to do anything—anything at all—to make me regret that decision? Something like continuing your investigation or telling anyone what you saw in that file?"

"I understand perfectly," Billy said. Sweat ran down his face.

"I think you do," said Whiskey Joe, pressing the blade even harder into Billy's neck until its teeth broke, barely, the surface of his skin.

"I really, really do," said Billy.

The shallow wound stung from the steady drip of sweat down his neck. Billy was trying his best not to fall apart completely when Whiskey Joe tossed the saw to the ground and assumed his usual air of bluff joviality.

"Very good!" he said.

Billy relaxed a little, aware this could be a trick. "That was a smart story," he said, "about me planting false information."

Whiskey Joe laughed. "Oh, that was your medium friend who fed the story to Lars."

Billy could see how such a move would suit Ilsa's purposes to a tee, getting him out of the way to finish her job and leave town unimpeded. At the moment, he was too relieved about his apparent escape from death to feel much of anything about this revelation.

"But our business here isn't done yet," Whiskey Joe said, and it was not lost on Billy that Barnes still had him tied to a chair.

"What can I do for you?" Billy said carefully.

Whiskey Joe moved in close, no weapon in hand this time but with danger in his eyes nonetheless. "Where's Helton's file?" he said.

Billy hesitated.

"Don't you dare lie to me." Whiskey Joe said.

And so Billy didn't. "I have it," he said. "Do you want it?"

Whiskey Joe smiled and took a step back. "I do."

"The papers are in my stockings," Billy said.

Whiskey Joe shook his head. "I thought the boys searched you."

"They were probably only looking for weapons," Billy said. "Also, they're amateurs."

Whiskey Joe didn't disagree, and as he untied Billy, he

reminded him that Lars and Patrick were outside the door, should he decide to try anything funny.

"No need to worry," Billy said, and removed from his stockings the papers Gus Helton had given his life for.

Whiskey Joe took them, leafed through the small stack, and then, with a lighter he procured from a vest pocket, lit them on fire.

Billy rubbed his wrists where they'd been tied. He suspected he could still make the séance if he left right away. He watched Whiskey Joe return the lighter to his pocket, his weathered face absorbed in the simple task.

He saw Billy watching and said, "I'll come up with a story for Lars, and, of course, I'll pay you for bringing me the file. You can pick up the money tomorrow morning. I'll give you an address."

"Fine," said Billy. He took a breath. "Can I ask you something?"

"I may not answer," said Whiskey Joe, "but go ahead."

"Why are you working for Snaith?" he said. "I mean, what made you switch sides?"

After carefully coiling the rope that had bound Billy to the chair, Whiskey Joe set it on the table of old tools and turned to look back at him. "I got tired of the fight," he said. "Bone-goddamn-tired."

There was, in Whiskey Joe's face, a frightening weariness.

"Fair enough," said Billy, gingerly putting his weight on his legs as he stood from the chair.

"I hope it goes without saying," said Whiskey Joe, "as soon as you pick up the money tomorrow morning, you get the hell out of town."

Billy said that wouldn't be a problem.

# 59

Back downtown in the crawlspace where Madame Ilsa had concealed her earlier that evening, Francie Bream lowered herself into a sitting position. She'd been shifting periodically between sitting and squatting to keep the blood circulating, but also to alleviate her nervous boredom.

She'd brought a watch but of course, couldn't read it in the dark and had no idea if she'd been there for five minutes or five hours. It certainly *felt* more like hours than minutes, for whatever that was worth.

Yet again, Francie checked to make sure the Smith & Wesson was loaded—it was something to do—and again felt cartridges in all five chambers. She returned the gun to her overcoat pocket and thought of the two men she'd already killed: old Amos Boylan, smothered with a pillow, and Adam Wolfe, face smashed in with a shovel.

She reminded herself she was doing all this for a reason. She had to speak the language of the powerful, the language of violence in order to make the world a better and safer place for people like her mother, and the shoeshine boy murdered by Matthew Stockwater.

She wasn't a bad person, or if she was, she'd become one for a good reason.

She considered again her previous killings, trying to decide if ending the life of another human being was easier than she would have expected, or more difficult, and she thought the answer was a little of both. The physical act itself had not been so hard in either instance— holding down a pillow and driving down a shovel were relatively straightforward actions—but the emotional aftermath had been profoundly destabilizing, raising questions about her own nature she had yet to resolve.

Which brought her back to the troubling question of whether she was a good person or a bad person?

A bad person or a very bad person?

The people she'd killed had been bad people, or at least powerful people who'd harmed others, and Francie hoped—she still hoped—that once these killings came to light, and especially once *she* came to light as the perpetrator, powerful men everywhere might think twice before abusing their station to harm weaker people, might hesitate because who could say when the next Francie Bream would strike, punishing them for the harm they so thoughtlessly caused.

In truth, though, Francie was scared. She knew she might not survive this final task tonight, might join her targets in the oblivion of death, a thought that chilled her in spite of the stuffy air of the crawlspace. She thought briefly that death couldn't be worse than this cramped darkness, but no, at least in here she had her mind. She existed, which would not be the case once she was dead. She would simply be no more. A final and eternal nothingness.

The proximity of death made her feel like a child again, helpless and frightened in the face of mighty forces beyond her control.

She decided it was time to switch from sitting to squatting before these grim thoughts overtook her completely, but then, from out in the abandoned dressmaker's workshop, she heard footsteps. The séance would begin soon.

Francie removed the gun from her pocket and, gripping it tightly in her chilly hand, tugged down the sleeve of her overcoat to conceal the instrument of Roger Marsh's imminent destruction.

# 60

Night had fallen on Salt Lake City, bringing with it darkness and a greater permeability between our world and the next. Madame Ilsa von Hoffmann was back at the abandoned dressmaker's shop, this time accompanied by Roger Marsh and a woman several decades his junior.

"This is my wife Diantha," he said.

"*Former* wife," the woman was quick to correct.

Ilsa responded with the necessary pleasantries and surveyed the room as if seeing it for the first time.

"Brother Howard Benson will be bringing a table and chairs," Roger said. "I assume you'll want us sitting in a circle?"

Ilsa wondered again where Adam Wolfe was, but she wasn't about to complain about his absence. Looking out through the front windows of the space, she noted with relief that nobody had repaired the streetlamps she'd sabotaged earlier that evening.

"No, actually," she said. "I'd like the table over there." She indicated the darkest corner of the room. "And the chairs facing it in two rows."

"Of course," said Roger.

"Is that your typical arrangement?" asked Roger's wife, or ex-wife, Diantha.

Ilsa couldn't quite discern in what capacity Diantha was serving tonight. Roger hadn't mentioned her at all before this evening, but she spoke as if she were intimately involved with this whole enterprise.

"I allow the energies of the room to influence every element of a Summoning," Ilsa replied. "Buildings have memories, preferences, and dislikes."

She couldn't tell what Diantha thought of this; here was a woman well practiced in concealing her true opinions.

At the sound of heavy footsteps on the stairs, all three turned to the open doorway.

"That will be Brother Benson," Roger said, and moved to greet him.

"Wait," Ilsa said, and he paused.

She pointed at the worn carpetbag in his hand. "Is that my fee?"

"It is," said Roger.

"May I see it?" Ilsa said.

Diantha watched this exchange with interest.

"If you must," said Roger. He opened the carpet bag, and Ilsa saw bundles of currency inside.

"I'd like to hold onto it," she said.

"After the Summoning," Roger said.

Before she could respond, a big man carrying a stack of chairs stepped through the doorway. Ilsa was so relieved it wasn't Billy Lovelace that she didn't press Roger on the money issue.

While it had seemed that Lars Arnasson had taken her bait, Ilsa had no idea if the rest of her plan had played out as she'd hoped. But if Billy showed up now, she'd be sunk. He would examine the room, and he would find the concealed Francie Bream with no trouble at all.

While Marsh, Benson, and another man freighted the rest of the chairs and a long, wooden table into the dressmaker's workshop, and Diantha sat writing something in a bound notebook, Ilsa plotted various escape routes from the lamplit space, each one featuring a stop at Roger Marsh so she could grab the carpetbag filled with money.

Soon, the tables and chairs had been arranged to her specifications, and Ilsa needed to make her own physical preparations. She carried only a moderate sized handbag—at least, it was all she *visibly* carried. Her dress was custom-made and heavy, concealing a vast array of tools, tricks, and apparatuses. For now, though, Ilsa opened only her handbag and removed five simple candlesticks in five simple candleholders and arranged them along the edge of the long wooden table.

As the rest of the attendees arrived, an even dozen, Ilsa was again caught off guard by how polite and tidy these religious fanatics appeared to be. Perhaps she'd expected wild-eyed men with trailing beards and gaunt, haunted women clad in dresses even more outdated than her own.

Here instead were apparently respectable members of the bourgeoisie who happened to believe that tonight God would send the ghost of their founding prophet to command them to continue practicing polygamy. Ilsa felt a pang of guilt for her complicity in this enterprise but brushed it aside. It was almost time to begin.

At Ilsa's signal, Roger Marsh moved among his milling disciples, speaking in low, reassuring tones, and in response, the attendees sat in the chairs facing the table behind which Ilsa stood holding a single, lit candle. One of the men extinguished all other sources of illumination, as instructed, and Marsh opened his mouth to speak but was interrupted by unexpected footsteps on the stairway.

It had to be Billy Lovelace, and Ilsa prepared to flee as a tall, thin man about Roger's age entered instead accompanied by an armed U.S. Marshal with a moustache as ostentatious as his prominently displayed badge.

"Dowland," Roger said. "What are you doing here?"

A U.S. Marshal could be just as dangerous as Billy Lovelace, and Ilsa considered taking advantage of the distraction provided by their entrance to quietly leave with the bag of money, but the two men stood between her and the door.

"We're only here to observe the proceedings," said the tall, thin one—Dowland, apparently.

"If you're here to arrest me, then take me now," Roger said. "Although, I didn't think even you would sink so low as to involve a U.S. Marshal."

Dowland looked more annoyed than anything at this outburst, and the mustachioed Marshal merely looked uncomfortable. He shifted the rifle cradled in his arms and looked down at the floor.

"Save the theatrics, Roger," Dowland said. "I've brought Marshal Rooney only as a precaution. As long as you break no laws and don't, for instance, encourage the practice of polygamy, then the marshal here will have no quarrel with you."

Even in the relative darkness, Ilsa could see Roger trembling with fury.

"Iscariot," he hissed at Dowland, because maybe every story does need a Judas.

Dowland shrugged.

"I suggest we begin," Madame Ilsa said, wanting to move things along.

Roger let out a long, loud breath as Dowland and the Marshal took a place against the wall to the side of the chairs. Thankfully, Ilsa noted, the entrance to the crawlspace was in the opposite wall.

"Yes," Roger said, composing himself. "Let's begin. I would ask everyone present to say a silent prayer that the will of the Lord may be carried out tonight. Madame Ilsa, I turn the time over to you."

"Thank you," she said, and walked slowly around the table so she was standing directly in front of the audience.

Though the emotions on the faces of the attendees varied from suspicion to hope to eagerness to fear, they were all fixed on Ilsa with considerable intensity.

"I will first speak," she said, keeping her voice deliberately low so her audience would have to strain to hear her, "of the dangers inherent in tonight's undertaking."

A clatter of running footsteps momentarily broke the mood, and a sweating Billy Lovelace burst into the room. All eyes turned, but when he saw the Marshal, tense now, rifle half-raised, Billy seemed thrown.

"Please," he said, as much to the law enforcement agent as to Ilsa. "Go on. I didn't mean to interrupt."

He joined the Marshal against the wall, and after a brief, murmured exchange, each man seemed satisfied with the other's presence.

Ilsa waited a beat to see if Billy would speak, but when he didn't, she let the silence grow heavy before she proceeded.

"To rend the veil between this life and the next is to defy vast and incomprehensible forces," she said, "and while I have successfully undertaken this glorious transgression many times over the years, it is not without its perils. I must ask you, then, to empty your minds of animosity and anything that might attract the more sinister denizens of the afterlife, who feed on human wrath and misery. I will give you a moment now to prepare your inner selves."

She had won over this audience, she could feel it, though she deliberately kept her gaze from the face of Billy Lovelace. A look of skepticism from him right now could shake her confidence and break the spell she was casting over the room.

"Have you swept your minds clean as I have requested?" she said after an appropriate pause.

Several people nodded.

"I must also remind you that no matter what you see or hear tonight, you must not leave your seats. There is safety in unity and protection in the ancient and everlasting symbols formed by the two rows of chairs in which you sit," Ilsa said, improvising a bit, as the chairs had been arranged in no prescribed order.

She noticed several people reach down to clutch the seat of their chair. Then, right on cue, the five candles she'd arranged on the table behind her flickered to life. Her audience responded with a collective gasp.

"Ozymandias?" Ilsa called into the darkness. "Is that you?"

As she turned, as if searching for her spiritual guide, Ilsa slipped a hand into the capacious pocket sewn into the skirt of her dress and palmed the items necessary for the next phase of the Summoning, her broken finger hindering her only slightly.

After a significant pause, she turned back to address her audience. "Ozymandias is a long-dead Sumerian nobleman who serves as my liaison to the land of the dead. I felt a shimmering of his presence, but he must be explicitly invited into this space to manifest himself more fully. Please, each of you, extend a silent invitation from your hearts to Ozymandias, while I perform the necessary incantations."

Ilsa lifted her arms and tilted her head back to look skyward.

"Ozymandias!" she called and slowly stomped her foot once, twice, three times, four times.

This was Francie Bream's signal to un-tack the wall they'd constructed and creep forward to wait at the door for her next cue. Ilsa hoped the journalist was still up to the task.

"Ozymandias!" Ilsa called again. "We invite you to grace us with your spectral presence this night. Please feel the welcome in the hearts of those gathered here, and for our sake, undertake the crossing between your world and ours."

Ilsa walked around so she was standing behind the table and gave a dramatic shudder. "Yes!" she cried. "I am beginning to feel your presence. Allow me to assist you in making the final crossing."

Ilsa raised her arms higher in the air as her body began to convulse and guttural, animal growls escaped from her throat. She could feel the tension in her audience and increased the convulsions until her body was practically jerking from side to side.

At the sound of concerned murmurs, she flung her body onto the table and, retching noisily, coughed up a pool of glowing ectoplasm from her mouth and nose. Then she lay perfectly still and waited ten beats before leaping to her feet behind the table and opening her eyes as if nothing had happened.

"Ozymandias," she said, her voice weaker now. "If you have completed your crossing, please raise one of the candlesticks before me."

For a long, long moment nothing happened. And then, almost imperceptibly at first, one of the candles rose and levitated several inches in the air before slowly lowering back onto the tabletop.

"Thank you for making your presence known," Ilsa said amid the frightened twittering of her audience. "I've invited you here tonight, Ozymandias, on behalf of a group of the living who wish to communicate with one of your compatriots in the land of the dead. Would you be willing to facilitate this communication? Please raise one candlestick for yes, two for no."

After a pause, the same candlestick rose in the air and slowly returned to the table.

"Thank you, my friend," said Ilsa. "Now, the shade these souls wish to contact is a man by the name of Joseph Smith, a great prophet who was killed in the previous century. Do you know this spirit?"

Again, the candlestick rose.

"Can you invite him here, please?" she said.

Another *yes* from Ozymandias.

Addressing the audience, Ilsa said, "I will lend some of my own energy to assist in your prophet's crossing. Do not be alarmed by what you are about to see."

She took a deep breath, her eyes rolled back in her head, and she rose several inches into the air. Letting out a low moan, she then returned to the floor, and responding to the audience's shocked silence, closed her eyes, and then opened them to show they were back to normal.

"Was the crossing successful, Ozymandias? Is the Prophet Joseph Smith here with us?" she said.

The candlestick levitated.

"Wonderful," Ilsa said. "Would the Prophet be willing to visibly manifest his spirit to us?"

This time, two candlesticks rose from the table.

"Ozymandias, please tell the Prophet his presence is of the utmost importance to those who have summoned him," Ilsa said, and waited. "Now, please ask again whether he will manifest his spirit to us."

After a pause, two candlesticks levitated.

Ilsa turned to the audience. "I ask you all," she said, "to focus with the greatest intensity you can muster on your desire to see the Prophet Joseph Smith."

A few in the audience nodded, and others lowered their heads.

"Ozymandias," Ilsa said, after a pause, "will you please implore the Prophet one final time to appear before us tonight?"

At this, the long wooden table itself trembled, and a blinding flash of light filled the room.

# 61

Though the Summoning had gotten off to a rocky start—Roger was still furious about the arrival of Hyrum Dowland and that smug Marshal—Madame Ilsa had quickly laid his greatest concerns to rest. Roger had no doubt this woman was in command of supernatural forces, the only question now, especially as he watched her rise from the ground with her eyes showing nothing but white, was whether she was allied with the Lord or the Devil—or perhaps even with some murky force between the two.

That ambiguity was resolved when von Hoffmann's liaison, Ozymandias, indicated the spirit of the Prophet Joseph Smith had arrived; Roger felt a tingle down his spine, followed by a crackling warmth in the center of his chest and an overwhelming joy that the prophecies he'd received were finally and truly bearing fruit.

He felt only a moment's concern when the Prophet Joseph initially declined the invitation to appear, but that concern was replaced with a greater ecstasy when the room was filled with an astounding flash of light, here and gone in the blink of an eye. The darkness that followed was nearly impenetrable; the five candles on the table had gone out, and all eyes in the room were overloaded by the burst of light.

Roger blinked repeatedly, trying to restore his vision.

Then Madame Ilsa's voice cut through the darkness: "Spirit, I invite you to make yourself seen."

Roger was not the only one who audibly gasped when a face and then a torso flickered into view behind the table.

"We thank you," said Madame Ilsa, who stood a few paces away from the apparition, "for your presence here tonight."

The figure inclined his head toward the medium. "It cheers my soul to be here among my brothers and sisters in Christ," he said. His voice was bright and otherworldly.

The figure had fair hair, light, joyful eyes, and a countenance of dignified benevolence.

With all his heart and soul, Roger knew this was the Prophet Joseph Smith.

"Would to God I had forty days and nights to tell you all I have been taught since my bloody assassination," continued the Prophet. "The kingdom of the dead is a kingdom of learning and progression and feasting upon the sweet and everlasting truths of the Father."

Roger saw smiles on the faces of several listeners and realized he, too, was smiling. His spirit was brimming with joy. To look upon the face of the Prophet Joseph Smith and hear his teachings straight from his lips more than made up for the months of suffering Roger had undergone in the name of truth.

The Prophet moved soundlessly around the table as his discourse proceeded. "It is impossible," he said, "to say much more on the subject, as an unseen angel with a drawn sword threatens me with destruction if I speak further. I will, therefore, say only that, for the righteous, the life after this one is more wonderful and more glorious than you have ever supposed."

But then the Prophet's face grew troubled, and Roger could practically feel the impulse in those around him to reach out and comfort this beloved spirit.

"I want your prayers and faith right now," the Prophet said.

"To my great sorrow, I have been charged to speak this night on a subject that will be far less pleasing to your ears."

The Prophet paced across the space between the table and his listeners, watching them as he moved back and forth.

"We have learned by sad experience," he said, "that it is the nature and disposition of almost all men, as soon as they get a little authority, as they suppose, they will immediately begin to exercise unrighteous dominion. Such is the case with one among you tonight, and I have been sent by the Lord to rebuke this brother for his works of iniquity."

Roger drew in a breath. The condemnation of Hyrum Dowland was certainly near at hand, and he almost felt pity for his former colleague for the stinging rebuke he was about to receive for impeding the work of the Lord. Roger resisted the urge to turn and look at Hyrum.

"Roger Marsh," the Prophet said, and an icicle of fear pierced Roger's heart.

The prophet stood only a few feet away, and his disapproving gaze fell upon him like a bolt from heaven.

"Roger Marsh," the Prophet repeated. "As a young bishop, you used your position to serve the wealthy and powerful of this world at the expense of one of the least of God's children when you wrested an innocent babe from the arms of her vulnerable mother and presented her to a pair of ravening wolves in the clothing of sheep."

The Prophet was looming above Roger now, and from the corner of his eye, Roger could see Madame Ilsa edging warily away.

"For this most ungodly of acts, Brother Marsh, prepare to receive the punishment the Lord has sent for you," said the Prophet, raising his hand to the level of Roger's chest.

That hand held a gun, Roger noticed, just as a shot rang out through the darkened space.

Roger's hands flew instinctively to his chest. The gun fired again and again, but miraculously, he felt no pain. He looked down at the front of his shirt as the gun continued firing, but no telltale stain spread across the white fabric. As he patted his chest, he felt no warm wetness, no bullet wounds.

The gun clicked, apparently empty now, and Roger looked up to meet the eyes of the Prophet. For an instant, before the room burst to life, the two men shared a look of utter bewilderment.

Then everything was in motion, and Roger watched what unfolded as if from a great distance.

Several men in the room converged on the Prophet, shoving him to the ground, and in the process, knocking loose his hair—a wig—and Roger saw that this was not Joseph Smith, but a woman whose face he vaguely recognized.

# 62

As chaos blossomed in the dressmaker's workshop and everyone responded in their own panicked way to the unexpected gunfire, Madame Ilsa recalled a conversation she'd had back in her vaudeville days with The Elusive Damiani, Master of Escape. Like most performers of her acquaintance, Damiani was second tier at best, a cut-rate Houdini, but not without some cunning and a well-developed knack for survival.

The conversation concerned the difference between a stage escape (say, from a straitjacket, or a man-sized safe) and a real-life escape (from an unpaid hotel bill, for instance, or a retribution-minded theater owner after a much-promoted stage escape went awry).

A stage escape needed flamboyance, Damiani said, something the audience couldn't look away from so when the performer liberated themselves from their bonds, the spectators would feel they'd witnessed a miracle.

A real-life escape, by contrast, had to be executed with consummate sangfroid; both skulking and scurrying would draw the bystander's eye, so to move invisibly, the escapee had to conduct themselves as if they had every right to be doing exactly what they were doing, as if God and the universe willed it so.

With The Elusive Damiani's advice in mind, Madame Ilsa calmly walked across the room. To her left, Francie Bream scurried for the door in her felt-soled boots while the ostentatious U.S. Marshal aimed his rifle in her erratic direction, shouting at the other milling occupants of the room to get out of the way. Before the Marshal could get a clear shot, though, Francie was out the door, running down the stairs.

Meanwhile, Madame Ilsa picked up the carpetbag of money from where Roger Marsh had been sitting and then dragged a chair across the room and heaved it through the window she'd previously designated as the best means of emergency egress. She tossed the carpetbag through the shattered glass and was about to make a successful escape when a pair of strong hands grabbed her from behind.

When Billy Lovelace spun her around to face him, he looked so pleased with himself that Ilsa's first reaction was not fear but annoyance that her former friend had managed to outplay her. Hot on the heels of that annoyance came the fear, the instinctual terror of confinement.

"Billy, you need to let me go," she said, pulling one arm free from his grasp and pivoting away from him.

Billy opened his mouth to reply, but his words were preempted by the crack of a gun firing. Feeling at the same time a sharp tug at her shoulder, Ilsa looked behind her and saw the U.S. Marshal aiming his rifle at her.

She'd been shot, she realized, and suddenly felt dizzy. Her legs threatened to give way beneath her, but Billy took her by both arms and moved to hold her upright.

"Out of the way!" the Marshal called to Billy, who was now blocking the man's shot.

Ilsa's mind reeled, and Billy stepped aside, giving her a surreptitious push as he did so, sending her tumbling through the broken window as the Marshal fired another shot.

# 63

The moment the U.S. Marshal shot Ilsa—the sickening crack of gunfire, that look of animal terror on her face—Billy recognized he'd taken his revenge too far. He hadn't forgiven Ilsa for what she'd done—far from it. Instead, Billy realized he'd just violated one of his foundational moral precepts, namely: never side with an officer of the law.

True, he'd made exceptions to this rule in the past, but tonight he should have been on the side of Madame Ilsa, regardless of their complicated shared history.

For all the times they'd found themselves at odds with each other, at the end of the day, they were part of the same loose community of petty criminals, a community that looked out for each other whenever possible and who held as common enemies people like the Marshal and the outraged audience members already putting together a search party.

All of which was to say, Billy wasn't going to let this gang of upstanding vigilantes hunt down his dear nemesis Madame Ilsa von Hoffmann.

Some of the men were already brandishing guns and dividing the city into quadrants, vowing to catch the woman who'd tried to kill Roger Marsh, as well as the fraudulent medium.

Billy recognized that, to an untrained eye, Ilsa and the other woman appeared to have been working in concert, Ilsa a willing accomplice to the attempted violence. But he could tell by the way Ilsa had handled herself in the chaos that this was not the case. He believed they were uneasy allies at best, but there was no way to convince this angry little mob of that, and so Billy would utilize instead his considerable talent for duplicity.

"I think I hit her again before she fell," said the Marshal, looking to Billy for congratulations, which probably meant he hadn't clocked Billy pushing Ilsa through the window to relative safety.

"Good shot!" said Billy with false heartiness, clapping the other man on the shoulder.

They both approached the shattered window and looked down at the carriage beneath them that had broken Ilsa's fall, and at the quiet street surrounding it. To Billy's relief, Ilsa was nowhere in sight.

"Dammit!" said the Marshal. "She escaped."

Billy couldn't help but admire Ilsa's resilience. "She can't have gotten far," he said, and the Marshal seemed to take comfort in this.

Billy heard someone say that the police were on their way, and then someone else pushed a nickel-plated derringer into his hands.

"I hear you're a detective," said the man.

"That's right," said Billy.

"You'll join the search party?"

Billy watched the Marshal run out the door in pursuit of Ilsa and the failed assassin. "Of course." He looked around at the outraged, armed men and silently vowed to find Madame Ilsa before they did.

# 64

Francie Bream's fury as she slipped from shadow to shadow in the nighttime streets of Salt Lake was the stuff of myth, a blazing, God-cursing fury that gave her feet wings and her heart enough hatred to fuel a locomotive.

She'd anticipated either death or a nocturnal flight such as this one, but all her plans included celebrating the much-deserved assassination of Roger Marsh. Instead, she was evading the retribution of vigilantes while Marsh continued his lifelong campaign of self-righteous dominion over the lives of others.

Voices sounded in the night, and Francie ducked into a dark alleyway, running until she emerged onto an empty city street. Avoiding streetlights, she walked down the sidewalk, trying to decide how angry she was with Madame Ilsa von Hoffmann, who'd almost certainly been the one to load the gun with blanks.

Francie recognized this for the act of self-preservation it was, but still, the medium's trickery had destroyed what otherwise would have been the perfect fulfillment of her plans.

Madame Ilsa could wait, though. Right now, Francie needed to speak with her long-lost sister.

# 65

Though just an hour earlier the séance had seemed a failure of epic proportions, Roger's near assassination had somehow been transmuted into an unmitigated success. Diantha wasn't sure which attendee of tonight's gathering first uttered the word *miracle* in relation to Roger's escape from death, but the label had stuck, and among those who had witnessed the journalist's attack, Roger's survival was now viewed as God's protection of His chosen prophet, and a token of a heaven-sanctioned message.

As shaken as she still was by everything that had happened, Diantha couldn't resist the opportunity to rub this unexpected triumph in the face of that officious double-dealer Hyrum S. Dowland.

The few attendees who hadn't joined the police in their search for Francie Bream and Madame Ilsa clustered around Roger, eager disciples feasting on his words. A handful of policemen, here for the protection of those still in attendance, stood in clusters, waiting to escort their civilian charges home.

A short distance away, Hyrum Dowland watched this tableau with what might have been envy. Her own face a mask of graciousness, Diantha approached the Apostle.

When he saw Diantha, Hyrum's face assumed the expression of ecumenical solicitude he wore whenever performing official business of the Church.

"Is there anything I can do for you, Sister Marsh?" he said.

Something about Hyrum's defensive formality and the complicated emotions that seemed to hide behind it made the vindictiveness drain out of Diantha, and she gave him a civil answer. "I'm glad the excitement has passed," she said.

Dowland nodded, and something in his face softened. "Yes," he said. "I'm very relieved Roger wasn't harmed."

"Are you?" she said.

Dowland looked in Roger's direction. "Of course," he said. "He's one of my oldest friends."

"A friend you seemed eager to consign to the infernal realms earlier this evening," Diantha said.

Hyrum exhaled heavily. "It's complicated, Diantha," he said. "You know that as well as anyone."

They both looked at Roger now, practically glowing with joy as he spoke to the small handful of men and women hanging on his every word.

"I think his new church may have legs," said Diantha.

"I think you're right," said Dowland.

"What are you going to do about it?" she said. "You and the Brethren, I mean."

"Well," he said, "Roger will do whatever he thinks is right, regardless of what the rest of us think."

"So, you plan to leave him alone?"

"Absolutely not," said Dowland with a bitter laugh. "We'll do everything in our power to nip this thing in the bud."

Diantha nodded.

"For tonight, though," Dowland said. "I'm celebrating the survival of a man I care deeply for."

It was probably the late hour, but Dowland looked very old right then, older than his years. Still, Diantha did not pity the man.

He'd chosen this role of church enforcer for himself again and again and again.

He rested a paternal hand on her shoulder. "Goodnight, Diantha."

A pair of police officers followed him out the door, solemn protectors for the journey home.

"May my colleague and I escort you to your house?" asked a policemen, clearly eager to discharge his duty so he could go home.

"Yes, please," said Diantha, glancing at Roger and disciples. "But would you mind waiting a few minutes?"

"Whenever you're ready," said the policeman, with only a hint of impatience.

Diantha thanked him and moved closer to Roger. She was relieved he hadn't been murdered by that unhinged journalist Francie Bream. Truly, she was. She didn't love him, at least not in the way a wife might love a husband, but she did care about him, as much as he troubled her. So, yes, she was glad he hadn't been murdered.

And while Roger lacked the political savvy of a Hyrum Dowland, lacked the good sense to keep his mouth shut when it could keep him out of trouble, a trait which had cost him dearly over the past few years, her ex-husband was no fraud, which gave him considerable power when conditions were favorable.

Right now, for instance, he believed every word he spoke to this small but adoring crowd, and they could sense that. Tonight, the wind was in his favor and, Diantha suspected, it might continue to be for some time.

She caught Roger's eye and, mid-sentence, he stopped speaking to shine a ray of his glory in her direction.

"Diantha," said Roger, directing the attention of his little coterie her way. "I can't begin to describe how essential you've been to the work the Lord has called me to do."

She sensed the next words out of his mouth would subtly (or explicitly) reduce the role he'd already offered her in the new church, and she wasn't about to let that happen.

"Thank you, Roger," she said, stepping forward so she stood right next to him. "I'm grateful for this opportunity to address a select few of our fellow disciples."

Roger looked startled, but before he could contradict her, she spoke to those assembled. "When the Lord called me to lead this church alongside Roger, I was overwhelmed and humbled," Diantha said, marveling at the certitude she felt, the Spirit prompting her to continue, even as some murmured in confusion. "I won't at this time recount all the events and experiences that led me to ultimately accept this calling, but I will say that our Father in Heaven has made known that the time has come for my faithful sisters to step up and assume the mantle of authority prepared for them since before the foundation of the world."

The murmuring had subsided—Diantha suspected the others were now feeling the influence of the Spirit as strongly as she was—and while some of her audience still looked at her with skepticism, the majority listened with love on their faces.

"That expansion includes me, of course, and so when you look at Elder Marsh and myself at the head of the church, you will be looking at two co-prophets, equal before God and the world. Please also know that by accepting this role as Co-President of the Reformed Church of Jesus Christ of Latter-day Saints, I am pledging to be your servant. And so, I ask for your prayers as Elder Marsh and I continue in this sacred work, and I leave this with you in the name of Jesus Christ, amen."

Diantha had never felt the presence of the Spirit as immediately as she did right now.

"Amen," said the disciples, each of them now gazing at her with love and devotion, all of them having received, presumably, the same confirmation from the Lord.

Roger looked at her with wonder and maybe a little fear, and Diantha felt the full power of her new office, the power to speak something and make it so.

# 66

As soon as he could, Billy Lovelace split off from the main civilian search party, telling them he meant no disrespect, but he preferred to work alone. The men, doubly abuzz over the miraculous salvation of their new prophet and the opportunity to avenge his near martyrdom, barely seemed to register Billy's departure, which was probably for the best.

If he knew Ilsa as well as he thought he did, Billy had a pretty good idea of where she had gone after he'd pushed her out that window, and so, after making sure he wasn't being watched, he turned around and headed for the building where the séance had been held.

He could still see lights on in the second-floor dressmaker's workshop and moved with caution to the back of the building, where he found a fire escape that zig-zagged up the brick wall.

Billy lowered the bottom-most ladder as quietly as he could and began to climb. He didn't know what he would do if he found Ilsa. He wasn't sure how he *felt* about Ilsa right now, other than confused. He still wanted to hurt her for the way she'd betrayed him in Seattle, and also wanted to protect her from the men who were hunting her down, and also wanted to ask her advice on the Whiskey Joe case, and also wanted to buy her a drink at a bar in some paradisaical city and spend the evening shooting the shit like the old friends they were.

When he reached the roof, at first Billy saw no one there, but as he crept across the tarpaper surface, a lumpen bundle gradually came into view, a figure lying in the corner against a row of exposed pipes.

"Ilsa?" he whispered. "It's me, Billy."

The figure didn't stir, and for a horrible moment, Billy worried that Ilsa—because it had to be Ilsa, he'd recognize that dress anywhere—was already dead.

"Ilsa," he whispered again, drawing closer, and this time, she turned her head and looked at him with glassy eyes.

"Here to finish the job?" she croaked, and Billy remembered he was holding the little derringer.

"No," he said, and tucked the gun into the back of his pants.

He was already annoyed with her self-pitying tone and also worried she was on the cusp of death. Even in the darkness she looked terrible, her face damp with sweat and her body visibly trembling.

Of course, she was also a consummate performer, fully capable of feigning this level of incapacity. To be safe, Billy maintained about a yard of distance between himself and his ex-partner.

"What are you trying to do here, Billy?" Ilsa's voice was so weak that Billy had to crane his neck to hear what she was saying.

"I'm here to help you, I think," he said, carefully sitting down on the rough surface of the roof.

Ilsa propped herself up on her good arm. "So, first you almost get me killed, and now you're here, you say, to help me? Forgive me if I'm a little confused, but what's your game here, Billy?"

This speech had clearly cost her, and she leaned her body back against the makeshift headboard of pipes that ran up from inside the building and down the outside wall.

Her question was a fair one, and Billy didn't have a good answer to it. He felt many conflicting things about Ilsa right now, but the one thing he did know was that he didn't want her to die.

"Let me get you to a doctor," he said, "and we can sort the rest out later."

"Meaning what?" she said. "Once the police arrest me, you'll put in a good word for me?"

"I can help you avoid the police," he said. "Let me get you to a doctor."

"You have a doctor in town you can trust?" she said. "One who's not going to balk at a gunshot wound?"

He didn't, and she knew he didn't.

Ilsa closed her eyes, and Billy could see by the rise and fall of her chest that her breathing was growing more erratic. He could also see blood seeping from the edges of the makeshift bandage she'd tied around her shoulder. He took off his jacket and vest and tore the vest into thick strips.

"I'm going to bandage you up some more," he said. "All right?"

Ilsa shivered and nodded. Billy scooted over so he was right next to her, and then Ilsa moved like lighting, and Billy understood he'd been duped. In the time it had taken the penny to drop, Ilsa had handcuffed Billy—both hands behind him!—to her headboard of pipes.

"Do I need to gag you?" she said, crouching just out of reach, "or can you manage to keep quiet on your own?"

She held his borrowed derringer, having managed to snatch it, apparently, as she'd applied the cuffs.

"I wasn't lying when I said I wanted to help you," he said.

"That's not what I asked," she said.

He thought about it for a minute. "No gag."

"All right," she said, and Billy could see it hadn't *all* been an act, that Ilsa *was* seriously hurt. Her face was dangerously pale, and blood seeped through the sleeve of her dress.

"You've got fast hands," he said, "even with that bad arm."

"It's part of my job."

"And the cuffs were in your secret pocket?"

Ilsa picked up the carpet bag resting near her feet. "As much as I'd like to talk shop right now, I need to get moving."

"How much did he pay you, by the way?" said Billy, nodding at the bag.

She opened it and pushed aside the top layer of bills to reveal stacks and stacks of cut newspapers.

"Oh," he said. "I'm sorry."

Ilsa shrugged.

"It's enough to get me out of town, at least," she said. "In fact..." She picked out the genuine bills and slipped them into the pocket of her dress.

"No use toting this whole thing around," she said, dropping the carpetbag and kicking it to the edge of the roof.

"What's the plan then?" Billy said. "Even if you make it out of Salt Lake, you can't work, at least not for a while."

"Don't worry about it," she said. "I have something lined up."

"What is it?"

But then her face softened. "Lucy Lammermoor has a farm in Wyoming," Ilsa began.

This rang a bell—Billy had heard something through the grapevine about a group of female impersonators he'd known on vaudeville starting some kind of commune together.

"You're not going to that farm with the Crimson Swans, are you?" he said.

"Why shouldn't I?" she said.

Somehow, living on a farm with a bunch of failed vaudevillians seemed an even sadder outcome for Ilsa than what Billy had previously imagined.

"You know communes never work, right?" he said.

"I do, Billy," she said. "Thank you for that insight."

"It's probably already defunct."

Moving in a shaky crouch, Ilsa leaned over the edge of the roof to survey the streets below. "I'm leaving now," she said, stepping back from the edge of the roof.

"Aren't you going to uncuff me?" he said.

She slipped the derringer into the hidden pocket of her dress. “I taught you how to get out of those cuffs that time when we were in Bismarck.”

“That was so long ago,” he said. “I’m not sure I can still do it.”

“You better get working then,” she said, and picked up a few of the strips he’d torn from his vest.

Staying clear of his legs, she gagged him with the fabric and then patted him on the shoulder. “Can you breathe well enough?”

He grudgingly nodded his head.

She stepped back and looked him in the eyes. “Sorry about the gag, but I can’t take the risk,” she said. “And for whatever it’s worth, I’m sorry about Seattle. I really am.”

Billy paused and then nodded. She left him alone on the roof.

# 67

On the floor of Diantha Marsh's coal cellar, Francie Bream lay concealed behind a broken table. A minute earlier, a negligent policeman had shined a lantern across the space from the top of the stairs, doing such a shoddy job that the light had come nowhere near Francie.

She waited until she heard the slam of the front door, then a single set of footsteps moving across the house. She assumed the policeman was now stationed outside keeping a lookout for the likes of Francie, leaving Diantha alone upstairs.

To be honest, Francie didn't have much of a plan. Nevertheless, she crept up the dirty cellar stairs and opened the door at the top, emerging into the kitchen. The house was dark, save for a sliver of light at the bottom of a bedroom door.

Moving through the darkness, Francie considered what she might say to her long-lost sister. When she reached the bedroom door, she hesitated and then—why not?—knocked.

"Roger?" came Diantha's voice from inside.

Francie slowly opened the door.

"It's me," she said.

Diantha sat on the edge of her bed in a cozy-looking dressing gown. Her eyes widened in terror, and as she opened her mouth, presumably to call for the policeman, Francie waved her hands.

"Please don't yell," she said. "I'm not here to hurt you."

Diantha looked at Francie's empty hands and pleading eyes and slowly let out her breath. "There's a policeman outside," she said.

"I know," said Francie, lowering her arms.

"Keep your hands where I can see them, please," said Diantha, and Francie re-raised her arms.

"Truly," she said, "I'm not here to hurt you."

"Then why *are* you here?" Diantha looked ready to spring at Francie at the slightest provocation.

"Can I put my hands down, please?" Francie asked. "My arms are getting very tired."

Diantha considered this and then nodded at a desk and chair at the other side of the room. "You can turn that chair around so that it faces the bed," she said, "and sit down with your hands on your knees. But do it slowly, do you hear?"

"Yes," said Francie. "Thank you very much." She followed Diantha's instructions to the letter, and, once she was facing the other woman, she answered her question. "I came here because there's something you need to know. Something important."

Diantha looked skeptical. "What could you possibly have to say to me?"

"The story I told you earlier," Francie began, "was all true, but I left out one important detail. The woman I heard it from was my mother. She gave birth to me a few years after you were stolen from her. Which is to say, Diantha, we have the same mother. We're sisters, you and I."

Francie wasn't sure how she'd expected Diantha to react to this revelation, but it certainly wasn't with the stone-faced indifference she was projecting.

"Did you hear what I said?" Francie asked.

"We share the same mother," Diantha said. "That's very interesting." She clenched her jaw and looked defiantly at Francie, who couldn't believe what she was hearing.

"*Interesting*?" Francie said. "*Interesting*? Don't you care that we're sisters?"

Diantha, hugging herself through her soft dressing gown, said, "I don't think *you* care we're sisters, not really."

"That's ridiculous," Francie said.

"No," she said, "it's not. The whole time we've known each other, you've not only deceived me, but treated me as a means to an end, as a way to get to my husband."

The accusation stung.

"That is *not* true," Francie said.

"Which part?" Diantha said. "That you lied to me about our real relationship, or that you were planning to kill Roger all along?"

Francie felt that Diantha was being deliberately obtuse now. "Yes, I did those things," she said, "but I did them for you. For *us*."

"No, you didn't," Diantha said.

"Yes, I did," said Francie.

Diantha shook her head. "Let's say one of the men at the séance this evening had been quicker on the draw," she said, "and shot you dead. I'm assuming you anticipated that possibility?"

"I did," said Francie, "but—"

"But nothing. If you'd been killed, who would have told me that your mother and my mother are the same person?"

This stopped Francie short. She hadn't thought of that, actually, but that didn't mean Diantha was right. She *did* care about her sister, but she'd had so much to think about, and this detail had merely slipped through the cracks.

"An oversight, it's true," Francie said, "but that doesn't change how I feel about you."

Diantha sighed heavily. Francie looked down at her lap, feeling more disappointed now than at her failure to kill Roger Marsh.

"What do you want from me, Miss Bream?" Diantha said.

Francie didn't know what to say to this.

"Answer my question, please," said Diantha.

Francie looked up, doing her best not to cry. "I suppose I thought we might run away together," she said weakly.

Diantha looked horrified by this confession, and Francie's cheeks burned with humiliation.

"Why would I do that?" Diantha asked. "Why would I run away with some...some madwoman who tried to kill someone I care about? Why would I want to do that?"

Francie wanted to crawl beneath Diantha's bed and weep. "Because we're sisters," she said instead.

Diantha laughed. She actually laughed at this. "Not in any way that matters," she shot back. "You're nothing to me but a homicidal lunatic. Now get out of my house."

# 68

By this time of night, Gilbert Snaith was really feeling sorry for himself. He was bothered less, he'd decided, by Diantha Marsh's rejection of his suit (though he was, he had to admit, quite bothered), and more by the wholesale deception she'd perpetrated.

Here he'd thought Diantha was one kind of woman—gentle, strong but demure, innocent—when in reality, she was a mocking harpy who didn't respect him at all. Gilbert had a hard time believing he'd ever been attracted to her; currently, the thought of Diantha repulsed him.

On top of that situation, the inept Lieutenant Mainwaring had stood him up for their scheduled evening debriefing.

Awash in melancholic resentment over the world's indifference, Gilbert sat in bed eating black licorice laces and listening repeatedly to Caruso sing "Vesti la giubba" on his bedside phonograph player.

He drew some comfort from the fact that, if he wanted, he could ruin Diantha Marsh's reputation—such as it was. In the wrong hands, the letters she'd written him could give the impression of a more salacious relationship than they'd had. He could set those wheels in motion right now.

But no.

Gilbert was a gentleman and would eschew vengeance, choosing instead the higher path men like him traveled by pure instinct. Who was it that said virtue is its own reward? Anthony Comstock, perhaps? Or was it Jesus?

Basking in the warm glow of his native goodness, Gilbert was further rewarded by a knock at his bedroom door.

"Yes?" he called out.

The butler opened the door and stepped inside. "Lieutenant Mainwaring to see you, sir."

"Thank you, Bernham," Gilbert said from his nest of misery.

He waited for Bernham to leave and then rose to dress for the meeting.

Downstairs in the greenhouse, Gilbert found Lieutenant Mainwaring sitting amid a cluster of potted lemon trees, looking sweaty and exhausted. When he saw Gilbert, he sprang to his feet.

"Sit down," Gilbert barked. He remained standing, towering over the lieutenant. "You're three hours late."

Mainwaring looked up with the sorry eyes of a basset hound. "My apologies, Mr. Snaith," he said. "A crazy woman tried to kill Roger Marsh, and we've been in pursuit for hours."

Gilbert couldn't say he was surprised; this seemed like exactly the type of thing that would happen to Roger Marsh.

"You haven't found her?" Gilbert said.

"Not yet," said Mainwaring.

"Of course you haven't." Gilbert examined the frond of a Boston fern.

"You'd be interested to know, however," said Lieutenant Mainwaring, "Diantha Marsh is perfectly safe."

Gilbert spun around to face the lieutenant. "Why would that interest me, Mainwaring?" The lieutenant shrunk back into his chair.

"Hmm?"

"I just thought..." Mainwaring began.

"No," said Gilbert. "Never mention that woman's name again."

"Yes, sir."

"And stop cringing," said Gilbert. "What news do you have for me?"

The lieutenant extracted a folded document from his coat pocket and handed it to Gilbert. "Mr. Barnes wasn't happy to see me," he said. "He said it's much too risky making direct contact."

"Well, desperate times," said Gilbert.

"Yes, sir," said Mainwaring. "On a different subject, I don't think the Helton business will cause any more trouble."

"Helton business?" said Gilbert. "Who's Helton?"

Mainwaring stiffened. "He's the man we discussed earlier today."

This was maddeningly vague.

"Be more specific," Gilbert said.

"Gus Helton is the man you asked us to, uh, to take care of," Mainwaring said.

And then Gilbert remembered; it had been such a hellish day that the whole incident had slipped his mind.

"Yes, *Helton*," he said. "Of course."

Mainwaring rubbed the back of his neck, and Gilbert wished the lieutenant would just disappear.

Gilbert said, "I'm going to read the message now, if that's all right with you, Mainwaring."

The lieutenant looked away as Gilbert unfolded the paper, which read as follows:

*Killing the detective would cause more problems than it would solve. We've come to an understanding, and he poses no threat to us.*

Gilbert crumpled the paper when he'd finished reading and shoved it into the pocket of his dressing gown. "Wait here," he said to Mainwaring and left the room.

At his office typewriter, he composed a response:

*I'd prefer the detective to be permanently dealt with, but I will defer to your judgement this time, with the understanding that if anything goes awry, you will face significant consequences.*

Back in the greenhouse, Gilbert handed the folded paper to Lieutenant Mainwaring and summarily dismissed him.

It was all so tiresome, Gilbert reflected as he returned to his bed and his resentment over Diantha's insidious deceptions. But no: hadn't he wallowed enough? After all, Diantha wasn't the only woman in town, nor was she the only polygamist who'd caught Gilbert's eye. Though not as young as Diantha, Eliza Williams, the fourth wife of a minor Mormon official he'd met at a recent city function, had a certain knowingness about her, a gleam in her eye that suggested a warm affection for the ways of the flesh. There were possibilities there, great, untapped possibilities.

Gilbert turned off his bedside lamp, and dimly erotic visions of Sister Williams danced in his head until sleep overcame him, and he dreamed the dreams of the innocent.

# 69

Madame Ilsa needed someplace to lie low until morning and decided to test the hospitality of Rose Montague and the Stockade, as she had no other semi-reliable contacts in the city. On her way there, she made a detour to retrieve the escape bag she'd stashed on the grounds of the Salt Lake City Cemetery.

She moved through the streets with care, as the civilian searchers conducted their patrols with such festivity that she could hear them coming from a block away. The professionals—the police and the U.S. Marshal—were few and far between, having positioned themselves, Ilsa suspected, at the train depot and the main roads out of town so they could contain Ilsa and Francie until daylight tipped the odds in law enforcement's favor.

As she stepped into the dark cemetery and retrieved the concealed bag from the shrubbery, she was feeling good about circumstances (well, relatively good: her shoulder was throbbing, she grew dizzier and dizzier with each passing moment, and she was so, so tired) until a voice whisper-called from a nearby grove of trees.

"Ilsa," came the voice again, and Francie Bream stepped out of the trees, still dressed as Joseph Smith, though the wig was long gone and her own tangled hair framed her drawn face.

Madame Ilsa crossed the grass, pulling Francie back into the cover of the trees.

"What do you want?" she demanded.

Francie looked surprisingly hurt by Ilsa's tone. "You know, some might say I'm the one who should be mad at you," said Francie. "You replaced the bullets in my gun with blanks."

"I did," said Ilsa. "And you made me an accomplice to attempted murder."

Francie looked away. "None of this has gone how I'd hoped."

Was Francie really responding to her with *self-pity* right now? "What do you want?" Ilsa asked again.

"I thought I'd find you here," Francie said, "because I saw you hide that bag. I was watching from over there." She pointed to the street that ran along the south side of the cemetery.

"I don't care how you found me," Ilsa said, and suddenly her dizziness intensified, and it took some effort to remain upright.

"I thought we could help each other," said Francie. "You're probably the closest thing I have to a friend right now."

Ilsa looked Francie in the eye. "What could you even offer me?"

"I have someplace we can hide, at least for the night," Francie said.

"So do I," Ilsa said, though that was far from certain.

"Where?"

Another surge of dizziness made it hard to focus, and Ilsa found herself telling the truth. "The Stockade."

"Where the prostitutes work?" said Francie. "That place will be crawling with police."

Ilsa knew the journalist wasn't wrong. "Well, do you have anything better?"

"Yes, I just told you I do," said Francie.

Ilsa's head was really spinning now, and then she was sitting on the sidewalk with no memory of how she got there.

"What's wrong?" Francie crouched down next to her. "Are you all right?"

Ilsa shook her head. "The Marshal shot me in the shoulder."

Francie looked truly sobered by this information. "Are you able to walk?"

Ilsa recognized she wouldn't be going anywhere without assistance, and so extended her good arm to Francie, who helped her to her feet.

Ilsa leaned heavily against the journalist and said, "So where's this hideout?"

"Down that way," Francie said, nodding southward

"I hope you're telling the truth," said Ilsa. "Now don't let go of me, please."

She could keep walking, barely, with the help of Francie, but Ilsa felt her body revolting with each step, begging her to stop and lie down. She became less and less aware of her surroundings, relying entirely on Francie Bream to steer clear of the merry vigilantes who would likely shoot them on sight.

Finally, minutes or hours or days later, they stopped in front of a modest bungalow. Francie withdrew a key from the pocket of Joseph Smith's coat and unlocked the front door. Ilsa tried to focus her vision as Francie guided her inside.

The unpleasant aroma of a butcher shop invading Ilsa's nostrils "Where are we?"

"Adam Wolfe's house," said Francie, pulling Ilsa onward. "The bedroom's back here."

The bloody, meaty smell grew stronger.

"What?" said Ilsa. "This isn't safe at all. What if he comes back?"

It was then that she caught sight of the source of the terrible smell, the naked body of a man lying on the dining room floor, his face smashed beyond recognition.

"You killed him," she said, turning to look at Francie. "You killed Adam Wolfe."

The expression on Francie's face told Ilsa she wasn't wrong. The smell—that smell!— was stronger than ever now. The room began to rock dangerously, and Ilsa fell to the floor.

# 70

STANDING IN THE ABANDONED DRESSMAKER'S SHOP with a small number of eager listeners around him, Roger paused to recognize that he hadn't felt joy like this in months, not since the halcyon days before his illegitimate excommunication by the leaders of the now-fallen Church. This magnificent feeling confirmed he was doing exactly what the Lord wanted him to do, a synchronicity between himself and Almighty God brought about through the Gift of the Holy Ghost.

He'd passed through his Gethsemane of doubt and now here he was, a shining instrument in God's hands.

Roger didn't know how long he'd been speaking, and his listeners appeared no less rapt than when he'd begun to address them following the miracle of the failed gun.

Off to the side, the handful of remaining policemen repeatedly checked their watches, more than ready, Roger supposed, to escort him and his valiant band of disciples safely back to their homes.

He would leave when the Lord notified him it was time to leave, and not a moment before.

The police in this case were like the Roman soldiers in attendance at the crucifixion of the Lord, unaware they were in the presence of Deity. Not Roger himself, of course, but the palpable

Spirit of Christ made manifest by the faith of Roger and the other followers of this new, re-sanctified iteration of God's one true church.

This gathering was something precious and powerful. Here, verily, was the stone carved from the mountain without hands, destined to roll forth and crush the mighty idols of this world, and so Roger ignored the increasingly impatient gestures of the policemen and continued to teach the honey-sweet words of the Lord.

# 71

In the hallway of Adam Wolfe's house, Francie dropped to her knees to assess Madame Ilsa's condition. The medium couldn't die right now; that would be exactly the kind of incidental harm she couldn't bear to be responsible for. A cursory examination revealed, to Francie's relief, that Ilsa was still breathing evenly and her heart was still beating, and so she turned her attention to Ilsa's arm.

The shoddy bandage Ilsa herself had presumably applied seemed to cover the wound only partially. It had slipped down, and the whole upper sleeve of her dress was soaked in blood. As Francie explored the area with her fingers, Ilsa's eyes fluttered open, and she tried to stand up.

"Wait," said Francie. "Let me help you, and we'll get you to the bed."

Ilsa muttered something she couldn't make out, and with some effort, Francie helped Ilsa to her feet. Ilsa could barely stand, even with help, and so they staggered with great effort into the bedroom.

With some miracle reserve of strength, Francie was able to help Ilsa up onto Wolfe's bed, where she immediately passed out.

After catching her own breath, Francie again checked Ilsa's

breathing and heartbeat— both steady enough—and set to work preparing supplies from around the house:

She filled a basin with soapy water and set it next to the bed. In a linen closet, she found a clean sheet to tear into strips for bandaging. And, after some foraging, she found a sewing kit that must have belonged to the late Adam Wolfe's late wife, and she set it next to the basin and the bandages.

Francie figured her basic first-aid training was enough to treat this particular wound, which was more than a graze but less than something truly serious. Sitting at the edge of the bed, she helped Ilsa out of the bodice and sleeves of her dress to treat the wound unobstructed. As she lowered the dress, though, Francie was confronted with a chest covered with a broad swath of dark, curly hair.

This unexpected sight gave her a moment's pause, but Francie quickly collected herself and began to clean the wound in Ilsa's arm.

# 72

It was nearly sunrise in Salt Lake City, and Billy Lovelace had finally managed—using the clip of the pen he kept in his jacket pocket—to pick the lock of the handcuffs Ilsa had slapped on his wrists several hours earlier.

He rubbed his chafed wrists and kicked the cuffs across the roof. Checking his watch, he saw that his appointment with Whiskey Joe was still some time away. Billy suspected the payment Whiskey Joe had offered was genuine, but there was still a chance their meeting would serve as an occasion to permanently eliminate Billy.

With his own fragile mortality at the front of his mind, Billy decided not to take the risk. Feeling tired and hungry, but also happy to be alive, he climbed down the fire escape and circled to the front of the building. He was astonished to see the second-floor lights still illuminated, with the shapes of people moving around inside, though, perhaps he shouldn't have been surprised at all. He imagined Roger Marsh would be taking full advantage of the excitement caused by his near assassination.

Thankfully, that was none of Billy's business anymore.

He looked around the empty streets and took in a lungful of chilly air. He considered simply walking to the depot to catch a train, but out of an abundance of caution—if Whiskey Joe or Gilbert Snaith *did* want to kill him, they might have someone watching the station—he decided instead to hop a freight train outside of town.

He'd need to get walking. Orienting himself in a roughly south-westerly direction, he crossed the street and mentally added Salt Lake to the growing list of cities to which he could never return.

# 73

SOFT, MORNING LIGHT FILTERED IN THROUGH DRAWN curtains, and Madame Ilsa heard a rhythmic, mechanical clattering. She was awake—tired, yes, but clearer-headed than she'd been the night before. She knew she was in Adam Wolfe's house, in Wolfe's bed to be precise, and that Francie Bream was the one who had brought her here.

Lifting her head, she identified the source of the clattering as a portable typewriter in Francie's lap. The journalist sat in a rocking chair in the corner, so engrossed in her writing she didn't seem to notice that Ilsa had woken up.

Ilsa's shoulder hurt, and her broken finger hurt, and her body felt weak from its exertions of the previous day, but she was also alive, which was not nothing. She propped another pillow behind her as she sat half up. "How long have I been asleep?"

Francie stopped typing and looked at her, and then at a small clock on the dresser. "Five or six hours."

"What time is it?" said Ilsa, who couldn't read the clock from the bed.

"A little after seven."

Ilsa sat up all the way, and her body protested. She wasn't sure where she stood with Francie, but the journalist hadn't killed her in her sleep, so that was promising.

"I need to get working," Ilsa said. "Where's my bag?"

"It's by the front door."

Francie nodded, and a heavy silence followed. Ilsa was trying to remember everything that had happened the night before, as well as plan her next move, as well as figure out why Francie was helping her.

"So," said Francie, eyes still on Ilsa. "You're a man, then."

Ilsa realized she was undressed, and that Francie must have been the one to undress her. She tensed and pulled the bed sheets up higher. "No," she said. "I'm not."

Francie looked like she might register an objection, but instead said, "I stitched up your arm with some sewing thread—I don't know if you remember that—but you'll want a real doctor to take a look at it."

"Thank you," said Ilsa.

"It's the least I could do," Francie said. "Considering."

Then Ilsa remembered the dead body in the dining room. Surely, Francie wouldn't let her leave this house alive considering all she knew.

"Do you have someplace you can go?" said Francie. "Someplace safe?"

Ilsa nodded warily. "Some old colleagues of mine are running a farm together," she said, "and they invited me to join them."

Francie wrinkled her nose. "A commune?" she said. "Communes never work out."

Ilsa didn't want to have this conversation again. "Maybe not," she said. "But I could use an honest failure right about now."

Francie seemed to consider this. "How will you get out of town?"

Ilsa supposed there was no harm in telling her. "I have a disguise in my bag," she said. "I plan to walk right into the depot, buy a ticket, and board a train. How about you?"

"I'm not planning on going anywhere." Francie's eyes traveled to the dressing table next to the rocking chair, on top of which sat the little derringer Ilsa had taken from Billy.

Ilsa didn't know what to say, although she could see now why Francie might let her go unscathed.

"I imagine you'll want to leave soon," said Francie, pushing through the awkward moment. "I wouldn't want to delay your preparations more than I already have."

"Of course." Ilsa scooted to the edge of the bed and put her feet on the floor. Slowly, testing the strength of her legs, she stood up. She took one cautious step, and then another, thankfully managing to stay upright.

"There's a bit of food in the kitchen if you're up for it," Francie said. "Bread, cheese, and a bottle of milk that's still good, I think. It was delivered yesterday morning."

"All right," Ilsa said, feeling more confident with each step.

Crossing the dining room with the gory corpse at its center was a challenge, more emotionally than physically, but Ilsa made it into the kitchen and found the food Francie had mentioned.

She ate carefully at first, and then avidly, washing down mouthfuls of stale bread and cheese with swigs of warm milk. She had to make herself pause after a minute so she wouldn't get sick from eating too quickly, and then she resumed more deliberately, already feeling stronger for having a little food in her belly.

When she finished eating, she retrieved her bag from its spot by the front door, and then, sitting down in Wolfe's modest parlor, took inventory of the bag's contents: clean underwear, a shirtwaist and dark skirt, a blond wig and matching false eyebrows, a small makeup kit, a few toiletries, a hairbrush, scissors, and a tin of Fig Newton cakes.

If she worked quickly, she could be ready to leave for the depot within an hour.

She started with a shave and a bath—both quite difficult with her bad arm—and then dressed and pinned up her hair. She took her wig, brush, and makeup kit to the bedroom and sat at the dressing table.

Francie paused her typing, reached out for the derringer, and tucked it next to her on the rocking chair.

"What are you working on, if I might ask?" said Ilsa, unpacking her makeup kit.

She felt less nervous if Francie was talking, as it gave her some indication of the journalist's emotional state.

"A confession, and a justification," Francie said, typing as she spoke. "I've mentioned in it, by the way, that you were only accidentally involved in my attempt to kill Marsh."

"Thank you," said Ilsa. She removed the pair of blond false eyebrows from her bag and laid them on the dressing table in front of her. She wanted to know more from Francie but wasn't sure how safe it was to ask.

"Tell me about your disguise," Francie said, still typing.

"There's not much to tell," Ilsa said, spreading spirit gum on the back of the eyebrow. "Blonde hair, respectable clothing, and the kind of makeup that looks like I'm not wearing makeup."

She carefully placed the false eyebrow over her real one and held it there.

"And that's enough?" Francie said.

"You don't want to look like you're wearing a disguise," Ilsa said. "If it looks like you're trying to hide, people will know you're hiding."

Since they were talking shop, Ilsa decided to hazard a question. "Why *did* you try to kill Roger Marsh?"

Francie stopped typing. Ilsa braced herself for an explosion.

Instead, the journalist said, almost sadly, "The story I told at the séance about the stolen baby? The woman Roger Marsh stole the baby from was my mother."

"Revenge?" Ilsa said.

The journalist shook her head.

"Justice, not revenge," she said. "I hoped that by killing Roger Marsh, I'd cause other powerful men to hesitate before using their power to hurt others. Violence isn't ideal, of course, but it's needed right now to jolt people to their senses."

Ilsa looked at her reflection in the dressing table's cracked oval mirror. There were many things she wanted to say, but she was unsure what the consequences would be if she said them.

Francie watched her carefully. "I don't care if you disapprove of my methods," the journalist said. "I'm committed to change, and I'm tired of waiting."

"All right, then," said Ilsa, and turning to Francie: "Are my eyebrows on straight?"

Francie looked. "Yes." She started typing again, and then almost immediately stopped. "I would like to know what you think, actually."

"Would you?"

"Yes," said Francie. "Sincerely."

Ilsa turned her chair so they faced each other. "I don't think killing Roger Marsh would have achieved what you wanted it to achieve," Ilsa said.

"And why's that?" said Francie tilting her chin upward.

"I've spent a lot of time in my life watching people respond to death," Ilsa said. "Generally speaking, people feel tenderly toward the dead and are willing to overlook a lot."

"But—" Francie began.

"You asked for my opinion, and I'm going to give it to you," Ilsa continued. "If you had killed Marsh, people would have sympathized with him, not you. I'm not saying that's right, or fair, I'm only saying that's how it is."

"But what *you* don't seem to understand," Francie said, "is that I'm happy to be the villain as long as it strikes fear in the hearts of men like Marsh."

Ilsa shrugged. She didn't want to push the armed journalist too far.

"What is it you want to say?" Francie said. "That I've become as bad as one of them?" She looked like a rattlesnake rearing to strike.

For several long moments, Ilsa barely dared to breathe. She hadn't felt closer to death in the past twenty-four hours than she did right now, but then something seemed to shift within Francie Bream, and her posture drooped, the threat dissipating into the cool morning air.

"I think," Francie said finally, "we'll just have to agree to disagree over the efficacy of the work I'm doing."

"Of course," Ilsa said eagerly, and Francie returned to her typing as if nothing had happened.

Ilsa waited until she seemed fully engrossed in her work again and then started putting on her makeup.

She needed to get out of here, and fast.

# 74

The young policeman, an Officer Simmons, wouldn't listen to reason.

"If we walk quickly," Roger explained again, "my associate's house is only ten minutes away."

They stood on the sidewalk in front of Roger's primary home—his only home, actually, now that he'd given the other house to Diantha—having walked together from the venue of the séance.

Young Simmons removed his cap and ran a hand through his pale, prematurely thinning hair.

Roger had spent the entire night in the dressmakers' shop imparting the word of the Lord to his fellow disciples, energized and inspired by an especial dispensation of the Spirit, and although he had insisted, when morning came, that he was more than capable of walking himself home and the Lord had already demonstrated the protection he'd enjoy from this point forward, the bleary-eyed policemen said that the matter wasn't up for debate; they were under strict orders from the chief to escort Roger and his associates to their homes. Those two madwomen, Francie Bream and Madame Ilsa, still hadn't been apprehended, which posed a real threat, the policemen claimed.

Roger had acquiesced and allowed young Simmons to walk him home.

Now, standing on Roger's front steps, they found themselves with another conundrum.

"It doesn't matter how close your associate's house is," Simmons said, replacing his cap. "I'm supposed to wait here until eight-thirty, when Officer O'Meara will take my place."

On the walk home, Roger had decided he needed to check in with Adam Wolfe as soon as possible. Something about Adam's communique of the previous morning wasn't sitting right, and though Roger couldn't say why—call it instinct, call it a whispering of the Spirit—he wondered if Adam had never left Salt Lake in the first place.

Perhaps his young associate had gotten cold feet (not likely, Roger thought) or had done something he shouldn't have in the name of the greater good (as he saw it) and could use some guidance from a trusted mentor.

If Roger was wrong—though he was rarely wrong about this kind of thing—he would be out nothing more than a pleasant morning walk. But if he was right, perhaps he could provide some much-needed relief to his faithful friend.

But Simmons wasn't budging.

"If you need to stay here," Roger responded, "let me visit my friend by myself."

"You know I can't do that," said Simmons. "I have..."

"I know," said Roger. "You have orders to keep watch over me until Officer O'Hara relieves you of duty."

"O'Meara," said Simmons, and checked his watch. "And he'll be here in less than fifteen minutes. Why don't you wait inside, Mr. Marsh, and when O'Meara gets here, *he* can take you to your friend's house."

Roger could tolerate this for only so long. "Have I been arrested?"

"What?" said Simmons.

"Have I broken any laws?" said Roger. "Am I under arrest? Which is to say, if I simply walk away from you right now to visit my associate, will you attempt to restrain me?"

Simmons's eyes took on a distant, tragic look. "Of course not," he said. "If you left, I'd just have to follow you."

"Exactly right," said Roger, and he set off for Adam's house.

# 75

Madame Ilsa had left Francie Bream alone in Adam Wolfe's house with her typewriter and derringer and made her way to the nearest trolley stop without anyone noticing anything amiss about her, much less recognizing her as one of the two women being hunted by the city's entire police force.

Now, Ilsa sat in a streetcar bound for the train depot, wincing every time someone jostled her injured shoulder. Though she was grateful for the small victories she'd enjoyed so far this morning, her greatest obstacle still lay ahead. The depot would be lousy with policemen, each one looking for her. And while her disguise had sufficed up to now, her precarious physical condition threatened to counteract all camouflage her careful getup had provided.

She needed to maintain an expression of detachment, even entitlement—this was truly the most effective component of a disguise—but it was getting more and more difficult to keep her face from twisting into a permanent rictus of pain.

Some of her fellow passengers stole glances at her now, not, she hoped, because they suspected her of being a wanted woman, but because they could see she was in agony. This attention was dangerous. She needed to be invisible. She needed to be one of them.

Fretting would help nothing, so she thought instead of what a successful escape from the city might look like: If she made it past the police and boarded a train—it didn't matter which one— she would be home free. She could sleep on the train, building up her strength and the peace of mind that would come from leaving Salt Lake farther and farther behind her.

There was also Francie's manuscript. If the police found it and believed Francie's assertion that Ilsa had been unknowingly embroiled in the whole affair, maybe they would give up their search. A lot of maybes, true, but not outside the realm of possibility.

She let her imagination continue in this vein and tried to imagine what, specifically, life on the Lammermoor farm might look like.

She pictured the lot of them—Lucy and whichever of the Crimson Swans had washed ashore onto the commune—crowded into a rustic kitchen at the end of a long day spent plowing the fields or nursing a sick cow or checking the hay stores for moisture.

She could see Lucy standing at the stove tending to one of her eccentric stews, while Nellie Chen sat on a stool with her Spanish guitar singing sentimental ballads about lonesome travelers and lovesick girls, while at the table, Princess Fontina and Daisy Fortnum argued for the two-thousandth time over which of them had pioneered the triple wig removal as the finale for their otherwise mediocre acts, while at one of the picture windows, Tiffany Cartier and Alexandria Lake stood hand in hand watching twilight creep across the quiet Wyoming farmland.

Obviously, Ilsa recognized this was an over-idealized portrait of life on the farm, that the reality would include brutal winters and hurt feelings, failed crops and illnesses, costly mistakes and petty grudges, mud and sweat and sorrow, but still, Ilsa would give anything—she was ready to admit—to make it onto whatever train would take her away from Salt Lake City and toward the messy, beautiful farm where her old friends waited (she hoped) for her arrival.

Ilsa's yearning was interrupted when, at a curve in the tracks, a fellow passenger bumped her, and she let out a cry of pain.

"Are you all right, ma'am?" asked a solicitous gentleman to her left.

"Yes, thank you." Ilsa adjusted the hat she'd pilfered from a closet of clothes belonging, presumably, to Wolfe's late wife.

Wearing the clothing of a dead woman (Ilsa had also borrowed a poorly fitting coat) seemed now like a terrible choice, an invitation to ill fate.

"Are you sure?" said the gentleman. Several passengers now watched her with concern and wariness.

"I'm perfectly all right," Ilsa said brightly.

In response, the gentleman and passengers looked away, but she suspected none of them really believed her.

# 76

To Diantha's surprise, she had fallen asleep fairly quickly after Francie Bream's departure the night before, and she felt truly rested this morning, sitting at her small bedroom writing table next to the window with a pad of paper before her and an excitement for the future she hadn't felt in quite some time. Roger's church seemed like it might actually succeed, and she had successfully, Diantha thought, positioned herself as a legitimate leader alongside her former husband.

The great challenge now would be eliminating polygamy. She couldn't do it right away; too many of the founding members had been drawn to this church as a vehicle to perpetuate plural marriage. She'd need to move in stages. She'd also, of course, need to get Roger to agree.

Through the window, she'd seen him arrive at his home a few minutes earlier accompanied by a weary-looking young policeman, but then he and the officer had left again almost immediately. She wondered where they'd gone.

She also wondered how truly amenable Roger would be to her presence as a co-leader possessing some very different ideas from his. Because if she was being honest, she knew Roger would *not* be open to the cessation of plural marriage; to him, polygamy was central to the restored gospel of Jesus Christ. There had to be a way to change his mind.

She considered the question for a time, tapping a pen against her teeth and watching autumn leaves blow down the sidewalk in front of her house. If ever a question merited prayer, it was this one. And so, she knelt down next to her bed and sought the counsel of the Lord.

At first, she felt only the usual, vague warmth in her chest, the whispered half ideas in her mind, but then it was like she was falling, tumbling through a great void, until she stood alone on a dance floor at Saltair (Coney Island of the West!) with the scent of the Great Salt Lake briny in her nostrils.

Before her stood a Being of Feathers and Fire, glorious to behold, and that Being held out a small, leatherbound book.

"Take," said the Being. "Eat."

And Diantha took the book, and she ate. It tasted like honeycomb and lavender, and Diantha could have lingered in its sweetness forever, but the Being of Feathers and Flames took her by the hand, and then she was far above Saltair, and the resort was in flames, and the lake was red like blood, and Diantha's cheeks were wet with tears. Filled with despair, she watched as the earth opened up and swallowed the flaming resort and the lake of blood, and below her Diantha now saw nothing but a vast and barren plain, and she was afraid.

The Being again took her by the hand, and then she was sitting on the dirt floor of a log cabin. The Being was gone, but a new Voice addressed her as if from the very wood of the structure that contained her.

"Feed my trees," said the Voice.

And Diantha, finding her own voice, said, "Your sheep, do you mean?"

And the Voice of the Cabin said, "Breed my sheep."

And Diantha said, "No, that's not right."

And the Voice of the Cabin fell silent, and Diantha was kneeling in a grove of living trees, and yet another Voice, this one a

Voice of Whispering Leaves, said, "And my sheep are as numerous as the sands of the earth and the stars of the sky, and they are the cedars of Lebanon, and the beloved of Solomon, and the clay of the potter."

And Diantha said, "No. The sheep are the sheep."

And then she was back on the empty Saltair dance floor, but this time she filled the space with the light within her until the Being of Feathers and Fire could bear it no more.

And the Being of Feathers and Fire said, "It is enough," and the space was filled with darkness.

Diantha came back to herself on the floor of her bedroom. She looked up at the clock. It was still morning; in fact, almost no time had passed. She wiped a trail of spittle from the side of her mouth, and sat up, shivering.

# 77

A SUICIDE NOTE/MANIFESTO/AUTOBIOGRAPHY WAS A difficult thing to finish, but for the moment, Francie Bream had run out of things to say, and time was running short. She set the manuscript—impressively thick for half a night's work—on the dressing table, removed her Joseph Smith coat, and went to the closet of clothing belonging to Wolfe's dead wife to assemble a disguise.

Some say an argument succeeds if it manages to change even one person's mind, and by that criterion, Francie's manuscript was already a success, as it had convinced her that she no longer wanted to kill herself, wanted instead to continue the work she'd begun, if not here in Salt Lake, then elsewhere, with other men who abused their power with impunity.

She would, she'd decided, take a page from Madame Ilsa's book: simply put on a different set of clothing and walk into the train depot like she had every right to be there. Mrs. Wolfe's clothes would fit her well enough, and now it was only a question of which ones to wear and what impression she wanted to convey.

As she examined first one dress, and then another, she thought back to the exchange with Ilsa. Francie had been surprised and a little hurt by the medium's evident skepticism of her quest for justice, but she didn't have time to dwell on it. She chose a dress, something sensible though a bit flirtatious, and laid it out on the bed.

She was untying her Joseph Smith boots when someone knocked at the front door.

Francie froze. There was a long silence, and for a moment, she thought she'd been granted a reprieve. Then came another knock, followed by the sound of a key sliding into the lock.

Francie picked up the derringer from the dressing table.

# 78

Young Simmons insisted on entering the house with Roger, despite Roger's repeated protestations that the presence of an officer of the law might alarm his friend, Adam.

"Mr. Marsh," began Simmons.

"I know, I know," said Roger. "You have your orders. All right. We'll go in together." He pushed the door open, and the two men stepped into Adam's parlor.

"Adam?" Roger called out. "It's me, Elder Marsh."

They listened for a response, but none came.

"Adam?" Roger called again.

Still nothing. Perhaps Adam actually had left town. Left town and forgotten to take care of his garbage; something smelled off in the house, warm and rotten.

"Do you smell that?" said Simmons.

"Yes," said Roger. "Unfortunately, Adam's wife died a while back, and so his housekeeping can be spotty."

Simmons sniffed at the air. "I don't like that smell," he said, drawing his gun.

Surely this situation didn't require firearms.

"Oh, please," said Roger. "You're being very dramatic."

Simmons took a step backward toward the front door. "I think we should leave."

The boy was obviously overtired and, as a result, overexcited. Perhaps Roger should have waited the ten minutes it would have taken for Officer O'Meara to arrive and let jittery young Simmons return home for some much-needed rest. But they were here now, and Roger hated to waste a trip.

He was feeling especially sorry Adam had missed the previous night's events. He'd done so much to facilitate that success, and it seemed unfair he hadn't been present to witness the miracle of Roger's preservation and to receive the subsequent outpouring of light and knowledge from the Lord.

Roger was feeling, in other words, gently grateful for the role he and Adam had been permitted to play in the preservation of God's one true Church, and he wanted to share that gratitude and quiet joy with Adam somehow.

"We can leave soon," Roger said to Simmons, who stood at the other end of the room. "I'll just leave a note for my friend."

Roger pushed open the door to the dining room.

"Wait!" Simmons yelled and sprinted towards him.

Before Simmons reached Roger, though, a figure moved into the doorway.

# 79

This time, Francie wasn't going to thwart herself with a grandiose speech to let Marsh know exactly who was killing him and why. Instead, the moment the dining room door opened and she saw his face, she emptied a bullet into his forehead from inches away, a live round, not a blank, its lethality confirmed by a spray of blood and bone and brain from the back of Marsh's head, a gory sludge that spattered the face of the policeman who was too late to intervene.

For an instant, Francie thought the bullet had hit the officer as well, but no, it had missed, and now he was raising his own gun to return fire. Luck was still on Francie's side, though, because the now-lifeless body of Roger Marsh fell right into the policeman, knocking the gun from his hand and throwing him off balance.

Seizing on this opportunity, Francie kicked his gun across the room and ran for the front door while the policeman regained his equilibrium. He hesitated—torn, apparently, between retrieving the gun, and directly rushing an armed assassin—which gave Francie just enough time to open the door and run down the front steps.

There was no conscious thought for Francie now, only an instinct to live and live and live. She almost tripped down the front steps but recovered her balance and ran. She turned when she reached the sidewalk and saw the policeman in the doorway, armed again, and she fired a shot in his direction. It missed but also forced the man to duck back into the house.

She threw aside the empty derringer and ran even faster.

"Stop!" yelled the policeman.

Francie didn't stop, heard a shot, felt a pain in her leg, and was suddenly unable to run, could only limp-stagger down the otherwise sedate residential street.

"Stop right there!" the policeman yelled.

Francie heard another gunshot, and this time felt the pain in her back, and then another shot, and more pain, and then she was lying in the street, or above the street, something vast and empty ballooning inside her.

# 80

THOUGH SHE'D MADE IT PAST THE HEAVY POLICE presence outside the train depot, Madame Ilsa was dismayed to find an even heavier police presence inside the depot: a pair of officers near every ticket window, a quartet at every exit, and half a legion milling through the crowd of Sunday morning travelers.

More dismaying still was the presence of the selfsame U.S. Marshal who'd shot her at the ill-fated Summoning the night before. He stood beside the ticket windows, his moustache as ridiculous as ever, his rifle still cradled in his arms.

Ilsa tried not to look directly at him—she didn't want to draw his attention—but in her attempts to observe without appearing to observe she lost focus on her immediate surroundings and was jostled by an over-stacked luggage cart.

The cart didn't hit her hard, but it did hit her right on her injured shoulder. Ilsa wasn't sure whether she yelled, but pain jolted through her whole body, turning her vision white and doubling her over.

As the urgency of the pain subsided, her vision cleared, and she found a pair of policemen standing on either side of her, asking if she was all right. She also saw, from the corner of her eye, the U.S.

Marshal watching, not with concern for Ilsa's well-being, it seemed, but with growing suspicion that he recognized this obtrusive woman.

Panic threatened to destroy Ilsa's composure and with it any chance she had of escaping this wretched situation, but she managed to compose herself, managed to thank the two policemen for their concern and assure them she would be perfectly fine without their assistance. The Marshal, though, still hadn't taken his eyes off her, and as she walked to a ticket window, she willed herself not to look in the man's direction.

She felt sick as she waited in line, a sitting duck for the Marshal to examine at his leisure. It had been dark at the Summoning, and her hair and wardrobe—her entire carriage, really—were entirely different. Still, she could feel the Marshal trying to match her features to his memories of the homicidal medium from the night before.

There were two ways Ilsa could play this:

Option one, she could double down on her mild-mannered citizen act and respond to any confrontation with meek confusion.

Or option two, she could raise the stakes for the Marshal, directly approaching him as the kind of person who would cause him a whole cluster of headaches if he wrongly accused her of being a fugitive from the law.

Both methods presented serious risks, and as she bought a ticket to Cheyenne, Wyoming—not the next train leaving, as that could raise suspicions, but one leaving soon enough—she still hadn't made up her mind.

When she stepped away from the ticket window, the Marshal had positioned himself directly in her path.

That settled it. She would raise the stakes.

Ilsa made a beeline for the Marshal, as if it had been her intention all along to approach him. The man looked intrigued by this move, and a bit worried. He adjusted his grip on the rifle, the more easily to swing it into action if this proved to be a physical assault.

The moment she reached him, Ilsa *did* launch an assault, though not a physical one.

"I understand there are two lady maniacs running amok in this city," she said in her best outraged citizen voice, commanding the attention not just of the Marshal, but of an adjacent policeman as well. "And I'd like to know why you haven't yet caught them."

The Marshal scrutinized Ilsa's face.

Ilsa felt dizzy with the challenge that lay before her. Pulling this off would require sheer nerve and more than a little luck.

"You look very familiar to me, ma'am," said the Marshal, peering carefully at her face. "I believe we met recently."

Ilsa tried to look both affronted and confused. "Where would we have met?" she said. "I'm Mrs. Robert McGuinness."

She paused significantly, waiting for him to recognize the name of her very important, very fabricated husband.

The Marshal frowned and shook his head, while the policeman glared at her.

"I don't know any Robert McGuinness," the Marshal said, "but have you attended any séances recently?"

He knew exactly who she was or thought he did. She needed to respond with real bravado.

"Excuse me?" she said. "My husband pays his taxes—pays your salary!—and I'm not sure what you're doing loitering around train stations while those women are still at large—"

"Ma'am," interrupted the policeman, "I can assure you we are deploying every tactic at our disposal to bring those women to justice."

The Marshal didn't take his eyes off Ilsa as the policeman at his side offered this reassurance.

"I don't care about tactics," Ilsa said, raising her voice now. "I care about results. And as far as I can tell, you're not getting any."

"I think the last time we met," the Marshal said softly, "you were wearing a black dress. Does that ring any bells?"

He was trying to rattle her, and he was succeeding.

Ilsa's plan was working insofar as the Marshal hadn't immediately clapped her in irons and dragged her down to the station, but at this point, her continued success depended on quelling the Marshal's suspicions before he could make her crack.

"I've already told you, Marshal," said Ilsa. "We've never met."

"I couldn't help but notice earlier," he said, with credible solicitude, "that you seemed to be in severe pain. Your shoulder, was it?"

"My shoulder?" said Ilsa, stalling as she tried to decide how a real-life Mrs. Robert McGuinness might respond to such a question.

"Yes," said the Marshal. "You cried out just now."

"Surely you're exaggerating," said Ilsa, "and anyway, what business is it of yours?"

The adjacent policeman was watching with amusement, but there was no merriment in the eyes of the Marshal.

"Only trying to help," he said. "It *is* your shoulder that's giving you trouble?"

Ilsa was running out of the energy she needed to maintain this indignant façade.

"No, it's not, if you must know," she said, pushing through the pain and fatigue. "I had a dyspeptic spell; my stomach ails me from time to time. Do you feel better having heard that?"

She must have conveyed more anger than she realized because a flicker of doubt crossed the Marshal's face for the first time.

Unfortunately, if Ilsa walked away now, she suspected the Marshal would continue to observe her, maybe even place someone on her train to keep an eye on her. She had to smother his suspicions entirely, but before she could do so, a new policeman jogged up to the Marshal and delivered a message that turned her stomach.

"I just called in to the station," said the new policeman, panting as he spoke, "and they got the journalist. She's dead, but she also killed Roger Marsh—"

The Marshal jerked his head in Ilsa's direction, and the panting officer got the hint, lowering his voice and delivering the rest of the news so only the Marshal and the other officer could hear. The Marshal maintained his poker face, but the policeman next to him looked alternately horrified and outraged.

"And the medium?" said the Marshal, loud enough for Ilsa to hear.

"No sign of her yet," said the new policeman.

Ilsa felt sad for Francie, and angry, and generally terrified. Grimly, she summoned the power of all those emotions to fuel the final act of her performance.

"You're going about this all wrong," she said, jabbing the Marshal in the ribs.

He looked down at his ribs as if he couldn't believe that someone had dared to prod them.

"Now, my husband used to be a dogcatcher," she continued, "which is nothing to be ashamed of, and he always said that the best way to catch a mad dog—which I assume can't be so different from catching a madwoman—is to put yourself in the place of the dog and think about what that dog wants."

She continued explaining her fictitious husband's theories of dog-catching, keeping a careful eye on the Marshal's face all the while. She watched his suspicion give way, bit by bit, to impatience and then exasperation.

Keeping in mind this could be a trap and he could be playing along until Ilsa let her guard down, she committed and then recommitted to this character she was playing until the blessed moment when the Marshal shot a covert eye roll to his fellow officers of the law and raised a hand to stop her.

"All right," he said when the hand alone didn't silence her, and then she paused, hoping to give every indication that she would start up again at the slightest opportunity.

"That's enough," the Marshal said sternly. "I appreciate your concern, ma'am, but right now you're keeping us from doing our job. We can't pay attention to you *and* everyone else in this depot."

"Well—" Ilsa began.

"No," said the Marshal, raising both hands now. "Enough."

Ilsa tried to look offended and must have succeeded because the Marshal again rolled his eyes, not even trying to hide it this time.

"Move along now," he said.

With a huff, Ilsa brushed past the Marshal, walked out to the platform, and boarded her train.

# 81

Two workers from the Salt Lake City Cemetery—both surly with the injustice of being pulled from their beds so early on a Sunday morning—loaded the three bloody corpses from the crime scene into the back of an unmarked wagon.

"What a mess," said one of the men as he considered their grisly cargo.

"We'll have to clean the wagon after this one," said the other as he covered the bodies with a canvas tarp.

And so it was that the earthly remains of Francie Bream, Roger Marsh, and Adam Wolfe traveled together to the site of their final resting place. In life, they would have been uneasy companions at best, but in death they rode uncomplainingly shoulder to shoulder, comrades in the work of decomposition and decay.

# 82

Gilbert Snaith was no late-sleeping sloven. No matter what time he went to bed the night before, he always arose at six the following morning, ready to face the world. This Sunday was no exception, which meant that by the time he took his customary nine-thirty coffee, he'd already been awake for hours.

He'd largely shaken off Saturday's foul mood and was plotting a meeting between himself and his new polygamist love object, Eliza Williams. Her husband was less of a fool than Roger Marsh, so Gilbert would need to proceed with caution this time.

Perhaps he could hire somebody to discreetly follow Eliza and learn her customary whereabouts, and then one day—*what a pleasant surprise!*—Gilbert would "accidentally" run into her and exercise his considerable charms. Where to go from there was a trickier question, but Gilbert was sure he would crack that nut in due time. First thing Monday morning, he would find somebody to track Mrs. Eliza Williams.

He felt confident about his prospects. Eliza, he believed, was no Diantha Marsh, no two-faced harridan who would draw him to her only to jeer at his most intimate dreams and secrets. No, that unpleasantness was behind him now.

He felt good today, buoyed by his success in eliminating the threats to his treasured labor spy, first in the form of that nuisance, Gus Helton, and then the detective, Billy Lovelace. They had both tried and failed to diminish his power, and now both were gone, Helton dead, and Lovelace run out of town.

Today was a good day—*another* good day—to be Gilbert Snaith.

# 83

Billy Lovelace, stowed away on a boxcar headed west, was feeling the sting of defeat. He'd achieved nothing in Salt Lake City and had been rewarded for his efforts with nothing but a new collection of bodily pains. He lay on the floor of the swaying boxcar, eyes shut tight, teeth clenched.

His ribs ached from the beating he'd taken at the hands of Lieutenant Mainwaring, the nerves in his back twinged from his being thrown out of the Alta Club, his wrists and ankles burned from being tied with rough twine by Whiskey Joe and his henchmen, his neck was bleeding from where Joe had cut him, his bad leg throbbed from general overuse, and his head pounded with one of the frequent headaches he'd been having ever since Anton LeFleur had nearly beaten him to death.

By this point in his career, Billy had learned to recognize a losing battle. He would walk away from the whole Salt Lake mess and hope his luck turned around someplace else. Now that he was no longer pursuing Ilsa across the country, he'd have time to take on more paying cases. That could be good. Maybe he'd even settle down someplace, who could say?

Repositioning himself in a futile attempt to lessen his pain,

Billy wondered if Ilsa had made it out of Utah in one piece, and grudgingly, he hoped she had.

# 84

Three years later, Madame Ilsa von Hoffmann was loading an assortment of gourds—butternut squash, pumpkins, acorn squash—into a wheelbarrow. Autumn's first hard frost was imminent, so this would be the final harvest. Not all the gourds had fully ripened, but enough had that Ilsa counted this crop a success.

On the whole, life at Swan Manor was less agricultural than Ilsa had anticipated, though they did have a milk cow, two horses, and a large vegetable garden of which Ilsa had taken unofficial ownership. It was maddening work, gardening, so fussy and unpredictable, but the triumphs, when they came, brought Ilsa a thoroughgoing sense of achievement.

She stood to stretch her legs and saw Nellie Chen approaching from the back of the two-story frame house. Nellie wore blue coveralls and a floral headscarf and carried a bottle of homemade apple cider. She waved, and Ilsa waved back.

"What a lot of pumpkins," Nellie said, approaching the garden.

She extended the bottle of cider to Ilsa, who brushed as much dirt as she could from her gloved hands before taking the bottle.

"It's no bumper crop," Ilsa said, "but it'll do."

She took a drink of cider, sweet and tart and cool, and handed the bottle back to Nellie, who wiped the mouth on her sleeve and took a drink herself.

The two women looked at the nearly empty garden.

"Would you like some help?" Nellie said.

"If you have the time," Ilsa said.

Later that afternoon, they were all going to the Falcon Gulch Hallowe'en festival, one of the high points of the year for the residents of Swan Manor. They would dance to the music of the hired brass band, eat pumpkin pies and popcorn, drink hot cocoa, swap ghost stories and gossip with their neighbors, dance some more, eat some more, and finish the night with the customary fireworks display.

"I have as much time as you do," Nellie said, and produced a pair of work gloves from the back pocket of her coveralls.

While they worked, they discussed Nellie's act. She was going on the road again in a few weeks (she hated the Wyoming winters) but was having trouble figuring out the transitional banter between a few of the songs. Ilsa offered some suggestions, and Nellie jotted them down in a notebook she always kept on her person.

"Do you want to move these to the root cellar?" Nellie asked once they'd filled the wheelbarrow with gourds.

Ilsa wiped her brow with the back of her arm. "I'll do it tomorrow."

Nellie nodded and took off her gloves. "Oh, by the way," she said as they walked back to the house. "Zeb Turner brought by the papers while you were in the garden."

On a weekly basis, the Swans received an array of newspapers from around the country, which they read not only for their own edification, but to enrich the acts of the Swans who still performed.

"Thanks," Ilsa said. "And thanks for the help."

"You too," Nellie said, and gave Ilsa a quick hug before going upstairs to change.

Ilsa found the dining room empty (everyone else was upstairs getting ready for the Hallowe'en festival) and the newspapers stacked on the table. She sat down, picked one up, and glanced through the headlines. An uprising in China, an airplane crash in Spokane, a visit by President Taft to San Francisco, the latest scores from the World Series: none of these stories much interested Ilsa at the moment.

Then, on an inside page of *The Denver Courier*, a headline caught her eye: *FORMER POLYGAMIST DIANTHA MARSH REVERED AS PROPHETESS BY FOLLOWERS.* Suppressing a shiver, Ilsa read on.

According to the article, in the time since Ilsa had left Salt Lake City, Diantha had reinvented herself as a roving mystic who—though she abjured personal acclaim—was attracting more and more disciples from all over the country. Whenever she arrived in a new city or town, she would station herself in some public place, like a park or a plaza, and once a suitable crowd had gathered, start to preach.

Every sermon began the same way, with Diantha instructing her listeners as follows:

*This is how a person should live*, she'd say. *Thou shalt love the Lord thy God with all thy heart, and with all thy soul, and with all thy mind, and thou shalt love thy neighbor as thyself*, and then she would recite the Beatitudes in full, followed by an injunction to eat no meat and no milk.

And that was all, in terms of moral instruction.

But the people didn't come to hear moral instruction from Diantha, at least not primarily. They came to hear about her visions, which she frequently received from God and relayed to her disciples with no exegesis, only a simple introduction. *Yesterday after lunch, the Lord gave me a vision*, she would say before recounting an otherworldly experience involving lambs and shipwrecks and enormous looms, or angelically piloted bicycles, or serpents and jelly jars and freezing fires that covered the Earth.

Some of her followers had taken to writing these visions down, and though Sister Diantha (as she called herself) had forbidden her listeners from founding a church in her name, they circulated collections of her visions among themselves, pondering them in private and discussing them in small groups.

Many claimed their study of these visions prompted visions of their own, even stranger and more oblique than Diantha's originals, visions that permanently shifted their view of the world, or left them with the lingering sense that something within them had changed forever.

There were also unverifiable rumors circulating of miraculous healings wrought on the hearers of Diantha's visions: a mother of three cured of an advanced case of tuberculosis, a poor farmer awakened from a three-day coma, the sight restored to a woman born blind, a young girl raised from her deathbed.

The Mormon Church had publicly distanced itself from Diantha and denounced her ministry as unauthorized by God, while secular skeptics called her a charlatan and a cheat. What Diantha herself thought of all this, no one could say, as she refused all interviews with the press.

Reaching the end of the article, Ilsa realized she'd been holding her breath. She'd met the third Mrs. Marsh only briefly, but the woman still served as an unwelcome reminder of the whole unpleasant episode in Salt Lake City; though the house was cool, almost chilly on this autumn afternoon, Ilsa had sweat through her shirtwaist. She certainly didn't *need* a reminder of that October misadventure of three years before. She still thought frequently of everything she'd witnessed, and how narrowly she'd escaped a bad end herself.

Following her getaway from Utah, Ilsa's first weeks at Swan Manor had been incredibly tense. Newspapers nationwide had covered the sensational murder of Roger Marsh, many of them specifically mentioning Ilsa's peripheral involvement. During that time, she'd expected a U.S. Marshal to come knocking at any minute, but none came. She guessed that with Marsh's actual killer dead, neither the Marshals nor the Mormon Church had worked up much appetite for further investigating the murder of a man they'd both viewed as a menace.

Eventually, the newspaper coverage had diminished and then vanished completely, the public's attention captured by other stories: the presidential election, the kidnapping of an oil heiress, the deaths of Butch Cassidy and the Sundance Kid in Bolivia.

Since those early, white-knuckle days, Ilsa had settled into a much steadier existence at Swan Manor. On realizing she had no interest in agriculture, Lucy Lammermoor (Ilsa's former mentor and the Manor's proprietress) had sold most of the land she'd inherited from her uncle to farmers in the area, and the proceeds from that sale largely funded day-to-day life at the Manor. The permanent residents all contributed to the household economy in various ways (cooking, cleaning, cheesemaking, occasional vaudeville tours), and the women were able to live simply but comfortably.

Ilsa no longer toured herself but had found a new career writing material for other vaudeville performers, female impersonators at first, but then, as word of mouth spread, all kinds of acts: magicians, singers, plate spinners, strong men, dancers. Her years as a medium had sharpened her stagecraft to a point where she could inject even the most tired routine with suspense, intrigue, and zest.

The writing didn't bring in a fortune, by any means, but Ilsa earned enough to put away a little money for herself on top of the contributions she made to living expenses at the Manor. For better and for worse, it was less immediate, less exciting work than being onstage herself, but there was a particular satisfaction in solving other people's problems like some very minor deity.

She also liked the town where they lived. Falcon Gulch was the kind of place, it turned out, where people came when they wanted to leave their old lives behind and make a new start of things, when they found the welcome of the world severely lacking. They were a careworn and tolerant populace, in other words, and embraced the Crimson Swans with open arms.

To her astonishment, Ilsa had friendly acquaintances in town and was romantically involved with a cheery and courteous farmhand named Washington Hart, who could imitate the song of any bird and coax even the most withered plant in Ilsa's vegetable garden back to life.

And now here was Diantha Marsh intruding on all that, resurrecting for Ilsa the most unpleasant weekend of her life. She felt a surge of anger, followed by a wave of shakiness.

The clip-clop of sensible shoes announced the arrival of Lucy Lammermoor in the dining room.

"You're not going to be ready for the festival in time," Lucy said, patting Ilsa on the shoulder.

Daisy Fortnum, Tiffany Cartier, and Alexandria Lake followed Lucy into the dining room, and the space came to life with the other women's preparations and conversations. Ilsa looked at the clock. She still had half an hour before they had to leave.

"I can make it," she said to Lucy, and ran upstairs to her attic bedroom.

True, the article in the *Courier* had left Ilsa feeling clammy and a little sick, as any reminder of her time in Salt Lake was wont to do, but also undeniably fascinated. With haste, she washed and shaved, considering as she did the strange trajectory of Diantha Marsh's life, from downtrodden polygamist wife to roving visionary.

She found Diantha's paraphrasing of the New Testament irritating for some reason, and the healings unlikely, but the visions—the visions intrigued Ilsa. She wondered if they were real, or rather, how real they were, though that was not the most interesting question to Ilsa. What she really wanted to know was what effect they would have on Ilsa herself.

If Ilsa missed anything about her life as a medium, it was her connection (artificial as it may have been) to the mystical. She could still almost summon that heady feeling of being in a room full of people who thought they were speaking with the dead, and she felt a sharp pang of loss for that sense of absolute mystery and possibility, that connection to something vast and unknowable.

She wondered if Diantha's visions had that kind of potency, or perhaps even more power than her own sham séances. What if they did? Would it be worth tracking the other woman down to try and learn her secrets?

No, it wouldn't, Ilsa decided almost as soon as she'd posed the question. She'd had enough of the Marsh family to last her a lifetime, and anyway, she had a Hallowe'en festival to attend.

Picking up a hand towel, she dried her face and, clean now, hurried into a fresh skirt and shirtwaist, and applied her makeup with the speed of the former professional that she was.

"Don't leave without me," she called down the stairs.

"Hurry!" someone called back.

Ilsa grabbed a coat and threw a few essentials into a purse, still feeling the slightest bit sick. She ran down the stairs and saw through the open front door their two horses—Huckleberry and Clive—hitched to the Manor's sturdy old wagon. Her housemates already sat inside, Lucy in the box seat, reins in hand, the others on straw bales.

The clamminess within Ilsa evaporated as she looked at her comrades. Alexandria had her arm around Tiffany, who was laughing at something Princess Fontina had said, while Daisy adjusted the feathers on Nellie's Merry Widow hat. There'd been a time in Ilsa's life when she'd been unable to even imagine a scene like this, let alone hope for something like it for herself.

"Are you coming or not?" Lucy said.

Ilsa stepped through the doorway and then put a hand to her head.

"My hat!" she exclaimed, and several of her housemates groaned.

She'd decorated the hat specially for the Hallowe'en festival and found it just inside on the back of a divan: a wide-brimmed straw boater trimmed with brown-and-white-striped ribbon and a small bouquet of goldenrods and asters. She put it on and ran back outside, closing the door behind her.

"That hat is stunning," said Princess Fontina, scooting over to make space for Ilsa on one of the straw bales.

"Thank you," Ilsa said, inordinately pleased by the compliment. She adjusted the hat's brim to keep the October sun from her eyes and felt something like contentment as she climbed into the wagon with her friends.

# SELECTED BIBLIOGRAPHY

Though the characters in this novel are fictional, the settings and historical contexts are based in reality. Here are some sources I found especially helpful in constructing the world of *A Bad Deal in Mormon Land*.


**General historical overviews:**

*A Fierce Discontent: The Rise and Fall of the Progressive Movement in America* by Michael McGerr

*The Gathering Place: An Illustrated History of Salt Lake City* by John S. McCormick

*Utah: A People's History* by Dean L. May

**The relationship between the Church of Jesus Christ of Latter-day Saints and polygamy at the beginning of the twentieth century:**

*The Politics of American Religious Identity: The Seating of Senator Reed Smoot, Mormon Apostle* by Kathleen Flake

*Prostitution, Polygamy, and Power: Salt Lake City, 1847-1918* by Jeffrey Nichols

**Whiteness and the LDS Church:**

*Mormonism and White Supremacy: American Religion and the Problem of Racial Innocence* by Joanna Brooks

*Religion of a Different Color: Race and the Mormon Struggle for Whiteness* by W. Paul Reeve

**Latter-day Saints in Dime Novels:**

*Dime Novel Mormons* edited and introduced by Michael Austin and Ardis E. Parshall

**Gender in the early twentieth century:**

*Manliness & Civilization: A Cultural History of Gender and Race in the United States, 1880-1917* by Gail Bederman

*Before We Were Trans: A New History of Gender* by Kit Heyam

**Vaudeville in general, and female impersonators in particular:**

*Vaudeville and the Making of Modern Entertainment, 1890-1925* by David Monod

*No Applause–Just Throw Money: The Book That Made Vaudeville Famous* by Trav S.D.

The University of Arizona's online Vaudeville Museum (https://sites.arizona.edu/Vaudeville/)

https://Vaudevilleamerica.org/

"Queen of the Dead: Bert Savoy" by Eve Golden (https://ladailymirror.com/2012/10/30/eve-golden-queen-of-the-dead-bert-savoy/)

"Bert Savoy" (https://queermusicheritage.com/jun2004b.html)

"Bert Savoy" by Kristen Chapman Gibbons (https://kchapmangibbons.wordpress.com/2013/05/18/bert-savoy-1888-1923-early-female-impersonator-vintage-photography/)

**Radical Politics in Utah:**

*A History of Utah Radicalism: Startling, Socialistic, and Decidedly Revolutionary* by John S. McCormick and John R. Sillitoe

**Miscellaneous:**

*Salt Lake City Underfoot: Self-Guided Tours of Historical Neighborhoods* by Mark Angus (contains delightfully gossipy and largely unverifiable historical anecdotes about Salt Lake City)

*Make Yourself Gods: Mormonism and the Unfinished Business of American Secularism* by Peter Coviello

(a fascinating read that helped me think about Mormons and Spiritualists existing together)

Historian Rachel Quist's Instagram (@rachels_slc_history)

(Full of great pictures, facts, and anecdotes of historic Salt Lake City)

*Marion Marlowe in Salt Lake City, or, A Bad Deal in Mormon Land* by Grace Shirley

(The 1901 dime novel that gave me the title for this book)

# ACKNOWLEDGMENTS

I got the idea for this novel from an anecdote in John S. McCormick's *The Gathering Place: An Illustrated History of Salt Lake City*, so thank you to him, and to all the historians whose work informed this book. They are true heroes of our time.

Thank you to Anthony Garrett, Hannah Montgomery, Nancy Radigan-Hoffman, and Mike Strayer for their insightful and supportive feedback on early drafts of this novel.

Thanks to Mary Vensel White for publishing this book, and for her keen editorial eye. The rest of the team at Type Eighteen Books has also been great: thank you, Katie Schwab, for the notes and first edits, Elisabeth Cunningham and Jaclyn Rodriguez for savvy marketing, and Sutherland Lovell for the eagle-eyed copy edit.

Thanks to Roderick Brydon for the lovely cover.

Thanks, as always, to J & A.

And finally, thank you for reading this book.

# ABOUT THE AUTHOR

T.I.M. Wirkus (they/them) is the author of the novels *The Infinite Future* and *City of Brick and Shadow.* Their novella, *Sandy Downs*, won the 2013 *Quarterly West* novella contest. Their short fiction has appeared in *The Best American Non-Required Reading* and elsewhere. They hold a PhD in creative writing and literature from the University of Southern California.

www.ingramcontent.com/pod-product-compliance
Lightning Source LLC
LaVergne TN
LVHW101603151026
850117LV00028B/169